BUZZKILL

A NOVEL OF TECHNOLOGY AND INTERNATIONAL TERRORISM

TOM HARRIS

DRONE WARS BOOK 1

Tom Harris Creations, LLC

Copyright 2024

Edited by
Lionel Dyck
And of course…
Nikko, the Grammar Dog

A version of this novel was previously published in 2014 as *Day of the Drone* by T.R. Harris.

All rights reserved. This is a work of fiction. Names, characters, places, brands, media and incidents are either the product of the author's imagination or are used fictitiously.

BUZZKILL...

This was the quintessential signature of drone warfare, what pilots call ...

BuzzKill.

Quote of the Day:
"It could have been worse..."

RIPPED FROM THE HEADLINES…

A new era of drone warfare has already arrived involving many more players. And the use of UAVs has moved from counter-terrorism or counter-insurgency warfare into full scale conventional combat. Indeed, up ahead, a new third age of drone warfare beckons as technology becomes ever more sophisticated and linked to artificial intelligence.

Jonathan Marcus, BBC
Feb. 4, 2022

The technology of today, while impressive, is developing the tactics and techniques of future terrorist attacks. The most prescient current technology that will enable future terrorist attacks is the drone. Drones have the ability of providing standoff, which can enable terrorists to conduct multiple attacks nearly simultaneously, rapidly magnifying their overall effect. A terrorist attack is meant to create an atmosphere of fear to influence a target audience—a civilian population or government—to force or impose political change. The massive increase in the number of form factors, capabilities, ease of access and ease of operation of drones at low cost will make them the weapon of choice for future terrorists.

The Role of Drones in Future Terrorist Attacks

Maj. Thomas G. Pledger

AUSA: Association of the United States Army

Feb. 26, 2021

PROLOGUE

Anastasia Beaumont heard the high-pitched buzz before she saw the tiny remote-controlled dune buggy slip past her and enter the bank. She watched with curiosity as the little toy, with the shiny silver canister taped to it, moved farther into the marble-floored and jade-columned vestibule before it stopped in mid-room and began to perform a series of radical three-sixty spins.

It was an odd scene, with people in the bank displaying diametrically opposed expressions. The two security guards wore scowls on their stern faces while the customers smiled, waiting for the bank promo regarding auto loans to be announced....

A small flying drone suddenly lifted off the dune buggy and climbed toward the ceiling. It hovered there as a tiny camera turned on its gimbal, scanning the scene below.

The guards approached the toy.

"Uh, uh … don't come any closer," said a tinny voice from hidden speakers.

Knowing this wasn't part of a bank promotion, the guards hesitated only a moment before spreading out and approaching the vehicle from opposite directions. Just then, a tiny servo motor began to whine, and the shiny, foot-long canister atop the dune buggy split open along a thin centerline. Robert Williams pulled his .9mm Glock—feeling silly to be pointing it at a toy—but he gasped when he saw what was inside the canister.

It contained three sticks of eight-inch, paper-wrapped dynamite, with a series of wires running from end-to-end and terminating at a glowing Samsung NTX-4 cellphone.

"What the hell?" Williams blurted. He and his partner, Gavin St. Croix, were less than ten feet from the menacing object.

"I can hear you, Mr. Williams," said the voice from the RC car, sounding almost giddy as he spoke. "Now, if you don't want Gavin to get hurt, or Joyce, or Kaitlyn—you see, I know the names of all the employees at the bank—then I suggest you holster your weapon and back away."

"What's this all about?" St. Croix asked just as bank manager Francine Howell came up next to him. Her expression was one of concern rather than the anger displayed on the faces of the guards.

"This is branch manager Francine—"

"Yes, I know who you are, Francine Howell," the voice interrupted. "To answer Mr. St. Croix's question, this is a robbery, pure and simple." The speaker paused to let the impact of his words sink in. Both guards shook their heads and smirked.

"Bullshit," said Williams.

"Watch your language in the presence of a lady, Bob. As I was saying, this is a robbery. I have three sticks of construction-grade dynamite wired to explode upon my command or if the device is tampered with in any way. Now I will ask that you look to the main entrance door...."

All eyes turned to the single, four-foot-wide glass door, now closed. Outside was another RC vehicle, this one a Tonka replica of the quintessential yellow quarry dump truck, with a round, 13-gallon plastic trash can sitting in the bed box.

"Please open the door, Mr. St. Croix, so my associate may enter."

"No friggin' way!"

"Ms. Howell, please have Gavin do as I ask. I would hate to stain the interior of your beautiful bank with the bloody body parts from your thirty or so customers and employees."

Panic swept through the cadre of customers, and a group of them lurched towards the exit. "Stop!" the voice cried out. "Stop ... or I'll set off the bomb."

Most people obeyed; others didn't. Fearing for their lives from the actions of the noncompliant, several of the bank customers grabbed onto the ones still rushing towards the exit and pulled them back by their suits and dresses. Scuffles broke out.

"Stop, all of you!" the voice from the toy car boomed out louder than ever. "All I want is some of the bank's money. Just let my associate in and then have the tellers fill the can with cash. After that, we'll be on our way, and with no one getting hurt."

Gavin St. Croix snorted. "You really expect us to fill your trash can with money and then just let you drive off?" He had his weapon drawn. "I bet that's not even real dynamite." He looked around at the frightened customers and employees. "This is probably some computer geek's scheme for making a quick buck by scaring the hell out of everyone here."

"Are you willing to risk the lives of everyone in the bank to satisfy your macho bravado? Just let me have the money. After that, it'll be the job of the *real* cops to find me. Don't be a hero, Gavin," the speaker growled. "Besides, the amount I'll take from the bank today won't even register as a rounding error on the ledger. Now, do everyone a favor…and open the damn door!"

One of the customers near the entrance pulled it open, and the RC dump truck quickly entered. In the ensuing confusion, the customer ran out, along with five others.

"Close the door, Gavin!" the tinny voice demanded. "If another customer leaves, I will set off the bomb. Doing so will only cost me a couple hundred dollars in material, as well as a few sticks of dynamite that I stole from the Greater East River Reclamation Project a month ago. I won't be harmed in any way, and I'll still have enough dynamite to come back here and do this all over again. Maybe then I'll be taken more seriously. Of course, I'll be dealing with a whole new set of employees—because all of *you* will be dead! Now get me my goddamn money…and no paint bombs, either! If I find any, I'll come back here with the sole purpose of blowing the hell out of this place."

The dump truck positioned itself between the original vehicle and tellers' row. Francine Howell motioned with her hands. "Hurry up, all of you. Empty the cash drawers and put the stacks in the can."

The eight tellers on duty obeyed, worry clouding their eyes and visible in their frantic movements; even so, in less than a minute, a fair amount of money filled the trash can.

"See, that wasn't too hard, now was it? And no one got hurt. Now, Mr. Williams, it's your turn to open the door so we can leave."

Robert Williams was now closest to the exit, and he bit his lip as a vein pulsed in his neck. The tiny, two-vehicle caravan took off for the front door, slowing to a stop as the guard stood firm with his left hand on the door handle and the other resting on the grip of his company-issued Glock. A standoff ensued.

"Don't be stupid, Williams," the voice said with steely purpose. "It's not your money, so don't die for it."

The guard took a deep breath before slowly pulling the heavy glass door in towards him.

"Good choice, Bob. Now step aside and let us leave."

Williams took a wide step to his right, and the caravan began to roll toward the door; however, when the lead car drew parallel to the guard, that's when things went tragically wrong.

The guard lunged forward, reaching down to grab a handful of the wires connecting the dynamite with the cellphone. He pulled hard, and the wires came loose. Next, he kicked the model dune buggy to his right, sending it skidding over the smooth marble tile floor.

"I knew it!" Williams declared. "It's all a fake."

The dune buggy spun around on narrow black wheels, the electric motor whining until it was face-on with the guard. The miniature camera mounted on the hovering drone focused on Robert Williams' smiling face.

"Do you think I'd be that stupid to build a bomb with only one way to detonate? Not likely. Now, say a prayer, Mr. Williams. You just cost all these people their lives."

The explosion blew out the fifty-foot glass front of the bank and shattered windows across the street along the entire block. Roiling clouds of white smoke billowed from the gaping hole on the ground floor of the twenty-seven-story building, with shards of glass and splintered marble blanketing the street.

Eight people died in the bank that day, along with two on the street outside. Both security guards were counted in the fatalities. Bank manager Francine Howell wasn't one of them, although she lost her left arm from the elbow down and suffered third-degree burns along the left side of her body. Three other people in the bank were permanently disabled, while every customer and employee in the bank that day experienced some level of injury or psychological trauma.

A week later, in Chicago, another remote-controlled car entered a bank. This time, all instructions were followed without question, and after the robbery, the two-car caravan left the bank and scooted along the sidewalk to an alley between the bank building and its neighbor. A buzzing, eight-bladed drone called an octocopter was waiting. Expertly, the unknown pilot snared the dual straps on the trash container and lifted it from the bed of the yellow dump truck. The UAV—Unmanned Aerial Vehicle—was rated for this heavy of a load, and soon, both the drone and the money disappeared over the crest of the building next to the bank.

A crowd of people, both from the street and the bank, had followed the RC cars to the alley. Now, they stood at the entrance, gawking and uncertain what to do next.

The remote-controlled dune buggy then turned to face the crowd. The tinny voice spoke for the last time. "All of you should take cover; I'm about to destroy the evidence."

Thirty seconds later, an explosion erupted from the alleyway and echoed throughout the downtown area, yet unlike New York, no one was killed in this event, just some rather extensive property damage in its aftermath.

The drone and the money were never seen again.

The first copycat robbery occurred nine days later, and by the end of the year, forty-two similar events had taken place. That was when banks and other public buildings in major cities across the country began to require entry doors to remain locked at all times until a guard gave customers and employees access.

And it was soon after this that the first terrorist-linked drone attack took place. Unlike the robberies, no amount of security or appeasement could keep the massive bombs carried by these remotely-controlled vehicles from exploding indiscriminately in just about any place a crowd assembled. A few months later, acid or fiery gasoline began to rain down on an unsuspecting populace from drones expertly piloted by remote operators, some of which were based in foreign countries thousands of miles away from the site of their deadly attacks.

These killer-operators were anonymous and often protected by sponsor nations, their identities a closely-held secret. This was a new breed of terrorist, a person who could pull a nine-to-five shift delivering death and destruction around the world, only to return home at the end of the day to his wife and children without risking a hair on his head.

It was out of a desperate need to respond to such attacks that the Rapid Defense Center—the RDC—was established at Nellis Air Force Base in North Las Vegas, Nevada, sequestered from the rest of the base in a low mountain pass five miles from the flight line.

Nellis was once the primary operations site for America's nuclear arsenal and, more recently—along with neighboring Creech AFB—had served as the home of the Air Force's Predator and Reaper drone programs. That program was absorbed into the more ubiquitous mission of the RDC, allowing the base to play host to the country's most-effective tool against a threat that, although individually on a much smaller scale than nuclear warfare, was nevertheless more prevalent, more personal and more deadly than anything the country had faced in recent times.

There was no deterrent against the use of unmanned aerial vehicles, as there was with nuclear weapons. From spiderweb-like international terror organizations, and all the way down to sick individuals with a single agenda, there was little that could be done to prevent drone attacks. And to make matters worse, the equipment and technology required to carry out such horrific acts of terror were readily available from Amazon, Walmart or hobby stores that carried remote-controlled cars, trucks and UAVs.

Without a doubt, the age of the Drone Wars ushered in a period of the most anxiety-producing paranoia ever experienced by mankind, and it was all the pilots and operators at the RDC could do to keep a dim flicker of hope alive for the innocent people of the world.

1

Xander Moore had just pressed down the top of the Keurig coffeemaker, puncturing the small container of Donut Shop brew, when the bug in his ear sounded: "M-9 Alert! Repeat: M-9 Alert. Red One, prepare; Blue Six and Red Nineteen, backup."

With the coffee machine located on a counter directly behind the pilot's console, all Xander had to do was turn toward the screens to comply with the order.

"Which one?" he asked the other two men in the room. He already knew from the alert code that this was an attack on a shopping mall and that it was occurring somewhere within zone nine, which was the state of Florida.

"The Dolphin Mall, Miami," replied Charlie Fox, his wingman. "Six seconds and counting, and it looks like we're first in line."

An array of preliminary information concerning the attack was already scrolling on the screens at each of the three stations, requiring only a couple of seconds to digest. Two UAVs, carrying bomb packs, had struck the Number One entrance to the mall—the main entrance—and detonated just to the left of the security maze. The breach was significant enough to allow twelve trailing combat drones to enter the mall.

"All autos?" Xander asked his scanner-operator, David Lane.

"These are," the young man answered, "...although an *RPA* just entered—and a huge mother, too!"

Xander paused for a moment as he received confirmation through his earpiece that his team was now the lead in the event. "Red-One confirmed, taking command." He glanced at each side of his station and at the other two members of his team. "Okay, boys, we're it. This is huge, so we should have backup on-site in seconds. Dave, post them to the exterior of the mall to take out any predators near the service exits. What about our assets?"

"Up and en route," Lane replied.

In the early seconds of an alert, David Lane was the eyes and ears of the operation, feeding crucial data to the other two from a variety of sensors under his control. "Units were offsite, but ten seconds out. Damn, we have eight rapid-response bunkers along the Dolphin Expressway, with a lot of targets within a few miles, including Miami International."

"Any simo's being reported?"

"Not yet; it looks like this is the only target being hit at this time."

"I have the Viper—assuming control."

With practiced and confident skill, Xander took control of the main defensive drone—an LSC Industries *Viper III*. Charlie Fox took command of the smaller JEN-Tech *Panther*, while Lane locked onto the tiny, yet extremely fast and agile, observation drone.

All three team members donned compact virtual reality goggles, placing them in FPV—First Person View—of their respective drones. Even after all the years of operating drones in FPV, it still took Xander a split second to adjust to the sudden shift in perspective; where one moment he was seated in a dimly-lit team room at a bank of sophisticated monitors and controllers to then suddenly zipping forty feet above a crowded parking lot in the brilliant, late afternoon sunshine of south Florida, twenty-three hundred miles away.

With the defensive drones launching on autopilot from their hidden bunkers only a few blocks from the mall, they were already quickly approaching the main entrance to Miami's largest shopping center by the time Team Red-One took control. Up ahead, they could see where the iconic banner sign displaying the words *Dolphin Mall* in large block letters had once spanned the outer concourse. At night, the panel would be illuminated in brilliant colors of art deco neon, in traditional South Florida fashion.

Now, the sign was split in two, with each half still swinging precariously from broken and twisted supports. Sparks popped from severed electrical wires, while fire burned off the remnants of bunting that had once proclaimed the arrival of the joyous Christmas shopping season. All the joy and promise of the Holiday Season had come to a sudden and tragic halt less than forty seconds ago.

Smoke billowed beyond the shattered sign where the main breach occurred. Most malls—as well as other large public venues in America—were now fitted with ingress and egress security mazes. These imposing, 'S-shaped' tunnels were designed to slow any attacking drones attempting to gain entry to the mall. They were equipped with heavy blast doors that could be closed at a moment's notice, trapping the attackers within the solid metal walls. At that point, even if the drones exploded, the damage would be contained within the maze.

Yet, in this particular case, the terrorists avoided the security maze altogether. The two enemy breach drones simply detonated their substantial payloads of high-grade explosive against the supposedly bullet-proof plate glass window to the left of the security maze. The resulting breach wasn't large—only about eight feet in diameter—but it was big enough to allow the other drones to enter the mall.

Most large public facilities now had their own defensive drone force onsite, yet Xander was surprised to learn that the Dolphin Mall did not. As David Lane had pointed out previously, there was a literal smorgasbord of likely targets dotting the ten-mile stretch of the Dolphin Expressway, running from the Florida Turnpike to the west and all the way to the cruise ship terminal on Biscayne Bay. This included Miami International Airport and American Airlines Stadium. Both of these facilities maintained their own extensive drone fleets, even as they relied on the additional RDC units hidden in underground bunkers nearby for backup. Because of the abundance of defensive units along the expressway, the Mall had skimped in maintaining their own drone force, relying on others to provide the response units.

It was also true that the pilots of the RDC had the authority to assume control over any and all defensive drones operating within a crisis area, whether they be private or government UAVs, including those from the airport and the stadium.

The three main drones in Xander's sortie were RDC units—the most advanced to be found in any defensive fleet—and now they shot through the same hole through which the enemy units had entered only seconds ahead of them. And Xander's defenders weren't alone. Trailing behind the three RPA's—Remotely-Piloted Aircraft— came a force of twenty autonomous defense drones. These *auto-controlled* units quickly dispersed, some turning left, others right, while four proceeded straight down the central concourse of the mall. Equipped with the most advanced sense-and-avoid software and scanners, the

RDC auto drones were designed to navigate tight quarters and home in on other UAVs in the vicinity through a combination of radio signals and audio pick-ups. Any aircraft not carrying the proper transponder code would be blown out of the air.

It was the responsibility of the live operators of Team Red-One to assess the event and coordinate the proper defensive response while also being on the lookout for any RPAs operated by enemy pilots. Actively piloted drones—remotely piloted aircraft or RPAs—posed the most problem for the defenders since they were unpredictable in their actions. Engagements between RPAs were when most of the head-to-head aerial combat took place.

It was nine days before Christmas, and the Dolphin Mall was overflowing with eager shoppers at the time of the attack. With a shake of his head, Xander knew that was why the mall had been targeted in the first place. More death and destruction … guaranteed.

With the unpredictability and spontaneity of drone attacks, the team's primary objective wasn't to *prevent* an attack but rather to *limit* the effect. They accomplished this through a combination of the quickest response times possible, followed by the systematic destruction of the attacking auto drones before they could target civilians and detonate onboard bombs. Time was the variable in the equation. The sooner the enemy robots could be neutralized, the lower the body count. Unfortunately, there was *always* a body count.

With a quick scan of data now present on his heads-up display, Xander Moore began assessing the situation at a location over twenty-three hundred miles from where he sat. He was tied into the mall's sophisticated security camera system, and with a flick of a toggle on his sixteen-function controller, he switched from scene to scene, looking for targets and damage.

The hostiles had come in shooting, which, to his relief, was better than coming in and detonating; however, he could already see a number of bodies sprawled out on the marble floor. Too often, drone attacks lasted less than thirty seconds, as three or four UAVs would fly into a crowded venue and simply explode: nothing fancy, just gratuitous killing for the sake of killing. Casualty counts for such events could be in the hundreds, and there was nothing the Rapid Response Center could do to mitigate the carnage.

Most autonomous attack drones operate on sophisticated pre-loaded programs, which basically instruct them to fly to a designated GPS location and then shoot anything with a specific heat signature—the heat signature of a human being. To combat this, malls and other public venues—where possible—would douse their patrons in water in order to soak their clothing and disguise the temperature readings. In addition, installed heating columns would activate during an attack, acting as decoys to distract the drone sensors from their primary targets. These towers were protected by thick, bullet-proof plastic and could withstand an onslaught from the lightweight, nylon-jacketed .5mm rounds most attack drones fired.

Of course, once these mindless killing machines depleted their supply of ammo, the next order of business was to detonate the small explosive charge each carried onboard. Drones were cheap and disposable weapons of destruction, and once the mission was complete, they usually went out with a bang.

However, by the time the auto drones reached the end of their usefulness—which could last as long as thirty minutes in some cases—most of the civilians in the area would have heeded the broadcast warnings and left the building or taken shelter. At the end of an *event*—as the RDC termed terrorist attacks—only additional property damage would result from the explosions. At least that was the theory.

Drone Alerts were becoming more common, with most being triggered by small-time events involving only a single drone or two and flown by lone-wolf terrorists or members of homegrown radical organizations. In one recent event, an attack was initiated by a man with a hefty bet on the sports team that was losing at the time. Out of desperation, he flew an unarmed drone into the sports arena to cause the game's suspension. Most of the time, these were spur-of-the-moment events, and the drones caused no real damage beyond the frayed nerves and tempers of over fifty thousand terrified spectators. In this case, the perpetrator was quickly apprehended, making his gambling losses the least of his worries.

If these events could be said to have a silver lining, it was that they emphasized the seriousness of the threat and helped quicken the public's reaction time when a Drone Alert was announced. For civil defense planners, the problem then became what to do with the thousands of panicking people the alerts set in motion.

The solution—at least temporarily—was found in the long, no-frills service corridors that were hidden from the main public concourses and used by vendors, employees and maintenance personnel. Now, they took on a dual purpose—as fortified bomb shelters. Once an alert sounded, civilians would have thirty seconds to enter the nearest, clearly designated service corridor, after which heavy blast doors would be shuttered. In some cases, a thousand or more people could be packed into these dimly lit and stuffy chambers.

Most often, patrons were not allowed to leave these shelters until all the exits were cleared of potential hostiles, including those that may be waiting outside for the mass of evacuees to reveal themselves. This made for a very uncomfortable half an hour or more, often producing its own set of tragic consequences in the process.

In addition to the service corridors, all inline stores at the major malls were retrofitted with heavy, automatic-closing security doors or grills, which allowed employees and customers to remain safely inside until the crisis passed. That was unless a drone chose to blow open a store's security barricade to get at the soft targets inside. This didn't happen often, yet when it did, the body count was significant.

After spending five years as the senior pilot at the Rapid Defense Center, Xander Moore had seen his share of carnage created by even the most basic drone attack, so he expected nothing less from this event; however, upon entering the mall, he was relieved to see that the main connecting concourse was clear of civilians, at least those who remained visible.

Xander knew that the few who hadn't made it to the shelters would be hiding from his drones—just as they were hiding from the enemy UAVs. This was understandable. Even though the RDC drones were painted with a distinctive red, white and blue motif, the bad guys had begun to paint their units in a similar manner, so to the people within the Dolphin Mall, all drones were considered the enemy. Fortunately, Xander and his team would experience no such confusion. The highly classified transponder signals employed by the RDC units would separate the good guys from the bad.

As Xander's huge Viper RPA cruised down the central concourse of the Dolphin Mall, he spotted another of the effective defensive tools being used to protect the public during drone attacks. These were the ubiquitous, twelve-foot-long, four-foot-wide seating partitions now found throughout most malls in America. Although fitted atop with an inviting four-inch-thick pad for seating comfort, these thirty-inch-high, 't-shaped' structures also served a dual purpose. Besides providing seating for weary patrons, their high-grade steel construction could be used to hide under and behind when enemy drones were in the area. They could also withstand a modest-size explosion.

So, as Xander's Viper led the three-drone phalanx toward the Bloomingdale Outlet on the north side of the mall, he knew that behind many of the seating partitions, dozens of terrified—and wet—civilians huddled, all of whom just had their joyous holiday season shattered by an experience that would haunt them for the rest of their lives.

"Autos are engaging," Lane reported. "Only three explosions recorded so far."

"Casualties?"

"I'm detecting seventeen people down, at least on the western side of the mall. No telling at this point the dead from the injured."

Just then, the team heard the distinctive pop-pop of small arms fire coming through the microphones on their drones. Xander's targeting display instantly locked red boxes on the heads of three men. They were poking out from behind a cellphone accessories kiosk in the center of the concourse, with weapons out and firing ... at Xander and his drones.

The RDC pilot wasn't worried. His drone was specifically designed for combat, with all components of the eight-bladed octocopters made of lightweight—yet virtually indestructible—composite materials; even the lens of the gimbal-controlled camera was made of half-inch-thick, shatterproof plastic.

Xander brought his huge drone to a hover in front of the men. The Viper carried .20mm dual machine guns mounted under the carriage, along with side-mounted .5 mm's. The UVA also carried two banks of pencil-missiles —a total of thirty in all. And now, all that firepower was pointed directly at the three men hiding behind the flimsy wooden kiosk.

"Cease your fire, dammit, we're from the RDC!" Xander called out through the speakers on the drone.

The men kept firing, even to the point where two of them had to reload.

"I said we're from the RDC! Now stop firing and take cover!"

"Bullshit!" one of the men cried out. "How do we know you're really from the RDC? All you damn drones look alike."

"How can you tell?" Xander asked. "You're still alive ... that's how! Now stop firing and take shelter immediately. The crisis will be over shortly."

The Viper hovered momentarily until the three men lowered their weapons, and then it sped off again.

"Everyone okay?" he asked his team.

"One of those dudes was a damn good shot. I took three hits. No damage, however," said Charlie Fox.

The trio of RPA's had now reached the end of the main concourse, which split off at ninety degrees to the west and east. This wide corridor formed the outer walkway for the mall, which was laid out in a huge, race-track-like configuration. Looking both ways, the team could see and hear the sounds of aerial combat taking place as battles raged between individual autonomous drones from each side, following their programming with regard to offense and defense.

Xander noticed that the majority of the enemy drones were basic quadcopters—four-bladed, box-shaped units that were painted to resemble the RDC units. Even a cursory knowledge of the units the government deployed, as compared to those used by terrorists, an observer could easily tell the difference. The government units were much larger octocopters, with blades hidden within protective rings. They were heavier, with double weapons platforms above and below, as well as forward and rear-looking cameras. The bad guys often used off-the-shelf civilian drones—which were mainly leftover inventory items now that the unregulated sale of over-the-counter UAVs had been outlawed a couple of years before.

However, even with their simple design, what turned these once innocent and harmless toys and tools into the lethal weapons they'd become was the installation of a tiny module within their flight controls called a *killbox*. Outlawed throughout most of the civilized world, these miniature, pre-programmed computers were manufactured by rogue nations such as North Korea, Iran and the Islamic State. Each compact device contained everything the aspiring terrorist or anarchist would need to turn their kid's toy or aerial photography platform into a killing machine, including simple plug-and-play operation through standard USB connections.

Several years ago, Congress passed a series of laws requiring that all drones contain restrictive programming covering flying altitude and limiting their access to certain public areas, such as airports, government buildings, sports complexes—and even shopping malls; yet as was common with such laws and restrictions, only law-abiding citizens and companies were impacted. Now, with a four-hundred-dollar killbox, those with evil intent could override any government-mandated operating restriction and carry on without skipping a beat.

Xander had no idea where the autonomous drones for this particular attack had come from. Even with drone sales highly regulated, they were still allowed to be purchased with the proper permits, screening, licensing and education; however, there were literally tens of thousands of older drones left over from the time when UAVs were the latest rage. In fact, Xander could see that most of the enemy drones they were facing today were *Phantom III's*, a popular and affordable quadcopter from about fifteen years ago. Although technology and government regulation had essentially killed off the civilian drone market, these surplus, and in some cases, homemade units still served quite well as killbox-executioners in raids such as the one taking place on this bright December afternoon in Florida.

In all honesty, Xander wasn't too worried about the enemy auto drones. His units were superior and would make short work of the enemy UAVs; however, it was the presence of the enemy RPA in the mix that had him spooked.

"Any location on the big boy?" he asked David Lane.

"Video surveillance had it turning right, heading for the *Dave and Busters* ... and the movie theater."

Xander cringed. He was afraid of that. Here was a large and heavily armed octocopter, guided by a skilled pilot, who could be located anywhere in the world and on the singular mission to cause as much death and destruction as possible. Even before he asked, he already knew the answer to his next question.

"Jamming?"

"Naw, picking up RFG indicators."

Through the use of the inaccurately termed Random Frequency Generators, piloted drones were able to get around the mission-ending prospect of having their frequencies jammed. RFGs were married radio units between pilot and drone, which constantly switched along a series of pre-determined frequencies unique to that pair, with dozens of switches taking place every second. RFGs were quite efficient, and all of the Center's RPAs employed the same technology.

And as for blanket jamming of *all* frequencies within the range of a drone attack? That would also result in the blocking of signals to Xander's defensive team, as well as the loss of GPS, cellphone, Wi-Fi and 911 calls. The bottom line: jamming was seldom used except in the most basic, rookie-generated attacks where RFGs were not involved.

"I have a video capture of the big dawg; I'm displaying it now," said David Lane.

The slightly blurred freeze-frame image of a gangly-looking drone came up on the left side of Xander's HUD.

"Is that what I think it is?" asked Charlie Fox.

"Sure is—a friggin *Ninja II*," Xander confirmed. "I guess that raises the threat level for this event up a few notches."

"Damn right," Fox said. "Besides being the most illegal drone around, it's also the most expensive. You don't bring one of those things to the game unless you have some very deep pockets and a serious desire to win."

At a cost of over a hundred thousand dollars each, the North Korea-manufactured killer drone was the best money could buy—unless, of course, you were the U.S. government. Xander's Viper was comparably priced, but for a terrorist organization to use a Ninja in a mall attack was unprecedented. Whoever was sponsoring this event had some major bucks behind them, and probably not from North Korea itself. Most nations shunned the country as a partner for their operations—even though they would still buy their lethal weapons from the boycotted nation.

The presence of the Ninja at the Dolphin Mall was sending a message and one that went beyond the potential staggering death toll of the event. It demonstrated to an already rattled population that no matter how tight the security of the nation may have become over the past decade, the masterminds of this attack still managed to get a Ninja II into the United States undetected and undeterred. The illusion of safety and security that the government tried to convey was just that—an illusion.

No one was safe from the drones.

Xander now steered his Viper along the northern corridor of the Dolphin Mall, knowing for certain that his day was about to get a whole lot worse. Beyond the relatively benign actions of the twelve auto drones currently serving up death and destruction throughout the rest of the mall, the Ninja would also end its mission in a fiery blast. However, with an operational time-on-station of up to five hours, there was still plenty of terror to be squeezed out of the drone's hundred-grand price tag before that moment arrived—unless Xander Moore could bring it all to an early conclusion.

The Rapid Defense Center couldn't prevent drone attacks, but it could do something to cut the duration, thereby saving countless innocent lives.

That was all well and good. It was just that Xander Moore had never gone up against a Ninja before....

With practiced confidence, Xander gripped the central control stick on his console with his right hand and placed the fingers of his left on the four toggle buttons controlling the drone's gimbals. His feet were also placed on peddles, allowing for even more agile operation of the Viper.

"Weapons hot. I'm coming up on the D&B's. I really hope it didn't make it into the theaters."

"Security cams show a solid lockdown of the Cineplex. Still, it's kinda ironic, isn't it, that the drone would be hiding in a Dave & Busters?" David Lane's comment was prophetic.

The popular restaurant and video game arcade chain was just the place the sadistic operator of the Ninja would choose. After all, to the three men in the stark and sterile team room at the RDC, they were essentially playing a video game, yet one with real weapons and real consequences.

"Holy crap!" Lane cried out. "Do you have the video feed from inside the arcade?"

Xander toggled the control until he came upon the scene that had his scanner-operator so upset.

"That monster just executed a dozen civilians inside the restaurant," Lane cried out. "He had them line up, telling them they could leave, and then cut them in half." Lane's voice was trembling. Even though he'd seen this level of barbarism many times before, it was something you could never get used to.

"I have the link, Dave," Xander said. "Son-of-a-bitch—now he's talking into the security camera."

The small screen in the upper left corner of Xander's display showed the image of the evil-looking drone hovering in the air while staring into the camera. The Ninja wasn't painted like the other attack drones, in the red, white and blue in the RDC units. Rather, it was silver and black, and with red swatches depicting dripping blood along the sides. There was a sinister-looking face painted on one of the facades, highlighting a hideous grin, and with the stereoscopic cameras serving as the eyes. A computer-disguised voice now spoke into the video display and was picked up by the security microphones.

"Merry Christmas to all Western infidels. I see that your desire for new designer jeans and shiny baubles has brought you out in public today and placed you within my sights. This is only the beginning of what, to me, will be a very joyous holiday season. And please note: what is happening here in Miami can happen anywhere. No target is too big or too small. We will strike at individual homes, at your clogged highways, at your dams and your power stations. We will crack your nuclear reactors and expose your pitiful nation to the deadly radiation from within...."

The recorded message continued yet trailed off as the audio sensors on the huge drone picked up the approach of Xander's Viper. He had entered past the shattered security grate the Ninja had demolished with a single compact missile fired from its arsenal and was in the entrance lobby, where customers had once been greeted by smiling hosts and hostesses. Now, the lobby was a smoldering mass of shattered metal and splintered wood. There were also two dismembered and barely recognizable bodies on the floor, and as Xander passed into the main dining room, he found the victims that the video had shown being executed by the combat drone a few minutes earlier.

After cutting short the recorded message, the Ninja sped off into the vast arcade arena beyond the dining section.

It's not easy hiding a six-foot-long combat drone within an enclosed space. The noise of the props and the wind they produced could be pinpointed by directional microphones aboard the Viper. Unfortunately, so could Xander's.

A thin line of white smoke shot out from behind a tall racing video game, streaking toward Xander's drone. With skill acquired over a lifetime of drone operation, Xander manipulated four different controls simultaneously and twisted his Viper in such a way that the missile missed it by less than two inches. The pencil-sized mini-rocket impacted the wall above the bowling games, blowing a two-foot-wide hole in the concrete block wall.

Xander now sent the Viper screaming through the center of the arcade area before spinning to his right to come up behind the racing game. "Charlie, cover on the right!"

"I'm on it!"

They had the Ninja boxed in—right up to the point that Fox's Panther came face-to-face with the evil-grinning black drone. Firing a split second before Fox, the Ninja operator unleashed a barrage of both missiles and lead at the RDC drone. At point-blank range, even the tough composite material was no match for the intense fire from the Ninja. The Panther was thrown back by the impacts, with four of its prop rings blown off and the flight control module shattered into plastic kindling. The drone fell to the floor and then sputtered for a few seconds before the power finally gave out, and the last of the spinning props wound down.

"I need a replacement—now!" Charlie Fox cried out.

A new voice spoke into the ears of the team. "Replacement on site ... switching now."

Suddenly, Charlie Fox was back in the fight, yet his new drone was still in the area outside the restaurant. He took control of the backup UAV and began the circuitous flight back to the arcade room.

In the meantime, Xander caught sight of the Ninja just as it blasted the Panther into the recycle bin. Now, it was his turn to send a burst of .5mm lead into the huge drone, striking against the rear buffer plate that protected the flight controller. The enemy UAV bounced forward from the impact and crashed into a bank of smaller video games. It recovered quickly, managing to do a complete three-sixty loop in the confined space of the arcade. The maneuver was incredible since drones normally had trouble making vertical loops, even when outside and with plenty of space.

This pilot was good.

Xander was caught off guard by the flip and now found himself ahead of the Ninja with his ass exposed. In the blink of an eye, he took several heavy hits, losing one of his eight props in the process. He could still operate, although at a slightly reduced speed, and he had to compensate for the skewed balance of the wounded drone.

The Viper zipped off at near floor level, dodging around rows of video games that all seemed to explode the moment he passed by. The Ninja was bleeding pencil-missiles at a prodigious rate, and so far, the Viper survived. Once the grinning UAV ran out of missiles, Xander would have the advantage.

But then the Ninja pilot led the speeding target just enough so that the blast and debris from an exploding arcade machine rained down on Xander's drone. For a moment, the Viper was pinned under a pile of metal and plastic, having to scoot along the floor to work its way out.

The Ninja zoomed up to his left, turning its guns on the helpless Viper. There was just a moment's hesitation before it fired … which was just long enough for Charlie Fox to lay a barrage of machine gun fire into the Ninja's right side. When the enemy drone eventually fired on the Viper, its aim was off slightly as a result of Fox's gunfire, sparing Xander's RDC defender. But then the huge enemy drone spun away and, in a flash, was back on Charlie's tail, lighting off the last of its pencil-missiles in his direction.

As before, the lighter-armored Panther broke up and crashed into the ticket redemption case, sending a geyser of glass shards and cheap plastic souvenirs erupting into the air.

What followed after that was a wild chase between the two major RPA's that began in the arcade arena before ripping through the restaurant and out into the main pedestrian corridors of the Dolphin Mall, with the Ninja leading the way and Xander's Viper close behind. Through swinging movements, the enemy drone managed to avoid the six missiles Xander unleashed in its direction. The missiles exploded into storefronts and freestanding kiosks, sending smoke and debris into the paths of the speeding drones.

Both pilots were top-notch and avoided the obstacles

with precision and finesse, and when the Ninja reached the corridor that cut across the mall to the left and back toward the main entrance, it made a steep banking turn and disappeared around the corner with no decrease in speed. Xander had the mall schematics up on his display; he made a sharp left turn of his own down a narrow side corridor before steering to the right down another. A split second later, he shot out into the main center concourse just as the Ninja passed by.

With no time to react, the two combat drones collided, tumbling to the right and falling to the polished marble floor before slamming into a mall directory display. The thin metal-framed sign shattered, barely impeding the path of the careening UAVs.

Both drones came to a rest, at least until their pilots fingered throttles and attempted to take flight once again. But there was a problem. The complicated maze of extended prop arms and weapons arrays had become entangled; the two drones were locked together.

Xander gunned his Viper and managed to turn the Ninja on its back. In his teens, he had been one of the top combat pilots in the Drone Wars circuit, so he had plenty of experience with what was basically hand-to-hand combat between drones, and turning your enemy on its back was usually a death sentence for your opponent. However, the Ninja was not your ordinary drone, and the pilot's skill was exceptional. The grinning black UAV reversed prop rotation—which was something normal drones weren't capable of doing—and with the incredible power of the Ninja, Xander's Viper was lifted into the air before being flipped on its side.

Both drones once again crashed to the floor.

"This is some bullshit!" Xander declared. "I'm taking this bastard down!"

Xander gunned the remaining seven operating props of the Viper, sending the death-locked pair of drones scraping along the floor of the mall, and then, just before slamming into the closed screen of a Sunglass Factory, he angled the Viper up slightly. With the combined thrust from both drones, the pair lifted into the air. Xander continued to press upwards, even as the Ninja attempted to pull to the right. Soon, they were nearing the soaring, arched roof of the Dolphin Mall above the wide central concourse.

And that was when Xander detonated his own onboard supply of explosives.

Xander jerked his head back from the sudden shock of perspective change as he was once again in the confines of the team room at the RDC; however, it only took a second for him to focus on the large screen on his console and the view being transmitted from David Lane's eye in the sky.

A fiery ball of yellow and black now filled the curved ceiling of the mall. The white structure above broke apart and rained down on the central passageway. Barely visible within the fire, smoke and falling debris were the remains of the two huge combat drones. Both were in pieces.

"Dang, man," Charlie Fox commented. "There goes almost a quarter million dollars in drones."

"So bill me," Xander said softly as he removed his VR goggles and fell back into the pilot's seat.

"I'll do the honors, if you don't mind, boss?" said David Lane, as he maneuvered his small observation drone closer to floor level. He fingered the switch on his controller, giving him access to the mall's P.A. system. "This is the Rapid Defense Center. The mall is now clear of enemy drones, and the threat is over."

Lane's drone was now in the central concourse, hovering about fifty feet from the pile of smoking debris that was Xander's final solution to the Ninja II problem. Xander watched as several dazed civilians crawled from behind the seating barricades; some recovered quickly and began to cry and hug one another—even complete strangers in most cases. Another group of angry-looking customers approached the Eye. David spun the drone around until he faced them.

"Local authorities will take over from here, so please don't leave the mall grounds until statements have been collected. Please obey all further instructions." And then, as an afterthought, the twenty-two-year-old drone pilot added: "And by the way, have a very Merry Christmas."

The jaws of several of the survivors fell open. "Fat chance, buddy!" one of the male customers called out. "You guys need to do more to stop this kind of thing from happening."

Several of the others around him began to protest against his statement, while others joined the man's side of the argument. Within seconds, the group was engaged in a heated debate.

"The cops better get here in a hurry," David said to the team. He then toggled the speaker switch again and addressed the crowd. "Please calm down. The RDC is doing all it can at this time. Rest assured, we are constantly upgrading our equipment and capabilities. This could have been much worse had we not responded as we did. Now, please calm down. Local police are entering the mall at this time."

Another man with a wet mop of long blond hair down past his shoulders stepped up to David's bot and stared into the camera. "Sounds good, man, but can you do me a favor? Can you get them to turn off the damn sprinklers?"

2

Xander rubbed his temples before letting loose with a hearty stretch. "That has to be one of the biggest this month," he said to the other operators at his side. "I count over fifty dead."

David Lane listened in on his ear comm as someone spoke to him. "Sixty-four—so far, only London beats it."

Xander shook his head. "Worldwide, that's over a hundred drone attacks just this month alone."

Charlie Fox placed a hand on Xander's shoulder. "That's called job security, man; what else can I say?"

"That's a sick way to look at it, even if it's true."

"Chill out, dude," Charlie said with a grin. "This came right at the end of our shift. Now, five days off. I'm heading over to San Diego for some surfing. There's a wicked winter swell coming in, and that's your old hometown, Xander. Do you want to come along? Let's go shred some waves together."

"I'd love to, but they're calling me back on Monday to meet with a reporter."

"Damn, how many times can you tell the same story?" David asked.

"I know, but it's part of the job," Xander replied. "One of those PR pieces about how we're protecting the innocent from the terror impacting society these days. And after what just happened in Miami, people are going to be even more paranoid than normal. They actually need to hear this stuff."

"I suppose so," Fox said with a shrug. "And better you than me, buddy!"

At only twenty-two, Fox grew up with the ever-present threat of remote-control terrorism. Even still, Xander, at thirty-two, wondered how the young man could so easily accept—and reject—the threat facing every human being on the planet. At any given moment, it could be Charlie Fox lying dead at the entrance to a shopping mall somewhere, blindsided by an event that no one could predict or prevent. Yet he seemed to go about life without a care, even though he—better than most—knew the true nature of the danger. The most law enforcement could do was *react* to such events and limit the damage while doing very little to prevent them.

Xander checked the clock. From first call to termination of the op, the entire Miami event lasted eight minutes and sixteen seconds. That was about average for a non-explosive event. Fortunately, Miami had an ample supply of rapid-response drone bunkers available to answer the call when the time came. If not, the death toll could have been in the hundreds.

As the senior operator on duty—hell, he was the most senior pilot in the entire Center—he would be credited with another successful operation, even though over sixty people died during the attack. The brass in D.C. had a strange set of algorithms that weighed the number of *potential* victims against the actual casualties, along with the property damage suffered, to determine whether an operation could be deemed a success or not. In Xander's mind, this wasn't a success, but he knew his supervisors would see it differently. The official statement often came down to this: It could have been a lot worse.

Xander cringed at the thought, yet when considering the five-thousand, eight hundred, forty-two people killed so far this year by remote assaults, it *was* a rather low body count, especially with a Ninja involved. And compared to the days before the RDC was created, there was a marked decrease in casualties, even as the number of attacks grew exponentially each year.

These thoughts didn't help how Xander Moore felt at the moment. He knew another psych eval would be called for soon; it was common for pilots of his age. He shook his head; as far as he could recall, neither Fox nor Lane had ever been called in for a follow-up eval, at least not beyond their initial employment screening.

Is the younger generation that jaded and that acclimated to the horror we face every day that it doesn't bother them anymore? Xander asked himself. *Do they really treat their jobs like a video game instead of real life?*

Xander had frank conversations with his government-appointed shrink about this very topic. Dr. Tricia Ainsworth explained how younger people had the unique ability to block out the danger they face by experiencing life in smaller segments, content to act in *episodes* rather than over the long term. It was a contributing factor to why most of them rented rather than owned such things as homes, music, videos, and books. They lived for the moment since, without warning, it could all come to a sudden and tragic end.

In the past, Xander tried to live by that creed but failed on each occasion. He was more of a long-term strategist, which required as a prerequisite the belief that one would live long enough for well-laid plans to be realized. This philosophy helped him accumulate more material goods than most of his counterparts—which they passively envied—yet it also helped to foster an underlying paranoia in him about leaving the house each day. He had too much to lose.

Maybe he felt this paranoia more acutely than the

general public because of his job. After all, he faced the reality of this new and growing brand of terrorism every day. It was his responsibility to fight such evil acts with equal deadly force, so he ate, slept and breathed the nightmare. For the vast majority of the world, the reality of this new phase of human debauchery was simply more headlines and news flashes, and something others experienced … but not them. Even though the danger was real—and they knew it—there was nothing they could do about it personally, so why worry? All they could do was continue living as best they could, content in the knowledge that there were people like Xander Moore out there protecting them. That was all they needed to know; that was all they *wanted* to know.

Yet the public also had to be constantly reminded of this fact; otherwise, they would become restless and demand more security from their leaders. And the politicians knew that if voters felt that their current crop of leaders couldn't provide that *feeling* of security, then maybe the next batch could.

Hence, another interview will be conducted to keep the masses placated.

As the Rapid Defense Center's senior operator—indeed a pioneering member of the drone corps itself—Xander endured these kinds of interviews nearly every month. His identity was protected—that was *the* paramount condition before an interview would be granted—even though he was becoming somewhat of a shadow celebrity to the media personalities who had access to the Center. His bosses preferred Xander to present the government's side of the story rather than some pimple-faced kid barely out of high school. His advanced age—for the profession—added a layer of credibility to the narrative, and his superiors knew it.

Eventually, Xander Moore would become too well-known to remain a pilot. He would then be bumped up to a more visible role within the organization—unless he opted for a new identity and a fresh start. After a particularly bloody op—such as today's—he tended to come down strongly on the side of a fresh start. To remain at the Center, yet without a controller in his hand, would be more than he could take. Even though he resented the fact that his job existed, he nevertheless acknowledged its necessity, which, bottom line, was his biggest gripe.

In the enlightened times of the late 2030s, why people still insisted on killing their fellow man was beyond him—and in such ruthless and savage ways. It seemed that the more technology advanced, the more creative people became with regard to killing their neighbors. Where these technological advances had once been lauded as the saviors of mankind, the naked truth was that many made it easier for sick minds to cause even more carnage. And now the most horrific crimes imaginable could be perpetrated against almost any target from halfway around the world, and with objects that were essentially toys.

Already this year, three attempts had been made on the life of the U.S. president, and the situation was so serious that he rarely ventured out in public anymore. After all, what would stop a radicalized activist located somewhere within the Islamic State from toggling a control knob, sending a suicide drone crashing into the President's podium during a speech at the annual White House Easter Egg Hunt? The answer was nothing. Nothing could prevent such an attack; all that could be done was narrow the time required to respond so the damage could be controlled.

The former president of Uganda had recently experienced such an attack, yet without the backup that an agency like the RDC offered. Even though the initial assassination attempt failed, the RPA attack drone then spent over twenty minutes methodically stalking the President throughout his palatial compound before eventually locating him in an upstairs closet. If there had been an RDC-type response to the attack, he might be alive today.

Nearly every month, a world leader was attacked in such a manner, with the fatality rate climbing rapidly as more sophisticated attack drones were built and deployed. Now, one in three leaders targeted by drones could expect to die in such an attack. First World countries, such as the United States, Britain and most of Europe, lowered those odds considerably. Yet that only meant attacks on leaders of less-developed nations succeeded in nearly every case. And these assassinations could be carried out notoriously and in plain sight, without fear of reprisal.

In the United States, that couldn't happen anymore, not with the Rapid Defense Center in operation. The average domestic terrorist attack now lasted less than eight minutes, sometimes longer if fleeing drones had to be pursued into the open.

The Center grew out of the unfortunate necessity to counter such threats. Although other governmental agencies still sought to *prevent* such attacks from happening, the RDC was there when they couldn't. And without the Center, once an attack began, the perpetrators would often have all the time in the world—or at least until the batteries ran dry—to wreak as much havoc on the crowd, facility or site as possible. Although he couldn't prevent the attacks, Xander Moore could *limit* the scope of the damage while saving untold innocent lives in the process.

It was this facet of his job that kept him coming back day after day. He felt like he actually made a difference. Whether or not he would feel that way in another position with the Center, he very much doubted. At least with a controller in his hand, he could stop others from dying. Serving as a mouthpiece for the Center wouldn't bring as much job satisfaction.

Yes, the need was great, and even as Xander and his team prepared to leave the Team Room, four other events were being reported and responded to across the country.

The twenty-two hundred pilots and scanners making up the teams at the RDC would be busy this holiday season. How this fact would impact their own personal celebrations depended on the personalities and, frankly, the callousness of the individuals involved.

3

The head of the Rapid Defense Center was an Air Force colonel named Jamie Simms. He met the team in the debriefing room, and after an hour-long session—eight times longer than the actual event—he let Fox and Lane go while asking Xander to remain.

"A hundred-thousand-dollar drone," Jamie stated with a smirk. "You're lucky our budget is the largest under the Homeland Security banner.

"Taxpayer money well spent, in my opinion," Xander replied, matching the smile.

"No argument there, it's just that I'm going to have to do some fancy footwork to pacify the bean counters in D.C. They've never been in drone combat before to know that sometimes you gotta do what you gotta do."

Xander shook his head. "A Ninja ... that was unexpected."

"You know, you're only the third pilot to go up against one and the first to come out the winner."

"Not sure if committing suicide counts as winning," Xander moaned.

"That drone still had hours of operating time left. It could have been a lot worse." Jamie Simms smiled broadly. "Now, on a more pleasant note...." He slid a manila folder over in front of Xander. "Feel free to keep the headshots. For the bikini photos, you'll have to go online."

Xander flipped open the file. "No shit? I've seen her before."

"Yeah, she's the type who, once you see her, you never forget."

The reporter Xander was scheduled to meet with the following day was someone new to the pool. Most of the regular reporters covering the RDC were known to him, but this was a first for this one. She was a hottie from Fox News named Tiffany Collins, and as was the case with most of the female talent on the network, she had been a beauty contest winner—either Miss USA, Miss Universe or Miss *You-Gotta-Be-Kidding-Me*—something like that; however she was also extremely talented and good at what she did, from what Xander could tell. He'd seen her dozens of times throughout the years on TV, and now, leafing through her file, he had to admit he was rather anxious to meet her in person.

"Don't let the pretty face and golden locks cause you to reveal any state secrets, buddy," Jamie said. "Although to a stud like you, she probably wouldn't even rank over a six or seven on the Moore Hotness Scale."

"You give me too much credit. I'm just a nerd with a high-paying job." He looked at the professional portrait of the broadcast reporter again. "But, with a few days off, I might be willing to go slumming."

"Off limits, Mr. Moore, and you know it. Save thoughts like that for some of your other conquests. Speaking of that, you still seeing that hot Asian blackjack dealer?"

"That's ancient history, Colonel. Although she did have great hands, she was asking all the wrong questions."

Simms stood from the conference table. "Sorry your deflation time is being broken up, but you know how important the PR game is these days. I'll see you back here bright and early Monday morning."

"Yes, sir, Colonel, sir."

4

The normal rotation for drone pilots at the RDC was ten days on and five off, with the teams staying in two-person rooms in buildings Four and Five of the six-building complex while on duty. With his seniority, Xander earned a private room, which wasn't much more than a ten-by-eight-foot box with a fold-up bunk, a desk, a media center and a hotel-size refrigerator. There were two huge mess halls in the buildings, along with a movie theater, a gym, a library and a TV room—all the comforts of home when you weren't chasing killer drones across a crowded football stadium or away from a fallen freeway overpass.

Since the Center paid very well—especially its civilian contractors—people like Charlie Fox could afford to take mini-vacations to nearly anywhere in the world during their time off. So, within fifteen minutes of being released, Fox and Lane were out the door and lined up for the next bus heading back into Las Vegas. Xander caught the third one after that.

The RDC complex was located in an isolated valley at the east end of Nellis Air Force Base, at the base of the craggy Sunrise Mountain. It was comprised of six structures: three five-story buildings housing Operations, Flight Systems and Communications, plus two employee apartment buildings, along with a three-story Research and Development facility. All the structures were connected by wide, low-profile canopies, ostensibly to protect workers from the brutal desert sun, but in reality, it was to keep them from being observed from space as they moved between the buildings.

The dirty little secret of the RDC was that what was above ground was just the tip of the iceberg. Two-thirds of the Center existed below the buildings, with some substructures extending down eight levels, such as was the case with the Research and Development building. R&D also had access to a mile-long underground runway tunnel that cut south under the mountain and exited at what appeared to be an abandoned mining operation. Here, fleets of top-secret UAV prototypes entered and exited the base without being readily observed, even though many were now the basis of dozens of UFO sightings in the area and had been for years.

There were three roads leading to the Center, which were used only by visitors and the small fleet of converted buses that shuttled the employees to and from the facility. With the highly classified nature of the work, as well as the documented intent of vindictive terrorists to rid the world of as many skilled RDC pilots and operators as possible, all employees were required to take the bus system to and from the Center. The routes changed constantly, with many of the buses traveling empty to serve as decoys.

Yet all trails began and ended at the Las Vegas Strip. Here, the buses would disappear into the massive parking structures under six of the largest casinos until they arrived at secure areas shielded from the rest of the tourists and casino workers. RDC employees were then processed through checkpoints before being allowed to blend casually with the thousands of tourists crowding the casinos every day. Casino ownership cooperated with the government, allowing the bus system to operate within their properties in exchange for licensing concessions and tax breaks, and as a result, the employees of the Center could come and go virtually undetected amidst the hordes of tourists crowding the Strip twenty-four-seven.

Once in the vast parking complex of the *Bellagio*, Xander drove his Jeep Wrangler out onto Las Vegas Boulevard and immediately donned dark sunglasses against the bright Nevada sunshine for the thirty-minute drive to the Anthem section of southwestern Henderson. He owned a sprawling thirty-two-hundred square-foot, single-level home overlooking the golf course and with a fantastic view of the Vegas skyline to the north. He bought the property five years before, just after joining the Center and at the start of the Second Depression, so he got it for a song. Although the Depression was short-lived, the deal he got on the home would last forever.

More than most, Xander enjoyed his days off. He had been playing video games and flying drones longer than most of his co-workers, and it was beginning to wear on him. The majority of the other pilots at the Center were between eighteen and twenty-five and so hooked on gaming that when they weren't doing it at work, they were at home sitting in front of a monitor. The last thing Xander wanted to do during his time off was work a controller. He felt sorry for this generation of Gen Whatever's, and if the Exceptional Skills Bill passed Congress, mindless gaming would be institutionalized and rewarded.

The Center was in desperate need of more pilots and scanner operators, and not just anyone, but only the most skilled at war games and combat drone strategies. Unfortunately, many of the top candidates for these positions were kids, those aged twelve to seventeen. The Exceptional Skills Bill would open up employment opportunities to youngsters fourteen and older to join the Center. Schooling would be provided part-time on-site, with the remainder of the day utilizing the phenomenal talents of these young operators.

Thinking about this, Xander felt a twinge of regret for the lost youth of these new recruits if the bill passed, and yet he'd also seen first-hand the results from the test groups run through the Center. These kids were good, and they could save a lot of lives, even if they did go about the task of fighting *real* terrorists with the same detachment and complacency as someone playing a video game. The surprising thing, however, was that the psych tests also showed these kids suffered no lasting effects from their participation in live-fire operations; they were already so desensitized to the games that they couldn't tell the difference between reality and make-believe. And with the current nature of warfare, these kids may never come face-to-face with the real world they were entering when the FPV goggles went on.

Yet the saddest thing, in Xander's opinion, was that the people running the Center—and others like it—didn't care. These talented children were simply assets to them, assets that begged to be used in the never-ending war against modern terrorism. The kids would also come to the Center already trained to an eighty-percent proficiency level, which saved the government both time and money. With all the support within the establishment for passage of the Bill, Xander was sure the legislation would become law.

How he would cope with managing a bunch of immature, inexperienced and emotional teenagers was something Xander chose not to dwell on. The benefits may indeed outweigh the consequences, so he would wait and see how it went, which was all anyone could do at this point.

And so Xander Moore left his other life behind—at least temporarily—and did his best to pretend he was just a normal guy, living in a normal neighborhood and with normal dreams. Few would ever know the truth....

Xander changed into a bathing suit and then, without hesitation, jumped headfirst into the deep end of his swimming pool. At first blush, the water was refreshingly cold, a by-product of the incongruity of winter in the desert. The outside air temperature was a very brisk forty-three degrees, and even with the pool heater set on low, the water still registered a crisp sixty-five degrees. It cast off a light cover of fog as his passage stirred the surface.

He had five days off—except for Monday's half day for the interview. As he rolled over onto his back and floated effortlessly in the crystal-clear water, Xander began to run through the list of female companions he could call upon to help take his mind off the job.

There was no shortage of extremely attractive women in the Las Vegas area, and Xander Moore was a favorite among those he met. At just over six feet tall, with curly blond hair and a well-groomed goatee, he looked more like a well-aging former surfer—which he was—rather than a highly skilled drone pilot fighting terrorist activities on a daily basis.

According to his cover story, he had a high-paying job in IT consulting, which required him to travel frequently. His female friends could count on him to show them a good time when he was in town, but they also knew he was not the kind to commit. Most accepted this fact and enjoyed the moment. The few who didn't were discarded, not out of some cruel aspect of his personality, but from the necessity to shield his profession.

In the early days of the drone program, when the emphasis was on ISR activities—intelligence, surveillance and reconnaissance—pilots could exist in the open more than they could today. Now, with the proliferation of mini-drones, every RDC operator was the proclaimed target of a variety of harmed groups, be they foreign or domestic. And it wasn't that taking out the occasional drone pilot would make a difference. It would, however, give the killers bragging rights while also serving to deter some skilled gamers from joining the Center.

And so the need for his secret identity.

His term as a pilot at the Center would probably last another five years at the most before he would be either bumped up or booted out. At that time, he would be in his late thirties and with plenty of time still left to think about settling down.

However, until that time, he had to keep secret the fact that he played video games for a living … real-life video games with real-life body counts.

5

Molly Snow—her real name—was the lucky lady Xander called up that evening for dinner, a movie and as much intimate play as they could both handle. Fortunately, the interview at the Center wasn't until one pm, Monday afternoon; even still, it was an ordeal dragging his body out of bed that morning.

He parked in the underground garage of Caesar's Palace this time before walking next door and down into the bowels of the Venetian. After passing by several screeners and through four secure entrances, Xander boarded the plush motorhome bus for the thirty-minute ride to the Center. This was an off-time for the shift changes, so only two other people were on the bus. Even though Xander knew them both, after a friendly acknowledgment, none entered into conversation. It was how it was done at the Center. Except for the teams, most others kept to themselves, choosing to remain anonymous and unconnected, separating their private lives from their professional personas.

In fact, except for an occasional surfing junket with Charlie Fox, Xander didn't associate with any of his co-workers. Over the years, Xander had come in contact with some of the employees at the infamous Area 51 military installation at Groom Lake, located not too far from the Center, and he knew the same held true for them. It was just better that way.

With a budget no one complained about—not in light of the horrific damage caused by domestic terrorist attacks—the five-year-old complex was a study in modern architecture, and visitors to the RDC, including politicians and contractors, arrived in limos leased by the government in a process designed to impress. Gone from the drone program were the dimly lit, drab trailers that once dotted nearby Creech Air Force Base and served as the control rooms for the two-man Predator pilot teams. Those facilities had been shuttered several years ago, and the program's mission was absorbed into the more all-encompassing Rapid Defense Center. Pilots now enjoyed the best the government could afford at its most visible—and frankly—most-needed national defense facility.

Colonel Simms met Xander in the corridor leading to the conference room located in the Operations Building.

"You lucky bastard," he greeted.

"That good, huh?"

"Hell, I thought she was a knockout on TV. In person … well, damn."

"Watch it, Jamie, you're a married man," Xander said with a smile.

"Which qualifies me to make such a definitive statement." Simms then turned to him with a sly smile. "So, how was your time off, stud?"

Xander frowned. "Have you been spying on me again?"

"Always," Jamie said, his eyes displaying a sinister sparkle. "It's for your own protection, my friend."

"That's what they all say."

The two men stopped at the door to the conference room. "Good luck in there. And remember, don't reveal any state secrets."

Xander looked up at the tiny camera lens pointed down at them from the ceiling opposite the doorway. "With Big Brother watching and listening, I wouldn't dream of it."

As he entered the conference room, the smell of perfume was the first impression Xander Moore had of Tiffany Collins. This was something one never experienced watching a person on TV, and this particular fragrance was simply intoxicating. It seemed that a chemist in a cosmetics lab somewhere had finally discovered the Holy Grail of fragrances, and even if Collins wasn't absolutely drop-dead gorgeous, her perfume would have convinced Xander otherwise.

Instead, he was hit with a double-whammy: a near-narcotic perfume scent, along with the sight of the most beautiful woman he'd ever seen in person. Tiffany Collins stood near the end of the conference table, a slight smile painted on her full lips as she studied him with laughing eyes. Measuring five-foot-eight—in stiletto heels—her silky blonde waves reached down to mid-back, with an explosion of yellow hair framing with perfection her tanned, balanced face and high cheekbones. Impossibly blue eyes, along with blindly-white teeth in perfect alignment, rounded out the experience.

She extended a delicate, tanned hand with exquisitely manicured nails sporting French tips.

Xander was no slouch in the looks department, but even he had to work hard not to gasp while in the presence of Tiffany Collins. He fought to keep a neutral demeanor, although he suspected from her humorous eyes that the woman saw right through his façade of indifference. Mentally, he gave her a pass. She was beautiful, and she knew others knew it, as well. In a flash, a strange feeling of respect filled his mind. Based solely on her looks, Tiffany Collins could have done anything she wanted in life—or nothing at all. But instead of taking the easy path through marriage to some aging billionaire, she chose the thankless job of a broadcast journalist, one that would set her up for ridicule by a majority who would consider her just another dumb blonde, an airhead hired only for her looks.

However, her resume told a different story. Sure, she participated in beauty contests, but mainly as a way to finance her higher education. She graduated from Columbia University with a master's in Broadcast Communications, along with a minor in International Affairs. So Tiffany Collins had both beauty and brains if anyone would notice the latter.

"Ms. Collins, very nice to meet you—in person—I've been a big fan of yours on Fox for years."

They shook hands—the strong, firm grip of someone with immense confidence. "So, here's the three-dimensional me standing before you, rather than the two-dimensional image you see on TV. Now all my imperfections become obvious."

"That would take someone with better eyesight than I have, and even then, good luck with that."

"You're too kind … Mr. Doe. Is that what I'm supposed to call you?"

"Smith will do just fine."

They sat down at the table; she was at the head, while Xander sat in the seat next to her on the left. At this distance, her perfume was evident, yet not overpowering. He made a mental note to save a container of air from the room after she was gone, just as a reminder….

Or he could take a more direct approach.

"Forgive me, Ms. Collins, but what is that perfume

you're wearing? I'm sure in most countries, it would be considered a narcotic."

Her laugh was genuine and unforgiving. "It's a special find I made in Italy a few years back, very rare and very exclusive. I could tell you what it's called, but then I'd have to kill you. Kind of like the conversation we're about to have."

"*I* wouldn't kill you, Ms. Collins," Xander said, meeting her bright eyes with a steady gaze of his own. "But I would have someone else do it for me."

"Please, if you don't start calling me Tiffany, I may have to kill myself … myself." She took a notepad from the pocket of her stylish blue pantsuit. "Simple pen and paper," the reporter said. "The basic tools of the trade before technology took over and made it more complicated, which, if I'm not mistaken, is what this interview is all about. The technology being employed today by terrorists is some of the most basic we have. They're essentially using toys to kill thousands of innocent people around the world each year."

Tiffany began to take notes, her flirtatious nature gone. She was a professional now, and the subject she was covering was of extreme importance. "Drones—and radio-controlled cars—have been around for a long time," she continued, "So, why do you think there's been this sudden surge in their use by terrorists and other radicals?"

"They're easy to obtain, they're cheap, and they're anonymous in most cases," Xander began. "Gone are the days of the suicide bomber. Today, we have the suicide robot. It allows for more frequent attacks and a much higher survival rate for the perpetrators."

"Do you believe they're simply following the lead of the US military with respect to the use of drones, such as the Predator and Night Hawk?"

"Without a doubt, although our drone attacks are not the reason they've begun to employ these tactics. The use of UAVs—Unmanned Aerial Vehicles—and RC vehicles has simply expanded their reach and opportunities."

"And yet we set the precedence for their use—"

"I don't accept that," Xander answered. He knew she was baiting him, but some comments couldn't go unchallenged. "The initial use of drones, by Obama and Bush Two—and even before that, with Clinton and cruise missiles—was primarily against known terrorists and aimed solely at them. Sure, occasionally, there was some collateral damage, and we suffered mightily for that. Yet the actions taken by terrorists these days are designed exclusively to cause panic within the civilian population through seemingly random acts of violence and to exact costly damage to our cities and infrastructure. The drone strike last year on the Hoover Dam was a perfect example of this. Granted, it was a rookie attempt, and no real damage was done, yet it still shows how indiscriminate our enemies can be and what lengths they're willing to go in their fight against America and our allies. The difference between them and us is that we target only the guilty, while they target everyone."

Xander noticed the slight up curling of Tiffany's lips as she looked down at her notepad. *You little minx*, he thought. *You're playing me just to get a reaction.*

She looked up and caught his accusatory eye. A flash of embarrassment crossed her face. "If I recall, didn't this latest surge in drone attacks actually begin as something not even terrorist-related?"

Xander welcomed the change of topic. "You're right. It was the robbery of the First National Bank of New York nine years ago."

"Tell me about that. The Rapid Defense Center wasn't even around at that time, was it?"

"That would come two years later, but the robbery started it all. A small RC—remote-controlled—car drove into the lobby of the bank."

"It had a bomb on it, didn't it?"

"That's right. Three sticks of dynamite, linked to a cellphone detonator. A second tiny drone stationed itself near the ceiling so the operator could watch the bank below. He then announced his intention to rob the bank and told all who could hear to place money in a container on a second RC vehicle that had entered the bank. Failure to act would result in the bomb being set off."

Xander could tell from the reporter's expression that she already knew how the story ended. Even so, she expected him to finish the narrative. "As you know, the people in the bank didn't take the robber seriously. The guards closed in, and that's when the robber or robbers—they were never caught, you know—detonated the bomb. Ten people died."

Tiffany waited patiently for him to finish the story. "A week later, another RC car entered a bank in Chicago, but this time it left with over one million dollars. The car took the container of cash around the corner to a waiting drone that lifted the money away, never to be seen again."

"And then the copycats came out," Tiffany prompted.

"Hundreds of them, many with nothing more than fake bombs and lousy pilots, but still, the precedent was set, and everyone was terrified. Guards were placed outside of buildings with orders to shoot any approaching RC car or drone."

"That's when a Fox drone was shot down in Boston," Tiffany said.

"That … along with the Greensboro incident."

"Please explain."

"That's when two guards opened fire on an approaching RC car, setting off the bomb it carried," Xander explained. "It was on a crowded sidewalk next to a traffic-clogged highway. Three people died from the explosion, and the guards were crucified for their actions."

"It could have been worse."

"That's not how the media and civic leaders saw it. They blamed the guards for reckless endangerment, and they're still rotting away in prison simply for doing their job."

"Maybe they should have let them have the money?"

"That was a problem in those days," Xander said, shaking his head. "There were just as many terror attacks as there were robberies. No one knew if anything would placate the attackers. The terrorists saw the devastation caused by the first bank explosion and thought it was something right up their alley. They began to place RPAs—remotely-controlled aircraft—in crowded malls—"

"Just like in Miami on Saturday," Tiffany interrupted. "Were you involved in that?"

"Can't say, Ms. Collins—that's classified—but as I was saying, the terrorists would strike at anything, as long as it was big enough and could get the most headlines. You couldn't negotiate with them, and no money was asked for in most cases. They simply wanted to kill. And kill they did. Before the Center was established to counter these attacks, there were nine thousand—I repeat—*nine thousand* Americans killed in one year alone. That's three times the number of people killed on 9/11 and more than died in the Iraq, Afghan and Ukraine wars combined. Because of our efforts here—and by others around the world—that number is down to just over five thousand in the latest twelve months, and that's worldwide."

"So let's talk about that, Mr. Smith." Her face remained serious, even using the obvious pseudonym. "With such a proliferation of attacks taking place, something had to be done. How exactly does the Center defend against such attacks?"

"Unfortunately, we can do very little to *prevent* attacks. That responsibility lies with other agencies within the government. The Center comes into play once an event is underway. As you know, just about every major building, monument, sports venue and mall now has its own defensive drone fleet. In addition to this, in communities across the nation—and soon to be around the world—the RDC has bunkers set up with fleets of the most advanced ground and air units, all remotely controlled from here. The moment we get a notification that an event is underway, our teams go into action and activate the closest rapid response units or civilian drones."

"Even the privately owned security drones?"

"That's right. Quite honestly, we have the best remote pilots in the world, and our civilian counterparts acknowledge this. They're more than willing to let us take the lead during an attack. We can deploy within seconds of a call and with state-of-the-art weaponry and equipment. We do our best to limit the damage caused by the attacks."

"And just how big is the Center?"

Xander knew his job was to provide just enough information to give the population a feeling of security. He had been through this before, and most of the information was available online. But still, the reporter insisted on asking.

"I can't be specific, but we are much larger than the military foreign drone program."

"Because of the need?"

"Mainly because of the scope of our operations. You have to understand we cover the entire United States and our territories, with literally hundreds of rapid-response bunkers ready to respond at a moment's notice. Also, the devices within these bunkers have to be maintained and tested constantly to assure their readiness when called upon. And then we need operators—pilots. In the past, we've had as many as ten simultaneous events taking place. That requires trained pilots and sensor-operators to cover all the shifts and be ready to react when needed."

"And all out of here?"

"We are the main center, Tiffany, yet rest assured, as it is with most government agencies, there are backups to the backups."

"As I mentioned before," the reporter continued, "drones have been around for a long time, but now they've been regulated so much that everyone assumes that a drone in the air is up to no good. There have been protests by hobbyists and others against these restrictions. What do you say to these people?"

"Hey, for a long time, I was one of those people. I got my first drone when I was eight. Then I began to build them. At that time, there were so many kits available, and in fact, you could buy a drone for less than twenty dollars back then."

"But they weren't the sophisticated UAVs we have today."

"Some were. Depending on how much you could spend, you could get units capable of being easily converted into killers."

"But there were—are—safety features in them."

Xander's smile was more of a smirk. "It's like everything else, Tiffany; the regulations are designed to keep law-abiding citizens from violating the rules. Criminals don't care about laws—that's why they're criminals. Sure, there are safeguards programmed into the flight controllers, but like any computer program, there are ways around it."

"The killboxes?"

"Exactly. I see you've done your homework. If someone has the money and the access, they can acquire a killbox, and in less than a minute, all safeguards are voided. But even more, the internals within the killbox allow for standardized reprogramming that can make even the mid-range drone into a killer."

"Please explain."

Xander hesitated. He knew all this information was available in the clear, but he was an official spokesperson for the government, so he couldn't make the situation appear too dire. His job was to comfort the public, not make them even more paranoid than they already were.

Tiffany sensed his trepidation. "My report will be screened through your security people, Mr. Smith. I'd just like to know … for background."

"Please use discretion, Ms. Collins. After what

happened in Miami, we don't want to do anything that will impact the Holiday shopping season more than it already has."

"I understand; please continue."

Xander nodded. "As you know, drones are controlled through radio frequencies, and in the early days, it was possible to jam these signals without too much difficulty, even though it was illegal for civilians to do so."

"Why was that?"

"Because drones operate on the same frequencies as Wi-Fi, cellphones and even 9-1-1 calls, so if a person built an illegal jamming device, they could disrupt the entire grid. In the case of civil emergencies, the government would take such drastic measures. But then technology changed, and the killboxes have allowed a whole array of additional operations to be programmed into the flight controllers, which are prohibited in most civilian drones, including the use of the misnamed Random Frequency Generators."

"Misnamed?"

"That's right because there's really nothing random about these units. An RFG is a matching set of *pre*-determined radio frequencies unique to a particular pair of drone-and-controller that are constantly changing. This makes it impossible to jam the drones unless you overload every known frequency."

"So there's no way to stop them?"

"Short of shooting them out of the air, there's not

many. A few years ago, they tried using focused electromagnetic pulses, but that only works outside and on unshielded commercial drones, not combat-rated UAVs. Some facilities have used drone nets, either shot from guns or dropped from the ceiling."

"I saw where one of these nets actually caused more harm than good."

"That's right. Malls began using them right at the outset of the crisis, but a net can catch innocent shoppers as well as knock a drone out of the air. Now, modern combat drones can cut through the netting and have a ready-made killing field of trapped civilians nearby. Or they could simply detonate an onboard bomb, killing every person within range who couldn't get away."

"Aren't killboxes used mainly in the automatic drones?"

"*Autonomous* drones, Tiffany. RFG and advanced satellite disruption are things we're always working on, but they only apply to controlled units. These days, a vast majority of attacks are carried out using autonomous drones, which are programmed with a predetermined route and then sent off to accomplish their missions without outside influence. There's no signal to jam, and since this class of drone is cheaper to purchase and operate, they're the weapon of choice these days for terrorists. The killboxes allow for the installation of sense-and-avoid equipment, which allows a unit to scan its surroundings and avoid obstacles. This allows auto-units to operate within buildings and far beyond the range of any pilot-controlled drone."

"Yet the one inherent limitation with drone warfare is battery life, isn't that right?"

"That's another thing that technology has improved upon. Even ten years ago, the most you could expect to get was twenty minutes to a half-hour of flight time. Now, with lightweight and long-lasting fuel cells, your average off-the-shelf UAV can run for a couple of hours, maybe longer. And let's face it, if any attack goes beyond half an hour or so, the effects will be exponentially worse."

"Won't they run out of ammo long before that ... or just explode?"

"There's not much that can be done to stop the suicide drone designed simply to appear on site and explode. For the others, there's a whole catalog of UAV-compatible armament available, from lightweight nylon and composite cartridges to miniature missiles and even lasers. And since most drone attacks take place at point-blank range, there's no need for a lot of range or penetrating power, so a decent-size combat drone can carry enough armament to last for a while, depending on how plentiful the targets are.

"That's the reason the RDC has become so important. Without some countering force showing up on site, these killer drones could just leisurely pick off targets as they're located. I know the death tolls always look high in most drone attacks—even to me—yet without us there to shut down an event, the numbers would be far worse."

"Thank you for sharing that with me, Mr. Smith. Now, I'd like to spend a few minutes talking about the operators—the pilots, as you call them. Are you really pilots?"

It was Xander's turn to smile. "That's what we're called. I can be honest with you and say I don't hold a pilot's license for traditional aircraft; however, I'm pretty good with a controller in my hand."

Their eyes locked for a moment. "I'm sure you are, Mr. Smith."

The moment passed, and she continued. "What about burnout and other psychological factors with your pilots? I know that was an ongoing problem with the military drone pilots."

"We don't have that problem here."

"Why not?"

"Because our mission is completely different. The operation you're referencing is actually the outdated foreign strike program. Those units have been retired. We now use the smaller UAVs."

"So what makes your mission so different?"

"Simple: We're completely defensive in nature. On background, Tiffany, the problem they had with the initial drone program came from the attachment the operators sometimes developed for their targets. They would often spend weeks surveilling a hostile before getting the order to take them out. They weren't given a reason, just the order. It's one thing to be in a firefight against an enemy across the street shooting back at you. You'll kill without remorse, justifying it as self-defense. Most of the PTSD live combat troops suffer as a result of the *fear* associated with such fighting, not from the act of killing itself. With the drone program, the issue became the killing. There was no direct feeling of self-defense or personal danger in these cases, and most moral and compassionate people have a problem with simply following orders to execute a person—any person."

"But the targets were enemy combatants."

"Or so they were portrayed. The pilots and sensors had a problem accepting that assertion, and so there was a lot of turnover in personnel in the early days of the program, as I'm told."

"But here at the RDC, you don't have that problem?"

"Not at all, since we *react* to an attack already taking place. It's our job to *stop* the event in its tracks by killing—if you will—inanimate objects. Our job saves lives; we don't take them. It's a completely different mindset, based on the mission, and our people take immense pride in what they do."

"And yet you stay secret, unnamed and hidden away."

Xander smiled again. "We're not looking for medals or ticker-tape parades, Tiffany. We stay anonymous because the enemy realizes our value. In all honesty, you can have thousands of advanced UAVs at your disposal, yet without skilled pilots and operators, they're just useless pieces of plastic and composite."

"Which brings us to the Exceptional Skills Bill; you know there's a lot of opposition to its passage—"

The door to the conference room suddenly burst open, and a grave-looking Colonel Jamie Simms stepped in, followed by an Air Force tech sergeant.

"Sorry to interrupt, but this interview is over," Simms announced in a voice that left no room for discussion. "The sergeant will escort Ms. Collins to a safe room until arrangements can be made for her departure."

"What's going on?" Tiffany asked. Her face was flush with anger. "Was it something I said or asked?"

"No, it's nothing like that—"

Just then, an alarm began to sound throughout the Center. Xander had never heard this particular alarm before. It was different from the normal drills that were run periodically.

"What *is* going on, Jamie?" Xander didn't care if Collins heard or not. He was a GS worker and not in the military, and this was totally out of the ordinary.

Simms looked at both their faces, seeing the matching concern. "This will be hard to keep secret as it is, so what the hell. The base is under attack, Ms. Collins, so it's important that you go with the sergeant until the crisis is over. Xander, you're back on duty."

"Who's doing the attacking?" Tiffany asked.

"The bad guys," Simms responded. "Now, please, no

more questions. Just go with the sergeant so Xander and I can get to work."

Tiffany looked at Xander. *"Xander,* your name is Xander?"

"Talk to my mother about that. Now get going, please."

6

Once the reporter was out of the room, Xander turned to Simms. "Are we really under attack?"

"That's a big-ass affirmative. A whole fleet of quads and octs have breached the outer perimeter east of the Center and are headed this way; somewhere over a couple of hundred of them, and they're swarming. According to the security images, they're Lightning Zee-Fours and Eights, equipped with full strike packages."

"How did they get past the countermeasures?"

"That I don't know, not yet."

The pair left the conference room and headed north toward the tactical section. They were in Building One, which housed the admin and command offices for the RDC, and all the corridors were full of determined men and women rushing about with concern on their faces.

This was not supposed to happen—not here—and they knew it.

Xander and Simms entered the main tactical command room for the Center, a huge chamber resembling a college lecture hall with rows of observation stations set high to the back of the room and a series of flight control stations on the main floor below. In reality, very few operations were run out of the room; it was used mainly to monitor the activities of the ninety individual combat stations located in Building Three.

Yet today, most of the stations were occupied, with over twenty pilots and operators just now lighting up their consoles. Xander took a seat at a vacant pilot station. To his left and right were a wingman and a scanner operator. Simms stood behind him, watching the screens as they came to life.

"How many bunkers have activated?" Xander asked.

Las Vegas had more than its fair share of rapid-response bunkers, not only because of its proximity to the Center but also because of the massive number of tourists who frequented the city each year, making it an ideal target for terrorists.

When no one answered, Xander looked to the scanner, a young Hispanic woman named Lydia Garcia. She was frowning deeply at the information on her screen.

"Report, Lydia," Xander ordered.

"I'm sorry, Mr. Moore, but I can't detect a single activation."

Xander's mouth fell open while Colonel Simms raced to a phone at one of the observation stations behind the control consoles. He began to yell into the receiver.

"That's impossible," Xander said to Garcia. "Maybe it's a communications problem—"

"That's not it," Simms said, still cradling the phone on his shoulder. "All of the Las Vegas and Henderson bunkers have been hit with drone strikes, apparently simultaneously with an attack on Nellis, too. We've been compromised and to the highest degree."

The noise level in the room rose significantly as officers, pilots and operators began to ask questions and demand answers.

"If the stations are gone, then how do we defend the Center?" Garcia asked. Her voice trembled, and her eyes were moist.

That was the problem with remote warfare, the lack of connection to the battlefield, Xander thought. However, when the battle is in your own backyard, the fear and anxiety associated with real combat suddenly manifests itself. Although Lydia Garcia had participated in literally dozens of *remote* battles, she had never been this close to the real thing, and she wasn't handling it very well.

"Don't worry," Xander said. "There are defensive measures here and at the air base. This is one tough place to penetrate."

Or at least he hoped so. He'd been with the Center

since two years after its inception, yet he wasn't privy to that part of the operation.

Simms replaced the phone in its cradle. "Listen up, everyone! Quiet!" After all eyes turned to the RDC commander, he addressed the room. "All the nearby bunkers are gone, so there'll be no countering force coming from outside. Also, the Nellis flight line is in shambles, so we can't count on them, either. The attacks were coordinated."

"This doesn't make sense, sir," a senior Air Force officer called out. "Drones are not designed to hold territory, especially autos like most of these. So we just hunker down and wait for their batteries to run dry."

"The problem with that strategy, Major, is that these units have an operational life of at least two hours. In that time, they could level every goddamn building in the complex."

"Not the underground facilities," the officer countered. "We need to evacuate everyone below ground."

Simms considered all the eyes looking at him. Ironically, the Rapid Defense Center was not designed to protect itself; instead, it relied on forces from Nellis and the local rapid-response bunkers.

The approaching fleet of heavily armed drones would be upon them in less than five minutes.

"Let's do it," Simms said decisively. "Get everyone down as low as they can go. And no one remains outside."

"Sir!" said a Marine captain. "We have automatic

weapons and a security force of forty-five. I say we take posts outside and blast as many of these fuckers as we can."

Before responding to the Marine, Simms nodded to the Air Force major. Immediately, people began to stream from the room as the major talked on a cellphone. Then Simms focused on the Marine officer. "There are over a hundred UAVs coming this way, Steve, with mid-range missile batteries and the ability to dart around at over sixty miles per hour. You may be able to take out a few of them, but then they'll just saturate your positions with enough firepower to make the outcome a foregone conclusion. These are mindless machines we're dealing with here. There'll be no surrendering, no breaking off the attack at some point, no fear. The drones will keep fighting until the last unit is gone. So, you'd be sacrificing yourself for nothing."

Xander watched as the veins in the Marines' neck pulsed. Simms continued. "Take your men over to Comm. Major Drake is right. The attackers can't hold the ground, but they can take out our communications capability. Without that, we won't have access to any of the remaining RDC facilities across the country."

"Yes, sir!"

The man rushed out of the room.

Xander and his two surrogate team members now headed for the door. "Mr. Moore, a word," Simms said.

The other two operators hesitated for a moment before leaving the room.

"We don't have much time—"

"There's more," Simms said, interrupting.

"More … like in more bad news?"

"Exactly. The security breach goes deeper than simply identifying the location of the RR bunkers in Vegas. There's also been a huge data dump on the internet."

Xander shook his head, not understanding.

"The download contains information about our operations, the locations of the bunkers, as well as our security codes and protocols."

"Holy crap!"

"They've also revealed personal data on all our pilots and operators."

"What do you mean *personal* data?"

"I mean everything: names, addresses, photos, next of kin, even bank account information."

Xander was stunned, even if he didn't have time to react, before Simms grabbed him by the arm and pulled him toward the exit. The attacking drones would be at the complex in less than two minutes, and the pair had to find shelter.

Even though there were several prominent awning-covered walkways connecting the buildings, each of the structures had underground access tunnels as well. Xander and Simms took the first crowded stairwell down to the sublevels of the Administration Building and entered a passageway leading to the communications center next door.

"Where could they have gotten that information?" Xander asked.

"It had to come from here," Simms answered. "It's all on the servers."

"I thought we couldn't be hacked?"

"We can't," Simms answered gravely. "It had to be an inside job."

With a few moments now to digest the impact of this new information, Xander's legs grew weak. As a pilot for the Rapid Defense Center, his identity—along with that of all the others—was some of the most sought-after information terrorists coveted, not only because of the skills the operators possessed but also because of their effectiveness in foiling countless operations initiated by these groups. It was now a matter of principle for the dozens of radical terror groups operating around the world to take out any and all RDC operators they could find.

"All of us?" he asked.

Simms nodded. "I was told on the phone that there are reports of individual homes being hit, as well as the bunkers."

"The pilots?"

"And anyone else who happens to be home at the time."

"But you said the information was just dumped on the internet, and they're already striking at the residences?"

"The info dump was an afterthought," Simms said. "These attacks took months to plan, including the ones on the pilots, so whoever's in charge of this operation has had this information for a while. Now, they're just adding insult to injury."

Simms's comment was punctuated by a massive explosion that rocked the building above them, reverberating for several seconds after the first jolt. Ceiling panels crashed to the floor, covering the occupants of the corridor in a fine white powder. The lights flickered on and off briefly.

"We have to protect the comm links at all costs," Xander said. "You were right. The only way an op like this can be called a success is if they take out our way to communicate with the remaining bunkers. Without the ability to launch and control, our entire inventory is useless."

There was a storm of ear-shattering noise as the fleet of killer drones reached the RDC and unleashed their relentless assault on the facility. With no defense for the buildings, the enemy UAVs wasted no time sending small yet powerful missiles through windows and doors, resulting in catastrophic damage and crumbling structures. In less than three minutes, all six buildings in the complex were nothing more than smoldering piles of concrete, glass and steel.

By now, Xander and Simms knew the external satellite dishes and arrays were also gone, but the guts of the comm center remained intact four stories underground.

The deafening cacophony from above was diminishing; however, that didn't mean the attack was over. Now, the drones would find their way underground.

Xander fell against a wall as one of the blasts from above rocked the building. He righted himself and found Simms bleeding from a head wound caused by a falling power conduit from the ceiling.

"Are you okay?"

"I'll live." Simms wiped the blood from his left eye. "They'll be coming down here next."

"Where are the Marines?"

"They should be directly ahead of us. Let's go!"

The corridor between the buildings was nearly deserted by now and littered with fallen debris from the overhead utility runners. Water pipes had broken, and the concrete floor was slick in some places and gooey in others, as the water mixed with the chalky remains of drywall and acoustic ceiling tiles.

"Colonel, over here!"

Through the dusty haze of the tunnel, Xander made out the first contingent of Marines guarding the entrance to the critical communications equipment for the Center. As the pair ran up to the line of heavily armed men,

Colonel Steve Harkness took a quick look at the blood on Simms's head. "Medic!" he called out.

"I'm all right. Are your men in position?"

"Yes, sir. We've locked down the upper access points. The only way in should be through here."

"Good," Simms said as a Navy corpsman placed a compress on the side of his face and wrapped a gauze bandage around his head to keep it in place. "Can you spare any weapons—"

The heat and concussion from the blast were incredible, and it threw Xander and—along with the entire Marine contingent—out into the connecting tunnel. Smoke filled the passageway, and visibility dropped to nearly zero.

"What the hell was that?" Xander yelled out between coughs.

A voice in the gloom answered him. "One hell of a powerful explosion."

Just then, Xander felt a stiff breeze pass through the tunnel, running from the admin building through to communications. The access way above had been breached, and now air flowed freely between the two buildings. The tunnel cleared of smoke and dust almost instantly.

"They're coming in from above!" a Marine sergeant reported.

Once the haze cleared, Xander assessed the damage caused by the huge explosion. His friend, Jamie Simms, was pressed up against the far wall of the access tunnel, his eyes open, yet with his head bent at an odd angle. Xander rushed to his side and pulled the body away from the wall. His neck was broken; he was dead.

Xander went pale. In all his years of drone combat, this was the first time he'd seen a corpse in person—and it was one of his closest friends. All the sounds of battle around him faded away as he held the inert body in his arms before a pair of strong hands lifted him up. Two bloodied Marines dragged him down the tunnel past the communications building and farther on toward the research and development structure.

As he regained his senses, Xander was able to better navigate the passageway himself. He looked around at the scant number of Marines around him. "Where's the Captain?" he asked.

"He didn't make it. It looks like those drones came equipped with a bunker buster to get into the Communications Building; it took out most of our force with the blast. Our position is indefensible, so we're falling back."

Xander Moore had been around drones since he was eight, yet when he detected the tell-tale sound of angry bees coming up from behind, it struck terror in his chest. This was the quintessential signature of drone warfare, what pilots called *BuzzKill*. Drones were in the tunnel, and they were capable of traveling much faster than the men could run.

Xander was now at the R&D Building, with three wide

access portals leading off to the left. The Marines slid into the first portal and fell into defensive postures. Xander was literally thrown into the wide vestibule. "Take cover!" one of the Marines yelled back at him.

Xander looked around. There was a series of utilitarian couches lining the room along with a circular reception desk where Audrey White and her reliefs would normally have been sitting. Now, the granite desktop was covered with broken debris that had rained down from the ceiling.

Xander ran for the protection of the huge, permanent reception desk. He jumped and slid on the smooth stone surface until he fell off the other side.

He was expecting to hit the hard ceramic tile floor behind the desk; instead, he landed on something that was soft—and it was cursing.

7

"What the hell!" a female voice cried out.

His face was buried in the fabric of a blue pantsuit, and even without looking, he knew from the scent of the perfume that he had landed on the Fox News reporter Tiffany Collins.

He rolled off the woman. Their shocked expressions mirrored one another. "What the hell are you doing here?" Xander asked.

The woman brushed white dust off her ripped and bloodied outfit. "Oh, except for a couple of cracked ribs, I'm fine. Thanks for asking," she said.

Xander leaned against the back wall behind the desk. "I wasn't expecting to land on someone. So sue me."

The swoosh of the missile came a split second later. Reacting instantly, Xander draped himself over the reporter and pressed her flat against the floor. She yelped from the sudden move but was instantly overcome by the explosion that struck the stone edifice directly above them. A shower of debris fell down, including baseball-size pieces of granite. They were nearly buried in the aftermath of the explosion, which was soon followed by three more, just not in such close proximity to their hiding place.

Through the din of battle, Xander heard the frantic bursts of automatic gunfire, along with the grunts and screams of Marines being cut to shreds by missiles and gunfire. The air was also filled with the gut-wrenching sound of whirling propellers whizzing by from all directions.

And then the scene grew quiet as the sound of the buzzing moved farther down the corridor, broken occasionally by sporadic bursts of gunfire or the release of small, solid-propellant missiles, followed by more rumbling explosions.

Xander attempted to move while shedding a pile of rubble from his back. That's when he noticed he was again face-to-face with Tiffany Collins. Gone was the even complexion and perfect hair. The woman was now caked in white dust, and her hair a mass of mangled yellow, infused with a variety of objects that defied identification.

"I think they've moved on," she whispered.

Xander blinked several times before comprehending her words. "Oh yeah, of course." He pulled away, and more debris fell from his back.

Tiffany sat up and fluffed her hair, sending a cloud of

dust into the air around her head, forming a halo effect. Xander smiled at the vision.

"So, we meet again," he said. And then, without waiting for comment, he continued. "What *are* you doing here? What happened to the sergeant?"

"Oh, him? He was taking me to some sort of safe room when the drones attacked. The next thing I knew, he pulled his gun and went running down the corridor, yelling like a banshee, leaving me to fend for myself. After that, everything started falling on me—literally—you included!"

"By the way, thanks for breaking my fall. I could have hurt myself."

"Don't mention it. But what do we do now? Hopefully, you're not going to run off and leave me, too."

"I wouldn't dream of it."

Xander rose to his feet and looked over the reception desk. It was what he expected: a horrific scene of dead Marines and utter devastation where the access tunnel met the R&D building. Tiffany now stood next to him.

"What's going on, Mister Smith …. I mean, Xander? This is some major shit happening here."

He nodded. "No argument there."

"So, who's doing all this?"

"It could be one of a dozen organizations with a grudge against the RDC or even a coalition of them. This took a lot of coordination, money and manpower."

"What do they hope to gain, except bragging rights?"

Tiffany asked. "Taking out one facility doesn't kill the program."

Xander looked at her with a wry smirk.

She noticed his expression. "You told me there were backups to the backups. Was that not true?"

"Unfortunately, we're victims of our own success. But I believe that's a conversation to be saved for later. If you listen carefully, you'll notice that the Buzzkill is growing louder."

"They're coming back! And what's the *BuzzKill?*"

"Later," Xander said. He looked down the nearby corridors. "They're probably prowling for survivors. And one other thing: These units have microphone pickups, so they can hear when you yell like that."

"Screw you!"

"Perhaps another time, Ms. Collins, but right now, we have to get out of the facility. By my estimation, these drones still have over an hour of flight time left."

Tiffany gnashed her teeth. "Fine, smartass, this is your neighborhood; how do we make our exit?"

Xander looked behind him at the main entrance to the R&D underground facilities. There had been several powerful explosions deep within the subterranean labyrinth, yet he held out a glimmer of hope for a plan that was percolating in his mind.

"Follow me … and remain quiet. There may be sentry units sitting idle, just waiting for someone to wander by."

Taking point, Xander led the pair out of the reception area and into the main part of the R&D building—what was left of it. The corridors were wide and the ceilings high, designed to accommodate a fleet of golf cart-like vehicles that frequented the building, transporting huge UAVs and ground units from one section to the other. At the end of this particular corridor was the entrance to the testing labs, where the prototypes were put through their paces. A battle took place here, with the damage mirroring that found throughout the rest of the facility.

There were also bodies, which didn't seem to faze Tiffany Collins. For Xander, that was a plus in her column. *She's probably covered several wars and terrorist strikes during her tenure,* he thought. That would condition a person to the horrors that humanity can inflict upon itself, much better than Xander's first experience with death in the flesh only minutes before.

Unfortunately, the research labs were much like the rest of the base, and Xander's spirit sank when he saw a number of the larger prototypes twisted in shambles throughout the room. He moved to a large steel door set to one side of the testing area. There was evidence of an explosion taking place near the door, and the electronic access panel now dangled from the wall, held only by a few orphan wires.

"Dammit!" he said. "This is just great."

"What's inside?" Tiffany asked.

"This is where they keep all the really neat gizmos. There used to be an advanced hoverbike inside, along with some of the deadlier drones. Even if my access card would still work, the controls are shot to shit." He turned to survey what was left in the large testing area. "There's nothing out here I can use. We're going to have to hoof it. It's only a mile to the other side of the access tunnel."

"Or you could help me open the door. This thing is made of six-inch thick steel, and it weighs a ton."

Confused, Xander turned back to the reporter. She was standing at the left side of the heavy vault door that he could clearly see was open slightly.

"So much for high-tech locking mechanisms," Tiffany remarked with a smile.

"Let's hope the drones didn't get inside first."

The pair struggled against the heavy weight of the door until it began to open more freely. Then, at one point, it was wide enough for Xander to get behind it and put all his weight into the effort, using the jamb for added leverage. The door eventually swung all the way open.

It was dark inside the vast vault room, but after a moment, his eyes adjusted enough that the filtered light from outside allowed him to see. The room was undamaged, and placed haphazardly on the floor were a number of strange-looking objects. Most were drones, either quadcopters or octocopters, with some oversized and measuring as much as twelve feet in length. These were the next generation of attack drones being developed for the military. They were capable of carrying up to a ton of weapons, ammo and sensing equipment.

An MQ-3 Predator—the P3—was in the room as well. Unlike its now outdated namesake, this was a nearly autonomous octocopter with an effective range of one hundred miles from its operator or relay station. This craft was of true drone design, deviating from the aircraft configuration of its predecessor. The P3 would have the ability to operate in a target zone for several hours, defending itself against counterattack while expanding its mission to eliminate multiple targets during its time on station.

Unfortunately, a few of the earlier versions of the P3 had found their way to Iran and other terrorist host nations, where crude yet effective knock-offs were being manufactured. A hotel in London was attacked by one of these units six months ago. The entire building was brought down before enough firepower could be brought in to take out the UAV.

Open-source technology, financed by rogue nations, was proving to be a deadly combination. If an American location was targeted by one of these killer drones, even the assets of the RDC would be inadequate to bring it down, at least until the P3s were deployed to the rapid-response bunkers—if any bunkers remained after today.

As impressive as the arsenal of next-generation drones may have been, that wasn't what Xander was looking for.

He gave out an audible sigh of relief when he found the prize.

He ran toward the back of the room.

"What the hell is that?" Tiffany asked.

"It's our ticket out of here."

The object sat on the floor and wasn't more than a foot thick in its forward and aft sections. It had four overlapping rings of metal with propellers contained in each of them, two in front and two in back, plus a small dual arrangement of small ringed propellers in the rear. Between the large double rings was a narrow platform with two padded seats placed in a row, and under the platform was a long, narrow black box on which the apparatus sat.

"This is the Mallory Systems H-59 Hoverbike," Xander explained.

"That thing can fly?" Tiffany's voice conveyed her lack of confidence in the vehicle.

"Not really fly, per se. The max altitude is about forty-five feet, and only for brief periods. But it can scoot along the ground at close to a hundred miles per hour, and it can even jump over small canyons and cross rivers."

"Groovy," Tiffany said as she jumped on the odd-looking vehicle and straddled the rear seat. Xander was taken aback, thinking it would take a lot more convincing to get her on board. "What are we waiting for?" she asked. Then, noticing his quizzical look, she continued. "Kentucky-bred farm girl, Mr. Xander; I've been riding horses since I was five. This is nothing I can't handle. So hurry, your playmates may come back at any time."

Xander sat in the driver's seat. "Strap in," he said over his shoulder. "I may have to do some radical maneuvers before this is all over."

With a flick of a switch, the quad rotors began to spin, producing a low-pitched hum much quieter than even the tiny drones that had attacked the base. Dust and loose papers swirled in the vault, causing both driver and passenger to cough and cover their eyes. But then, the strange craft began to lift off the floor. "There are pitch and yaw controls, but it's mainly steered by shifting your weight," Xander called out over the sound of the wind from the propellers. "It's just like on a motorcycle; lean into the turns, and we'll do fine."

Xander felt Tiffany's arms wrap around his midsection. "Just give me a little warning before you do any really fancy moves."

"I'll try. Now, hold on, we're heading out."

Xander leaned to his right, and the craft spun around, aimed at the door to the vault. The movement of the hoverbike was smooth, with only minimal bounce. He remembered the first time he'd tried one of these contraptions—a more primitive version than this one—and how the ride was like running the rapids on the Colorado River. Since then, the technology has become more refined to the point where you could thread a needle while riding on one.

With the tail rotors providing the forward thrust, the hoverbike proceeded out of the vault and down the long chamber toward the exterior doors set in a false façade of what appeared to be long-closed-down mining operation a mile through the mountain.

Since the RDC was an arm of the U.S. military, the Mallory hoverbike wasn't built simply for transportation. Instead, it hosted a full arsenal of both offensive and defensive weapons, including dual 45-caliber submachine guns mounted to either side of the lower battery box. The standard load would be two hundred rounds for each. These were real killer rounds, much heavier than those carried aboard a standard combat drone.

He also had at his disposal six miniature Talon missiles, which could be set either for heat-seeking or line-of-sight targeting. Since most attack drones operated on battery power, heat-seeking was not that effective against them. If need be, Xander could use the joystick and monitor at the center of his steering column to find and capture an enemy target. Once locked on, the missile was effective for up to twenty miles and at a speed of six hundred miles per hour.

Xander now had quite the arsenal at his disposal, which should make him nearly invincible against the smaller quads and octs roaming the Center. At least, that was the theory. In reality, this was only the third time he'd ever been on this particular model of hoverbike, and never was he allowed to play with the onboard weaponry. He was familiar with the controls, yet until you've actually engaged the enemy in live combat, you couldn't tell how things would react—meaning both man and machine.

Xander Moore had no false illusions that the desert outside the base would be clear of hostiles. In fact, as he neared the hidden entrance doors to the testing chambers, he found them to be open to the outside world, allowing free access to the base.

Xander squinted against the bright desert sunlight pouring through the gaping entrance, yet his eyes grew wide when he spotted four Maverick quadcopters resting on the floor near the doorway. These were RPA's, probably connected to the outside world and their pilots by portable relay stations often dropped by other drones or helicopters within an operational area. To Xander's relief, their propellers were still, so he hoped the pilots were off doing something other than guarding the entrance. With the main battle for the RDC winding down, he wouldn't be surprised if more RPA's were entering the base, allowing live operators to assess the damage and engage in specific mop-up duties.

However it turned out, the loss of the RDC was only temporary. Batteries would eventually drain—even in the guided units—and control would once again revert to the few remaining people in the Center. After that, restocking the facility with trained and competent personnel would take months, if not years, especially in light of the computer download of personnel files and other critical data. And with the computer and comm systems down, it would require a complete do-over before the RDC would be back to full operational strength and efficiency.

Xander slowed the hoverbike while simultaneously flicking open the end cap on the center joystick. He toggled the switch inside until the monitor located between the handlebars came to life. There was a circle at the center of the screen, and Xander manipulated the toggle until the circle was positioned on the first quadcopter.

"What are you doing?" Tiffany asked. "They're asleep; maybe we should leave them alone."

"They won't be quiet all the time. Their pilots could come back and then use their units to kill more of my friends. Besides, I need the practice."

He pressed the center button under his thumb, and a short burst of .45 caliber slugs rang out. The first drone shattered into a thousand pieces, even as the burst raked the second drone behind it. Xander then moved the circle over to the drones on the other side of the runway—just as they both came to life and shot into the air.

The two menacing drones climbed to the ceiling of the chamber and spun around until their weapons pointed at the hovercar. "Hold on!"

Xander leaned to his left and gunned the rotors, causing their ride to turn at an almost ninety-degree angle to the floor. A series of bullets ricocheted off the metal deck directly along the path that the hovercraft had just traveled. But now, the left side of the chamber was zooming up in front of them, and it took another radical lean to the right to change course enough to avoid a head-on collision. The hovercar turned nearly on its side, appearing to ride along the side wall until it swung back to the horizontal.

The two enemy drones dove for the deck, coming up behind the hoverbike. Xander rocked the vehicle back and forth as another series of bullets sped past. Then, suddenly, they burst out into the bright desert sunlight.

Once outside, Xander had maneuvering room, except for one issue. The bike was not designed to fly, and now it was shooting out the entrance at over sixty miles per hour.

The short patch of level ground outside the false mine entrance was only about a hundred yards wide, a distance they traversed in a matter of seconds. Beyond that was a nearly vertical drop off to the base of a canyon five hundred feet below. Without any solid surface to push against, the force of the propellers wasn't strong enough to keep the hoverbike aloft.

And so they dropped—maybe not like a rock, but like a very heavy feather.

With the air being pulled from their lungs by the sudden freefall, Xander managed to point the craft nose-down to follow the natural contour of the hillside, a maneuver that caused them to pick up even more speed. The ground rushed up below them until he leveled off and gunned the motors even more. A blinding cloud of sand

and dust was thrown up around them as the wind from the props finally found something to push against; however, the hoverbike still bounced on the ground, causing Tiffany to slip to the left and nearly out of her seat. Only the safety belt kept her on the craft. Now, she clawed at Xander's left arm to regain her balance.

Xander wasn't expecting this, and his arm gripping the steering column was pulled to the left, sending the craft into a violent and rapid spin. It made three full circles, stirring up a mushroom cloud of blown sand before Xander could right the craft.

"Dammit, Tiffany, you almost killed us!"

"Me? You're the one who flew us off the edge of a cliff."

Once the dust settled, Xander aimed the hoverbike down the remaining slope at a more reasonable angle, looking to the monitor screen for any signs of the two remaining enemy drones. They were still following, even though they could only go about forty-five miles per hour. The hoverbike was just outside their firing range, but that wouldn't keep the drones from reporting their position and calling for backup.

"Hold on; we're turning around."

"Are you crazy?"

"Just do it!"

Xander leaned hard to his right, and the hoverbike performed a tilting turn and lined up on a course aimed directly at the pursuing drones. He fingered the toggle for the missiles. A pair of foot-long projectiles dropped from the base of the hovercraft before lighting off and streaking away, leaving a trail of puffy white smoke in their wake.

Xander had line-of-sight control of the missiles, and he manipulated his thumb on the top toggle switch on the joystick with minute movements. The enemy drones were pilot-guided, and they darted off to each side to avoid the incoming missiles. Xander sent the left missile into a sharp turn that cut off the angle of the nearest Maverick drone. A split second later, a relatively small explosion off in the distance signified a kill.

But now the second drone had managed to spin away and was now lining up on their right side. Tiny puffs of gunfire erupted from the craft, and an instant later, Xander and Tiffany heard the high-pitched zing of bullets streaking by. Two of the bullets hit the side of the hoverbike just behind Tiffany's legs. She wrapped her legs around Xander's waist in a movement that was a little too late. Luckily, nothing vital was struck, even as the bike was twisted toward the right from the impacts.

Maintaining this new course, Xander gunned the hoverbike and sped away. He switched the toggle control to that of the second Talon missile, which was now in a long looping circle high overhead. He placed the targeting circle on the remaining enemy drone and brought the missile screaming down from almost directly above the Maverick. Even without the explosive charge, the tremendous collision would have destroyed the drone, which didn't even see the missile dropping on it from the Heavens.

"Good job!" Tiffany yelled from the rear seat. "I hope there aren't any more of those bastards out here."

"Even if there aren't, it's a sure bet they reported our leaving."

"So what? I'm sure they didn't expect to kill everyone at the Center. They had to assume a few people would survive."

"You're right." Xander looked out at the sides of the narrow desert canyon they now traveled, heading east. The mountain would soon taper out, and they would be in the vast, flat desert heading out toward Lake Meade. He looked at the power gauge.

"We're going to have to find an alternative mode of transportation pretty soon," he called back over his shoulder. "This thing is just about out of juice."

"Any ideas?"

"Yeah, one. I hope we can make it."

8

Six minutes later, the hoverbike hopped over a short, barbed-wire-topped fence and closed on a cluster of small hangars isolated at the northeast edge of Nellis Air Force Base. Xander slowed the vehicle as it swept in over an expanse of white concrete leading up to the largest of the four buildings.

As he set the bike on the surface and turned off the motors, a young Airman in blue and black camo fatigues armed with an HK M27 infantry rifle appeared at a small door set to the left of the hangar door. He had the weapon leveled at them.

"Stop where you are!" he commanded. "I *will* shoot."

Xander raised his arms; Tiffany followed with the same gesture a second later. "Relax, airman, I'm with the RDC."

"This isn't RDC property. You shouldn't be here."

"We escaped from the Center, and I assume by now you know what's going on."

The young man motioned with the barrel of his rifle to his right toward the main part of Nellis AFB, located five miles away. "Oh, yeah, I know what's going on."

Xander and Tiffany looked to their left as well, where they saw a wide curtain of black smoke rising up in a line.

"They took out the whole flight line in a matter of seconds. Came out of a couple of semi-tractor-trailers out on North Las Vegas Boulevard, tiny things with bombs that hopped the fence and slammed into the helos and planes—mainly the helos. Some of the jets got away, but what can they do against little basketball-size things?"

"What are you doing here?" Xander asked.

"This is my emergency duty station. I'm supposed to have backup, but no one else came."

"Lower your weapon, son," Xander said. It was the first time he'd ever addressed someone as 'son.' It just sounded right for the moment.

"You're on a drone of some kind. How do I know you're not one of them?"

"Think about it; all the attacking drones are unmanned, with their pilots hiding away somewhere else. We're here, in the open. C'mon, we're all on the same side here."

Slowly, the scared airman lowered his weapon. Xander and Tiffany slipped off the hoverbike and approached the hangar. "I'm Xander Moore, senior pilot for the Rapid Defense Center."

"Sam Reynolds, Airman First Class." He looked at the disheveled Tiffany Collins.

She reached out her hand to the airman. "Tiffany Collins, Fox News."

"Oh my god, I recognize you!"

Even in her current physical state, Tiffany melted the young man with her smile.

Xander poked his head inside the hangar. "This is General McKinney's private hangar, isn't it?"

"I believe so."

The three of them moved inside. The only thing in the hangar was a tall, oblong object covered by a large green tarp. Xander walked up to the tarp and pulled. With some effort, the heavy canvas began to slide off.

"What the hell is that?" Tiffany asked.

"That's the latest in hovercopter technology—the Jarvis XV-9. I've been helping the general with some of the fine-tuning. It's a prototype."

What they were looking at was an odd helicopter-like vehicle standing about twelve feet high. It sported six huge ringed propellers running along a line of three on each side, with a clear plastic dome underneath. A sleek, fiber-glass fuselage ran back from the passenger dome and helped support the aft rotors. All the props were horizontally oriented, and there was no tail rotor, which was found on standard helicopters.

"That's one big-ass drone!" Tiffany exclaimed. "It really flies?"

"That it does, and at nearly two-hundred fifty miles per hour."

Xander noticed a long, orange power cable running from under the fiberglass body to a boxy power source against the wall. "Mr. Reynolds, could you open the hangar doors while I unhook the power cable?"

"I can't let you take it," the airman said aghast. "You said it belongs to the General."

"I'm just going to borrow it. Besides, it will be safer with me. If it stays here, it could be destroyed in the next wave of drone attacks."

"I don't know, man..."

Tiffany stepped up to the airman. "It will be all right. You can come with us. The General will be glad that you saved his prized toy from destruction."

Sam gave a sheepish grin and then moved to the hangar doors. He pulled on the chains, and the door began to rise. The hangar was facing due west and the setting desert sunlight now flooded the chamber, temporarily blinding the three occupants. Xander unhooked the power cord and let it spin back into its holding compartment within the hovercopter.

Airman Sam Reynolds stood to the side of the large

opening, silhouetted by the brilliant sun. "Can you tell me what's going on, Mr. Moore? I thought you guys were supposed to prevent things like this from hap—"

In an instant, the young man was perforated at mid-torso by a powerful blast of gunfire. He fell to the concrete floor, the top half of his body barely attached to the rest.

"Get in!" Xander yelled to Tiffany as he pulled open the left side door to the passenger dome and jumped in. The reporter was only a few feet away, and she was inside the compartment in two seconds flat.

"I thought you said you didn't have a pilot's license!"

"This is a drone, not an airplane. You'll be fine."

Xander flicked the switches that activated the rotors. Being electric, they spun up to power a second later. Without bothering to buckle in, Xander pressed the controls forward, and the strange-looking craft began to move forward, scraping across the concrete floor on metal skids.

Squinting into the afternoon sun, Xander noticed five small, black dots in the glare. There were tiny sparks coming out of them, and an instant later, bullets ricocheted off the thick plastic bubble. A spider web series of cracks appeared just below Xander's pilot seat.

But then he cleared the doorway and gunned the throttle while also pulling back on the control stick, sending the odd-looking craft climbing into the sky.

More bullets impacted the undercarriage of the hovercopter, yet a quick glance at the control panel showed that nothing was awry. They continued to climb.

Glancing over his left shoulder, Xander caught sight of the small flight of enemy drones below. They were rapidly falling behind, and for a moment, Xander thought they were home free. But then he saw multiple puffs of white smoke, followed by lengthening contrails.

The hovercopter could easily outrun the drones; what it couldn't do was outrun missiles.

They were at nearly three thousand feet and climbing, with six missile trails streaking closer. Xander banked the copter sharply to the left, a movement that sent the unrestrained Tiffany Collins spilling into his lap.

"Dammit, Tiffany!"

"It's not my fault!"

Restricted from fully actuating the controls, the hovercopter continued to turn to the left, forming a full circle before Tiffany could extricate herself from Xander. She fought to quickly fasten the waist strap before Xander sent the craft into another wide spin.

The first missile shot past, missing them by twenty feet. Now, it was Xander's turn to fasten his seatbelt. Afterward, he banked the copter sharply to the right just as another missile whizzed past.

He noticed high above that the first missile was now changing course and heading back toward them while another array of white smoke trails approached from beneath.

"Is your life insurance paid up?" he managed to call out.

Tiffany looked over at him and opened her mouth to reply when Xander suddenly tilted the hovercopter straight up while applying maximum power to the rotors. Each of them felt their stomachs rise up into their throats as the craft continued along its arc until it was horizontal again, although now it was upside down.

The hovercopter was not designed for such a maneuver. It stalled at the zenith and began to fall toward the desert floor, now a mile below. Tiffany's yelp was ear-piercing as the craft tumbled to the right. It nosed down and began to spin headfirst toward the ground. Xander barely noticed as the remaining missiles shot past, completely off target, the controlling pilots taken off guard by Xander's radical move—whether intended or not—and unable to follow his descent.

Gripping the central control stick with both hands, Xander fought to find the right combination of twists and turns that would right the craft. Most of his efforts resulted in only heavier spinning. But then he managed to stop the spinning, yet still aimed toward the surface at a nearly ninety-degree angle. Xander pulled back on the stick with little effect. Then he cut the four rear propellers. The tail end of the hovercopter began to drop as the two front rotors continued to fight against the steep angle of descent. Slowly, the hovercopter began to pull out of the dive.

Straining even more, Xander felt as if the control stick was about to break off in his hands. He glanced at the altimeter: five hundred feet … four hundred … three hundred.

Then, the rate of descent tapered off as the propellers cut into the air. Xander activated the four rear rotors again, and at a mere sixty feet above the surface, the craft was once again on the horizontal.

"I think I peed my pants," Tiffany muttered from the passenger seat.

"A little too much information, madam reporter," Xander said once he could breathe again. He glanced out through the dome of the hovercopter to see if he could spot the enemy drones. In that brief moment, he couldn't, but he knew they were still out there.

9

The sun was just now hiding behind the mountains to the west, and the landscape around them was dark. Xander Moore piloted the strange-looking hovercopter just above the ground, skimming a scant fifty feet above the desert floor as they sped off to the east. The damn craft had regulation running lights, which was something he couldn't override, so there was a chance the trailing drones could spot the alternating green and red lights. He cranked the speed up to two hundred miles per hour.

Five minutes later, Xander made a wide turn to the right and entered a series of low canyons along the mountains between Las Vegas and Lake Meade, heading due south. A few minutes later—and with no sign of a tail—they came up on East Lake Meade Parkway, the main road between Henderson and the lake, and followed it west.

During most of the short trip, Tiffany rested her head against the side of the plastic dome, watching the scene fly past below. Xander gained more altitude and was now zipping along at around eight hundred feet above the roadway.

He took the craft's radio and fingered the controls. Nothing but dead air. He tried it again.

"It doesn't work?" Tiffany questioned.

"One of the bullets must have hit the antenna or the unit itself. Ain't that some bad luck? That's all right. We're only about three minutes from my house, and I'll call someone when we get there."

It was an eerie sight from the air, looking out at the wide expanse of the suburban city below. Henderson was the fairly upscale southern enclave of Las Vegas, featuring the planned community of Anthem, and even though it was growing dark, the pair could easily spot the ominous—and seemingly random—towers of black smoke rising into the air from a dozen locations or more. North, toward Las Vegas, many of the plumes were located near downtown. This was where the rapid-response bunkers were located. And yet there were also columns of smoke rising up from the Summerlin area to the west, as well as more to the south, including an inordinate number of columns in the area where his home was located.

"Why all the fires? Did you guys have bunkers located in this many places around the city?" Tiffany asked.

"No, we didn't." His tone was sour as he spoke the words. "The Las Vegas-Henderson area only has eight bunkers and mainly concentrated downtown."

"So, what's causing all these fires?"

For an answer, Xander approached a large column of black smoke rising up from a home located on a low bluff and overlooking the southeastern side of a perfectly manicured desert golf course. He brought the copter into a hover about three hundred feet above the fully engulfed structure, a fire which had now jumped to the neighboring house to the north. No fire trucks were on the street, just a gaggle of stunned spectators and the frantic occupants of the neighboring house trying to save their home.

But what was shocking was that half of the huge, single-story home below was completely gone, and not from the fire, but from what appeared to be a giant explosion. Debris trails fanned out from the point of detonation, and the fire that raged was in the remaining part of the structure since there was very little left where the bomb or missile had struck.

Tiffany was engrossed in the horrific scene below until she suddenly pulled her attention away from the side of the clear plastic dome and turned toward Xander. "Is that *your* home?" she asked breathlessly.

"It was," Xander replied in a whisper.

"I am so sorry, Xander. But why would they attack your home?"

"Because they're going after all the RDC pilots. Along with the attack on the base, data on the Center's operations, security protocols and personnel was blasted all over the internet today. Each of those smoke plumes is where a pilot and his family lived."

"Oh my god, are you married? Were there any children at home?"

"Fortunately, I'm a bachelor," Xander answered. "But most of the others are married and do have children, but I don't think the terrorists give a damn about that."

"But why destroy your home? You weren't even there."

"I was supposed to be. Whoever did this—whoever leaked the information about the Center—knows our schedules. The homes of those on duty weren't targeted, just those who weren't."

"That kind of information would have to come from someone inside the RDC unless you were hacked."

"We weren't hacked, Tiffany. Whoever helped coordinate this attack is one of our own."

Just then, the pair began to hear small arms fire—and even rifle shots—from below. Looking down, they noticed several of the occupants of Cedar Lane had taken up arms against the odd, hovering craft. In light of all that had happened today, any strange craft in the air was considered a threat.

Xander gained more altitude, taking them out of range.

"What now?" Tiffany asked.

"I don't know. Eventually, the bad guys will learn that I wasn't home. I'm sure that part of their overall strategy involved taking out every RDC pilot they could. It's been the ongoing goal of a number of terrorist organizations since we began operating. And without the RDC to help combat further attacks, they'll probably just keep coming until they get us all."

"Is there anywhere you can hide until this blows over?"

"Blows over? You really think this will just blow over?"

"Eventually, the RDC will get back on its feet, or the other agencies will step up to fill the void."

Xander shook his head. "There will be interim steps taken, but we're still looking at several weeks before even a modest defense can be mounted. In the meantime, the terrorists will have free reign throughout the country."

"What about the other bunkers? You have literally thousands of drones available, don't you?"

Xander set the hovercopter off on a course south, towards the California/Nevada border. He was tired of watching his home burn to the ground.

"The drones in the bunkers are basically useless at this time," he said, continuing with the answer to Tiffany's question. "We have some very restrictive transponder signals that pass between the drones and the command center. Without those transponder signals being activated, the drones will not respond to commands, not without lengthy and exhaustive reprogramming. They were designed so they couldn't be hacked or their controls overridden. With the servers destroyed and our communications capabilities gone, there's no way to gain control over the drones in the bunkers."

"So, they cut off the head of the snake," Tiffany said.

"They knew what to do … and how to do it."

"Coming back to my original question: Is there any place you can hide, at least until you can get in touch with the government for protection?"

"I know a few people in San Diego, but that would only expose them to danger, too."

"I have a place in Idyllwild where you could stay."

Xander looked over at the woman. "Then that would place you in danger."

Tiffany grinned—a wide, clown-like grin. "As if I'm not already in enough trouble? Just look at me; I'm a mess. It'll be fine. The cabin is secluded, and no one even knows I have it. It's been in my family for twenty years, and I use it as a refuge when I need a break from real life—like now!"

"Are you sure about this? You didn't ask for any of this to happen to you—just the wrong place at the wrong time."

"Mr. Moore—that's your last name, right—well, you know what I do for a living, and although certain security regulations may not allow me to report on all I've seen and heard today, I know eventually I'll be able to tell my story. And that has blockbuster written all over it. So, honestly, I'd like to stick around a little while longer to see how this story ends."

Xander looked out the window of the hovercopter and scanned the multiple black columns of smoke filling his view. "Let's hope it doesn't end up with one of *those* rising above your mountain cabin, Ms. Collins."

"You've managed to keep me alive so far. I'm sure you can do it for a while longer."

Xander smirked and then nodded. "Idyllwild, you say? I've always loved that area."

"Hey, don't get your expectations up. It's not one of those really fancy places down around the lake."

"I just appreciate the offer. And now ... California here we come."

10

Xander gunned the hovercopter while also descending to just over a hundred feet off the ground. It was eerily lit by a near-full moon in mid-December, but still, the ground-sensing equipment aboard the copter would keep them safe—and hopefully undetected—for the two-hour journey to the San Jacinto mountain community of Idyllwild.

Xander couldn't take anything for granted when it came to the masterminds behind today's attack. They could have access to live satellite feeds and also the ability to tap into radio and cell communications—even if there wasn't a cellphone between them. All communication devices, including iPads, Kindles and cellphones, were required to be checked at the entrance to the RDC. Xander noticed that even Tiffany's handbag was missing—assuming she came to the Center with one. Without the copter's radio functioning, they had no way to communicate with the outside world without landing somewhere and bumming a phone off some startled civilian.

In two hours, they would be at Tiffany's cabin. It would be good to fall off the grid for a while, giving their trail a chance to cool.

The hovercopter skirted along the high desert of California for a hundred miles, with Xander doing his best to stay within the ground clutter of radar and satellite observation.

During the trip, Tiffany took the opportunity to probe more into Xander's background. It was a distraction from the worry they both felt and helped pass the time.

"How did you get into this whole drone thing in the first place?"

"My older brother got me into it. He was always tinkering around with something, and then one day, he brings home this quadcopter."

"Is he in the industry as well?"

"No, he was killed in Iraq in 2008."

"Oh, I'm sorry, Xander."

"That's okay. He died doing what he truly loved, which is the most any of us can hope to say. Anyway, when he died, I inherited his drone. I thought it was kind of fitting that I keep flying it since he loved it so much. Then, after a couple of years, some friends and I formed a club called the Alpha Pilots, and we began having competitions between ourselves and other clubs."

"What kind of competitions?"

"You know, war games, that sort of thing. Crash and burn, chases, obstacle courses—we even put paintball guns on our drones and fired at each other. Anyway, there were formal leagues starting at the time, and we joined those, too. We would meet in huge warehouses and have combat fights."

"How was that possible?"

"They'd hang big nets from the ceiling, forming a box and two drones would enter and fight to the symbolic death. The goal was to knock your opponent out of the air. Turning them upside down on their propellers was a sure kill. Then, we moved outside, usually to paintball fields, and that's when things got really exciting."

"Where were you at the time?"

"San Diego County, mainly in San Marcos and Vista, north of the city. It's an area known to UAV warriors as Drone Valley, just as San Jose and Palo Alto are known as Silicon Valley to the computer geeks.

"About that time, a billionaire investor formed the first Drone Olympics, thinking this was going to be the next big thing. The Alphas joined, and wouldn't you know it, we ended up winning the whole damn thing the first year the games were held, going up against the best pilots from across the country; hell, there were even people from Japan and Europe competing. It was really cool."

"So, I'm sitting next to an Olympian! I'm impressed. So you got medals and everything?"

Xander's expression turned sour. "I did. Unfortunately, they were in my house back in Henderson."

"Damn, I keep stepping in it, don't I?"

"Don't worry, Tiffany. I'm a big boy; it takes a lot to affect me these days."

"So, you and your Alphas won the Drone Olympics. That must have been a big deal?"

Xander snorted. "Maybe to some people, but not to most. We won three of the team events outright, and then I took the silver in two individual contests."

"Which ones?"

"Heads-Up Combat and Seek and Evade." He laughed. "Again, don't read too much into it. It was the first and only year of the Olympics. After that, we got sued by the real International Olympic Committee, which happened to be about the same time the public started to turn negative on drones and their operators. That's when the bank robberies began."

"So, again, Mr. Moore, how did all this get you the gig with the government?"

Xander looked down at the dimming desert landscape that sped away past the odd helicopter as it skimmed not more than a hundred feet above the ground. The memories seemed so long ago.

"After high school, I went to San Diego State, pursuing a degree in avionics. While there, I was approached by some people who'd heard of my expertise with drones. They wanted me to head up a research team they were putting together to devise contingency plans against hostile UAV activities. Turns out they were with DARPA."

"Oh, damn, I've heard of them, I just can't recall what the acronym stands for."

"The Defense Advanced Research Projects Agency."

"Thanks, that's a mouthful."

"So, I packed my bags and my surfboard and headed off to Washington, D.C. I spent the next four years thinking up some of the worst uses for drones imaginable and then ways to counter them. At the time, the Rapid Defense Center was just being planned, and they came to DARPA looking for help in specific areas of contention they were running into. Have you ever heard of the *Posse Comitatus Act*?"

"This may surprise you, but I have. It restricts the government from using the military as law enforcement personnel."

"That's right, and at the time, the government was trying to devise some defense for the ever-increasing number of drone attacks taking place. They wanted it to be just an expanded function of the foreign drone program run by the military, but only domestic, and that was causing all kinds of resistance because of the Act. So, they started looking at a civilian solution. Since I was pretty well-known within the drone community, I was loaned to the RDC as a consultant to see if what the Feds had in mind would work."

"But the RDC *is* part of the military."

"That's right, but it took a lot of fancy footwork to make that happen. Our charter specifically restricts us from acting against individuals within the United States and its territories. We're strictly a defensive organization designed to target machines only—UAVs and other remotely controlled devices. That's how they got around the restriction. If an individual is identified as a target within the country, the FBI is called even before the locals. Now that the cat's out of the bag after this big internet dump, I can tell you that targeting citizens happens quite often. You'd be surprised how many of these attacks are carried out by people or groups operating from within the country and how few are carried out by remote operators overseas. Most terrorist organizations don't have the sophistication or the expertise to pull off long-distant operations."

"With the exception of The Arm of Allah."

"Even they're about ten years behind where the U.S. is in distant drone operations. You have to remember; we've been doing this for a very long time."

"But now the weapons are becoming smaller and more readily accessible."

Xander smiled. "So says the Fox News reporter, as she returns to the interrupted interview."

"After the day we've had, can you blame me?"

"Nah, but you do realize this is only the beginning, don't you?"

"What do you mean? Are there other Centers we don't know about?"

"Unfortunately, no. What I mean is that someone doesn't go through this much trouble to take out the most effective weapon against wholesale UAV attacks unless they mean to take advantage of the situation."

"More civilian attacks?"

"No question about it. And I've been thinking about this—it's what I do. The raid on the Center, along with the exposure of the program, has come right here at Christmastime and also during the transition period between administrations. With respect to the change in presidents, this is the time when we need decisive, effective leadership. That's not going to happen, not now. No one in the old administration is going to take responsibility for half-assed actions between now and January 20th, and the incoming administration doesn't have the authority to act. There's an outflow of political experience, and all are being replaced mostly by rookies, including even the presidency. When dealing with a major crisis like this, we're always guaranteed some level of clusterfuck to follow. But in this case, it's going to be so much worse.

"And as for the holiday season, one of two things could happen. Either people continue to risk their lives by going out in public—in which case a lot more people are going to die—or else they stay home, which wrecks the economy, not only here but around the world. How the American consumer spends money determines the economies of countless other nations, whether they want to admit it or not."

"So, how do *you* think the people will react? What about online shopping?"

"This should be a boom for Amazon, eBay and Alibaba, but then again, people are being forced into online shopping out of fear. That has to affect enthusiasm, both for the season and the feeling of security most of us require to function. Normally, I'd say people will continue to shop, but with the very public evisceration of the RDC, I now believe they'll stay home and basically write off the holidays for the year. The Center may not have been effective in *preventing* attacks, but we were really good at shutting them down within the first few minutes of the event. And if the country's infrastructure is attacked, that will impact delivery services, including roadways, airlines and even ports."

Xander sighed, his own words depressing him as he spoke. "Most people spend their days thinking that they're invincible and that bad things only happen to other people. That's why they still get in cars every day when their chances of being killed in a traffic accident are about a thousand times more likely than from a terrorist attack. I also think the RDC's success has been a double-edged sword. We boast about our success constantly and to the exclusion of all other assets and options available. We have the population believing that we're the *only* protection they need against drones. How do you think they'll react now?"

"There are other assets, as you call them. What are they?"

Xander's wry smile told most of the story. "In all honesty, there are very few. With the RDC's track record, there's been no big push to come up with alternatives, and definitely not enough money to fund them. In fact, our lobbyists fight hard against money being spent on anything other than the RDC, preferring to grab all they can so that more rapid-response bunkers can be built and more operators hired and trained."

"So there's no effective backup to the RDC?"

"Bingo! Even the FBI and local law enforcement have deferred to us. I know DARPA is working on solutions to the overall drone problem, but so far, they haven't let us in on any breakthroughs. It's our hope that one day they'll come up with something that can protect *against* drone attacks before they happen, not after."

A quick glance in Tiffany's direction revealed the paleness of her skin and the frightened look in her eyes.

"I guess I've been like most people in the country," she began. "I thought the drone problem was more isolated than reported. Being in the media, I know we have a tendency to blow some things way out of proportion. In my early days, I once reported on a school bus that caught fire. Sounds serious, doesn't it? As it turned out, a little smoke was coming from the rear of the bus; the driver pulled over, the kids transferred to another bus, and the fire was out before the fire trucks even arrived. The bottom line is that there was no story at all, but we sure made it out to be a lot worse than it was for the clicks and the ratings. That's how I've always seen these drone stories, especially since the RDC would usually sweep in and save the day. The report I'm working on has really opened my eyes to the true threat we face."

"Ms. Collins, I've spent my whole life around drones. I have played with them as toys, and I've operated them as weapons, so believe me when I say this: Drones are not the problem. It's the people operating them who are. Like all inanimate objects, it's what a person does with them that determines its utility. Unfortunately, there are way too many sickos in the world that even toys are being weaponized and sent out to kill. But unless you ban all *potential* weapons—which can be *anything* in the hands of a madman—this is the world we live in."

"It's also the world we die in ... and far too often."

"And yet people still tend to blame the mindless object rather than the person for the evil being committed."

"Yeah, things have flipped in recent years. What do you think about that? Are you for or against all the new regulations regarding drones?"

Xander looked at the reporter and frowned. "And the interview continues? I think I should plead the fifth."

"That doesn't apply in this case," Tiffany said with a smile. "But to answer *your* question, yes, we're always interviewing, asking questions and seeking answers, whether as a reporter or a drone pilot. It's how information is gathered and disseminated. It's how we learn."

Xander nodded in the dimly-lit cockpit of the hovercopter. Then he answered: "There have been hordes of people blaming the inanimate object for the harm it can cause when people choose to use it in a way it was never intended. It's the same with guns. A gun sitting on a table can't hurt anyone. It's only when a human picks it up and uses it for evil that it becomes a weapon. It's the same with drones. Restricting who can own drones—or guns—while attempting to regulate their use and operation only impacts the good guys. The criminals and crazies don't give a damn about rules and regulations. In fact, the fewer people out there with the means to protect themselves, the easier it is for the bad guys to do even more harm."

"That's why we have cops—and the RDC—to do the protecting for us."

"The authorities can't be everywhere. People should have the right to provide for their own protection."

"Are we talking about drones or guns?"

Xander smiled. "Sometimes, you need a gun to protect yourself against a rogue drone. But look at all the private entities that now employ drone defenses. Sometimes, the best defense against a drone attack is another drone. It really pisses me off that it's come to this. Drones are extremely useful in a variety of applications—and they're a hell of a lot of fun to fly. But now, there are so many obstacles to owning one that it's a miracle anyone—except for the bad guys—even has one."

"Do you have a better solution?"

"That's another thing that pisses me off—I don't. Last year, a disgruntled teenager, rejected by a girl he liked at school, flew a drone with a small pipe bomb aboard through her bedroom window. The UAV was a sixty-dollar unit over ten years old. Still, the media and advocate groups went berserk, calling for the outlawing of all drones everywhere. How about figuring out a solution to teenage angst first? If it wasn't the drone, this crazy kid would have used something else. It wasn't the existence of the drone that caused the kid to lose it, but his own instability; however, this story became a convenient scapegoat for the real problem."

"But now we have terrorists basically cornering the market on drone usage for evil," Tiffany said. "And in most cases, they're not using surplus or homebuilt drones, but rather sophisticated machines specifically designed and built for combat. Warfare is evolving to a point where huge floating airports and intercontinental ballistic missiles are far too expensive to build and deploy, especially when you can build a million killer drones for the price of one aircraft carrier and then spread your threat over a much wider area … and with no credible defense."

"Is that the lead to the documentary you're working on?" Xander asked, without his accompanying smile.

"Can you deny the truth?"

"No, I can't, but that's not the point. What you're saying is that humanity is reaching the point where anyone—and everyone—can become a mass killer or an international superpower. He who controls the most killer drones rules the world, right?"

"Don't get mad at me for cutting to the chase. It's not my job to protect the public from information that might upset them. I have a duty to let people know what's really happening, despite what the officials tell them."

"Wholesale release of information just for the sake of sensationalism isn't doing anyone any good. All it does is add to the paranoia. Is that what you want, a whole population scared to leave their homes for fear of a drone attack, or the latest disease outbreak, or that they might be hit by a piece of the space station falling from the sky? Is there any wonder why we have so many crazy people these days doing crazy things?"

"It's not my job to pick and choose the news, Mr. Moore." Tiffany's tone was as cold as the desert air outside the hovercopter. "When we start doing that, it's called censorship. Most of the criticism of the news media over the past twenty years has come not from a misrepresentation of the facts but rather from an omission of relevant data designed to mislead or to hide opposing views, so-called *disinformation*. And with the segmentation of the media we have today, it's become possible for a person to read, watch and hear only one side of an issue, with no opposing or countering viewpoints. This has polarized our population like nothing before, and it hasn't helped anything. How can people, operating on only half the information, make informed decisions? I'll put your views in my report, just as I will the opposition's, but then I'll let my viewers make up their minds. That's if you don't throw me out of this flying eggbeater first."

"Don't tempt me." Xander glanced out the side of the canopy. "But from this altitude, it might not kill you, and then I'd have a whole other set of problems to deal with."

Tiffany extended her hand. "Agree to disagree?"

Xander took the soft hand and held it for a moment longer than was necessary. "Just as long as you agree you're wrong."

"So, if two wrongs make a right…."

"Then I guess we're both right."

Tiffany withdrew her hand and looked out the window. "Are we there yet?"

Xander smiled. He liked to be challenged, both physically and intellectually, and Tiffany Collins—beyond the obvious reasons—was becoming more interesting by the moment.

11

Under cover of darkness, Xander piloted the hovercopter past the northern shore of the Salton Sea and then along the outskirts of Palm Springs before heading along Highway 111 toward the Palm Springs Aerial Tramway. He knew the small town of Idyllwild was located along the top ridge of the San Jacinto Mountains off Highway 245. Visitors to the Tram could catch rides from the top of the mountain to meet up with the highway, so he figured his quickest path to the town would be to travel up the same canyon as the Tram and then skim the treetops until he came to the road.

It was nearing seven o'clock in the evening when they entered the canyon and began to climb to the summit at just over seven thousand feet. The Tram wasn't operating at the time, even though he was sure there were workers around. Yet as the copter paralleled the long and steep cable line, he didn't see a soul, either at the base or at the summit. Even the Peaks Restaurant—where he'd dined on half a dozen occasions before—was dark. He began to suspect that most public facilities in the area had shut down early as a precaution against further terrorist attacks now that it was known the RDC had been hit.

There was a decent snowpack at the top, and the moonlit scene below was as beautiful as it was deceiving, making it appear as if all in the world was peaceful and pure. Xander knew better. The attack on the RDC was just the beginning. The terrorists didn't go through this much trouble to take out the Center without having a much larger goal in mind. And now America's eggs-in-one-basket-planning was coming back to bite them. The civilian defense forces at the individual venues would do the best they could, yet for too long, they deferred their responsibility to the RDC, saving money in personnel and training while even receiving a break on their insurance if they signed priority agreements with the RDC for the use of their drones.

Now, these mostly inexperienced pilots were about to get a crash course in drone defensive tactics. The terrorists had been planning this for months—if not years—so it was a good bet their pilots and auto drones would come at America with skill and overwhelming force, a reversal of the *Shock and Awe* campaign from fifty years before.

It was going to be a slaughter.

At just over seven thousand feet, they began skimming along the treetops, and after a few minutes, Xander spotted a curvy road below and followed it south for another five minutes.

"So, where are we going?" he asked.

Tiffany had her head pressed against the plastic side of the dome, intently watching the ground below. "I'm not quite sure," she said after a moment. "I've never had to find the cabin from the air."

"That's Highway 243 down there. We're just north of Idyllwild, I believe."

"Good. When we get to the town center, I can find my way from there."

A few minutes later, they came to a sprinkling of commercial buildings lining SR 243—The Banning-Idyllwild Highway—and with a couple of other roads splintering off from it.

"Follow that one," Tiffany said with confidence. "It should be Pine Crest."

Thirty seconds later, they came to a steep turn to the left. Tiffany pointed down. "There's a dirt road—see it? My cabin's up there. It's rather steep going up that way, at least by car."

Xander obeyed, and soon, the tiny copter was again riding the treetops with few roofs visible.

"To the right now, we're almost there."

The tiny cabin came into view, and Xander circled it twice before selecting a safe place to land. The cabin was set on a narrow ledge jutting out from the steep slope without much flat land around. The hovercopter didn't require the clearance of a traditional helo, so he set it down right at the front door, in the only place reserved for a vehicle.

Tiffany climbed out of the aircraft, and Xander met her a moment later at the front door to the cabin.

"I don't have my purse ... or the keys. Damn, everything was back at the Center."

"Do you mind?" He gently pushed her to one side and then placed his shoulder against the roughhewn wood of the door. He pushed, and the jamb easily splintered. The door swung open.

"You're going to pay for that," Tiffany said, smiling.

"Bill it to the U.S. Government."

The cabin was what one would expect to find at the end of a dirt road high in the mountains: basic and rural, with one large room combining the kitchen and living area and a single bedroom to one side with a small bathroom next to it. It was constructed out of half-logs and had a potbellied stove for warmth placed at one side of the living room. There was a wood-frame couch and a well-worn leather recliner facing the stove, along with a forty-two-inch LCD TV resting on a cabinet next to it. The windows were covered with paisley-print curtains, and there was a round area rug taking up most of the living area. A small dining table was the only separation between the living room and the kitchen area.

All in all, Xander liked the place. It spoke of a simpler time, a more peaceful time.

"I'm impressed, Ms. Collins. Not something I would have expected."

"You mean with my glamorous job and flashy lifestyle? I told you, I'm from Kentucky. Sometimes, I just want to escape the rat race and relax. The house has been in my family for years, yet none of the people I work with even know about it. My folks used it as a vacation home after they moved to California when I was sixteen."

Xander pointed at the T.V. "Do you get reception up here?"

"Starlink, with about a billion channels; I said I want to relax, but I still have to keep up on current affairs."

"That's what I'm interested in. I need to see how all this is being reported. Do you mind?"

"No, go ahead. I'll get the heat going and fix us some tea. After all, it is December. We don't get as much snow as we used to when I was younger, but still enough for a real *Thomas Kinkade*-like Christmas now and then. I'll also open a couple of cans of soup. I wouldn't trust anything in the refrigerator. I haven't been up here in about nine months."

Xander turned on the TV, which, to no surprise, was already tuned to Fox News. There was a scene of a burning building with a red framed chyron running across the bottom of the screen that read: *Major Terrorist Attack Strikes Las Vegas*. He sat on the edge of the recliner and watched the report until Tiffany handed him a cup of hot tea.

The room was small enough that she heard the report as well.

"So far, it's just Las Vegas," she said.

Xander shook his head. "Wait until tomorrow. Even if the terrorists don't begin hitting every target on their bucket list, some of our homegrown groups surely will, if only so they can blame it on foreigners."

"That's what the talking heads are saying. This certainly will panic the public, especially right here at Christmas. Who's going to go to a mall if the terrorists can strike at anything they want?"

"That's the idea."

Tiffany went into the bathroom and cleaned the caked blood off the side of her face. She came back into the living room with a damp towel. "Here, let me clean the blood off of you."

"Blood?"

"Yeah, you have some on your nose and upper lip. Are you hurting anywhere?"

"Anywhere ... how about everywhere? And you?"

"The same; I took some aspirin for the headache. I'll

get you some in a minute." She gently dabbed at the blood on his face, leaning in close as she did so. Xander noticed that her perfume was still present, even after all she'd been through, and for a moment, he was distracted from the seriousness of their situation.

That changed when the scene on the TV changed.

The President was speaking, addressing the nation from a secure room within the White House. Gone were the days of stepping up to a podium on the South Lawn; the danger was too real to take the chance. Now, he was trying to reassure a terrified nation that the crisis was coming to an end and that the limited battery life of the drones meant that the terror couldn't last. He acknowledged that the raid—as well as the information revealed on the internet—was harmful to the mission of the RDC but that measures were being taken to ensure that the facility would be back in operation within days. He also explained that most of the other remote drone bunkers across the country were still intact and functioning—which Xander knew to be a falsehood. Without a fully operational Rapid Defense Center, the drones in those bunkers were just collecting dust and would be for a long time to come. The President concluded his brief remarks with a reassurance that the United States still had plenty of capability to fight off future attacks and that people should go about their normal activities and enjoy the holiday season. America is strong ... the American people are strong ... and we will not cower to cowardly terrorists.

"Do you think anyone believes that?" Xander asked Tiffany.

"They still needed to hear it; besides, you're too close to the subject. Most people will believe it because they want to believe it. The alternative is not something they want to dwell on."

Xander watched as President Hector Ortega made a quick exit from the podium, refusing to answer the barrage of questions shouted at him by the press corps. Xander knew the man was as lame duck as a President could be, and now he had to deal with the largest national crisis since 9/11, and with only a little over thirty days left in his term to bring it to a successful close, otherwise, it would tarnish his entire legacy as Chief Executive. Xander snickered, knowing that that ship had already sailed. Ortega was screwed no matter what happens before the inauguration.

President Ortega had served two terms as the first Hispanic-American president, making it twelve consecutive years that a Republican had controlled the White House. Even then, his party had first lost the Senate, and then the House in subsequent midterms, and gridlock now infected the halls of government like never before.

His predecessor had enjoyed substantial majorities in all three branches of government, and the nation had prospered like never before. Ortega waltzed into the office, expecting to enjoy the same legacy. Yet ironically, it was the nation's newfound prosperity that caused him to lose control of the government. With the coffers full and businesses prospering, there came renewed demand for the government to give some of the prosperity back to the people in the form of more generous welfare programs, along with a resurrection of the national healthcare debate. When the Republicans in Congress refused to extend or expand many of these programs, the Democrats were once again able to form a unified opposition, and the dominoes began to fall.

Ortega's Vice-President, Peter Newman, had run on a platform of continuing with the prosperity of the past twelve years and ended up losing by a mere one-and-half percentage points in the popular vote and by five through the Electoral College. Newman was humiliated and blamed Ortega's failure to hold Congress as the reason he'd lost.

And now Owen Murphy was set to take over on January 20. Xander had considered the transition period between administrations as a major factor in the timing of the attack on the RDC, and even though he was a big supporter of Ortega, he knew the man was operating with a skeleton crew, a vindictive VP, and an incoming president who hated his guts.

But what worried Xander the most was that Ortega might not even try to resolve this new crisis and instead put in place some stopgap action that would carry it beyond his time in office and then lay the final resolution squarely at the feet of Owen Murphy. Xander had met the

President a couple of times during his time with DARPA, and he suspected that Ortega wasn't beyond such an act. In fact, he might consider it a symbolic middle finger to the bombastic and condescending President-elect. And from what Xander knew of Murphy and his politics, he had no doubt the man was not up to the task.

Once Ortega was off the screen and replaced with more talking heads, Xander sighed deeply and said quietly, "This is going to be a fucking disaster."

Tiffany looked at him, waiting for more to be said. When he remained silent, she asked, "So what do you think will happen next?"

He shrugged. "First of all, we have to accept the fact that the RDC is gone, out of commission for at least six months. In the meantime, crews are going to have to get into the bunkers and start reprogramming all the flight controllers to accept new transponder codes. Then, another facility will have to be set up where responses can be coordinated and acted upon while you round up a couple of thousand qualified pilots and sensor-operators for the job. Oh, and did I mention we'll all be living in caves and hunting with bows and arrows by then because there won't be much of society left after the drones get through with us."

"I thank you for that bright and cheerful dissertation, Mr. Moore," said Tiffany with a bite in her tone. "But what I meant is, what do you think will happen over the next couple of days with regard to terrorist attacks."

"Sorry," Xander said, feeling embarrassed for his emotional outburst. He glanced at his watch. "It's just past eight on the West Coast, which means the sun will be coming up on the East Coast in about eight hours. I would guess that there are already terrorist units in place and ready to strike, just waiting for the outcome of the raid on the RDC. Now, they'll be given the go-ahead. It all starts tomorrow, Ms. Collins. If ever we could place a date and time for the beginning of Armageddon, this would be it."

"All because *one* government agency was attacked?" Tiffany wasn't sold on Xander's grim view of the future. "I agree. We're going to see an increase in terrorist activities, and the Christmas shopping season will be impacted. But we weathered the pandemic in 2020, and that was global. I have to believe we'll get through this, too. And others will step up to fill the void left by the RDC. We still have the military, the National Guard, local police, the FBI, CIA, NSA and a whole lot more."

"I hope you're right," Xander said, "but the biggest question mark in this whole affair is what will Ortega do—what can he do—to make a difference? These terrorists know Americans, and they know our institutions. It's no accident that the attack happened when it did, and they couldn't have picked a better time for their purposes."

Tiffany got up from the couch and collected the empty teacups and soup bowls. Then she brought out a stack of thick cotton blankets and handed them to Xander.

"I take it I'm on the couch tonight," he said, acting hurt.

She leaned over and kissed him on the cheek. "You did a pretty decent job of keeping me alive today, but yes, you get the couch—for now. But seriously, thank you. I'm sure that if you hadn't literally landed in my lap, I'd be just another name on the casualty list at the RDC."

Xander grinned. "I couldn't let that happen, at least not until I learned the name of your perfume."

"*Bella Faito*—Beautiful Breath—I know, weird name, but it is pretty awesome, isn't it."

"That it is."

With a seductive smile, Tiffany retreated to the solitary bedroom, and Xander Moore was asleep within minutes of the lights going out.

12

After making the brief statement to the nation, President Hector Ortega walked back to the Oval Office with an angry and purposeful stride. His aides had trouble keeping up with him; this was his way of shedding some of the pent-up frustration he was feeling at the moment.

Why now? he kept repeating in his head. He was so close to making a clean getaway after a rather lackluster second term. And with no great accomplishments to offset this tragedy, he was about to be labeled for all eternity as the president who lost the Drone Wars to the terrorists.

As he entered the iconic circular-shaped room—now full of people from Cabinet members all the way down to porters—he was determined not to go down alone. That bastard Owen Murphy was due in the Oval Office any moment, and Ortega was going to get that SOB directly involved in every decision his lame-duck administration would make during the crisis. Just let him try to weasel out after that.

He could already hear the conversation:

"I inherited a mess left over from the Ortega Administration, so it's not my fault that things are so shitty. Blame Ortega!"

"But Mr. President, weren't you directly involved in all the decisions made following the attack on the RDC? Didn't you sign off on the actions taken by the prior administration?"

As he slipped into his large executive leather chair behind the Resolute Desk, Ortega let the fantasy fade away. Even though he would continue to consider politics in every move he made, he still had a major crisis to deal with. He was known for his level-headed decisiveness, yet even this early into the crisis, he knew he had to make some drastic moves.

"Everyone not cleared for Level One, get the hell out," he said in a normal talking voice. He didn't need to repeat himself. When the President of the United States spoke, people listened. Within seconds, only eight people remained.

"Admiral, what's the latest?" Ortega was amazed that here, at almost midnight, the Chairman of the Joint Chiefs of Staff, Admiral Gregory Hagar, was decked out in full dress attire, sporting an almost obscene stack of service ribbons on his left coat pocket and one wide gold band, accompanied by four narrower gold stripes on each sleeve of his Navy-blue uniform.

"The RDC is a complete loss, which compromises our ability to activate the units in the response bunkers. We're calling up every capable drone operator we can find within the service ranks and placing them on standby to assist civilian defense assets once an event is initiated."

"So, you also anticipate a surge in terrorist activity?" Ortega asked.

"Yes, sir, without a doubt. The field is clear—at least temporarily. It would be foolish to have taken such action against the RDC and then not act on it."

"How soon can we have a replacement for the RDC up and running?"

Acting Secretary of Defense Alice Grimes spoke next. She had been Ian Graves' assistant for only two years, and with him leaving the administration two weeks before to pursue a consulting job in private industry, she was a placeholder appointment until Murphy replaced her.

"Each branch of the military has a small drone program of their own, yet after the consolidation debate of four years ago, all major operations were shifted to the RDC." She looked to Admiral Hagar for moral support. "The most we can expect is about ten percent of the capacity of the RDC for civil defense, and that's through four specific chains of command."

"Bullshit! There's only *one* chain of command, and it ends right here," Ortega barked. "Admiral, assign your most competent senior officer to coordinate all military drone activity. All branches, everyone, will answer to him

… or her. If you hear any grumblings from anyone, can their asses and get someone in who will follow orders."

"Yes, sir."

"Go ahead, Alice; is there more?"

Just as Grimes was about to speak, the thick entry door to the Oval Office flew open, and President-elect Owen Murphy strode in as if it was his office already. He was followed by no fewer than six aides and advisors. Even though Ortega had invited him to the strategy meeting, his jaw still clenched at the arrogance and disruptive nature of his entrance.

Murphy walked up to the President's desk and extended an arm across the wide expanse almost before Ortega could get to his feet. The two men shook hands —briefly.

"Welcome, Governor, we were just starting."

"Thanks for inviting me, Hector."

Only Ortega's dark complexion kept the rest of the room from noticing the heat that rushed to his face as Murphy used Ortega's first name rather than his title. He hesitated a moment before speaking to let his nerves calm down. "With the seriousness and scope of this crisis, I thought it appropriate that the President-elect should be involved from the beginning."

Their eyes locked for a moment, which was confirmation that Murphy knew exactly what Ortega was up to. Whether he would let himself get trapped in a situation from which he couldn't escape was another question. It would take some deft politicking on the President's part to make sure he did.

Admiral Hagar gave up his seat in front of the desk to Murphy, who sat down without acknowledgment to the CJCS. "My people have been analyzing the current situation and have concluded we could be in for a period of increased terrorist activity. What steps are you taking to prepare for this?"

There was a large, ancient clock on the wall opposite where the President sat, and Ortega noticed that only thirty seconds had gone by since Murphy entered the office—and already Hector wanted to toss the man out on his ear. It was not the President's role to answer questions directed at him, at least when the cameras weren't on. It was *his* job to ask the questions and demand answers. So he took a full five seconds before responding, sending a subliminal message that he would answer only questions he wanted to answer and only when he damn well pleased.

"I've directed Admiral Hagar to set up a joint services response center to consolidate all our military defense assets and prepare for triage once the sun comes up. I'm sure we won't have to wait long to see the after-effects of the RDC attack."

"That's our belief, too," Murphy condescended to say. "Have you opened a dialog with the various terrorist organizations to see if there is any way to reach an accommodation?"

"That *I* haven't done," Ortega said forcefully, emphasizing the '*I*' in the sentence. "We're not about to be blackmailed by radicals when we don't even know the full extent of the crisis or even who's behind it."

An aide handed Murphy a sheet of paper. "We believe the Arm of Allah is behind the RDC attack. Their leader, Abdul-Shahid Almasi, has the expertise with distant drone operations, and he's very well connected with the other groups operating in the Middle East."

"I know who Almasi is, Owen," Ortega said. "And that's what the CIA and others have also concluded. Yet, so far, we have no confirmation of his involvement. This attack was on a larger scale than anything before it, so even if Almasi's group is behind it, they've brought in allies. It's also apparent that the information needed to carry out the attack had to be acquired from inside the RDC."

Murphy pursed his lips. "That's our conclusion, as well. A major security breach at the most significant national defense organization in the country. How could this have happened … Mr. President?"

Ortega pushed away from the desk and leaned back in his chair. He gave Murphy a thin smile. "There'll be plenty of time to assign blame, Owen, but right now, we have to gather our resources and prepare for what's coming. The RDC was effective in shutting down ongoing events—as they call them. We—all of us—have to come up with an effective alternative to the RDC." He looked to his Chief of Staff, Jack Monroe. "Jack, you've been looking into the economic impact of the situation. What can you tell us?"

Jack Monroe had given his notice a month ago and was scheduled to leave the administration the following week, a few days before Christmas, before beginning an extended vacation. He was the longest-serving member of Ortega's team, having been with him for his entire two terms. Earlier in the day, he withdrew his resignation letter. He would be with Ortega now until the bitter end.

"Prior to this, three malls were hit by drone attacks in the last week, and already year-over-year sales were off fifteen percent in the brick-and-mortar stores. In spite of this, online sales have been booming, so overall, it was shaping up to be a pretty decent holiday season. The people I've spoken with this afternoon are taking a wait-and-see attitude, depending on what happens over the next few days. There are only nine shopping days left before Christmas, which is the time when most transactions take place. Pressing the experts for a worst-case scenario, if attacks on the malls pick up, they can see a fifty percent drop in sales compared to last year."

"Holy crap," Ortega said. "What will that do to the rest of the economy?"

"Just as you suspect, Mr. President," Monroe said. "All sectors will be impacted—retail, financial … all of it. And then the ripple effect around the world would be catastrophic."

"We can't let that happen, Monroe," Owen Murphy

said, acting as if the Chief of Staff had some control over what the terrorists might or might not do. "This makes it imperative that we make contact with Almasi and his backers. It's not a matter of whether this is blackmail or not; it's a matter of economic survival. He wants something, and anything he wants is better than the alternative."

Ortega glared at the President-elect. "You're advocating premature capitulation, even before we have a chance to react?"

"We may not get a chance to react," Murphy countered. "Even if the attacks are not as prevalent, or we can counter some of them, it's the psychological effect this will have on the population that matters. If they're scared, they won't shop, and then everything goes to hell in a handbasket."

All eyes were on Ortega as he remained quiet for several moments after Murphy's comment. Then he calmly leaned forward again and placed his elbows on the desk. "Admiral, please go and begin the coordination of all military resources for a response to the anticipated attacks coming our way. Morgan," he said, addressing the head of Homeland Security, "begin making preparations for FEMA's response to catastrophic events and get with the CIA and FBI to determine if we can locate the head of the serpent behind all this. Jack and I will see if there is a political solution, following the very sage advice offered by Governor Murphy. We will look at all options—nothing will be off the table. Jack, see to it that the Governor and his staff are given accommodations within the White House for the duration of the crisis—"

"That won't be necessary, Mr. President."

"I insist, Owen. I want you by my side throughout all of this, and free to offer any suggestions you deem appropriate. Now, it's getting late. Let's break for now and meet back up at nine in the morning unless circumstances dictate otherwise. That will be all."

Both the President and President-elect remained in their chairs, smiling thinly at each other until the room was empty.

"Well played, Hector," Murphy stated once they were alone.

"I wish we could put party aside and just work together on a solution," Ortega replied.

"Party has nothing to do with this," said Murphy. "The quickest way to head off the coming disaster is to give Almasi what he wants. It doesn't have to go public."

"And then we set a precedent."

"What precedent? That was done long ago with hostage swaps and nuclear treaties. The old Reagan Doctrine of not negotiating with terrorists is a thing of the past. Now, all that matters is saving American lives."

"Your plan may be what's ultimately put in place, but I'm not about to lead with it."

"Well, I'm glad you have an open mind, at least." And then he smiled—a sly, devilish expression. "And Hector, don't think you can outmaneuver me. You came out of the business world, but I've been a product of political infighting my entire life. I've seen it all and done it all. I'll be covered no matter what happens. So, play whatever games you think you must, but I won't be harmed by them."

"You know, Owen, you are one nasty son-of-a-bitch."

"Oh, I know. That's why I'll be sitting in *that* chair in a little over a month. Then, the real professionals will be back in control of the government. We already have the Congress, and on January 20, a new era in government activism begins, and then you'll see what a government is truly designed to do."

Ortega shook his head. "And that is my worst fear of all."

13

Xander awoke before daybreak, and when he looked out the window to check on the hovercopter, he found that another generous coating of snow had fallen during the night. He stepped outside and took in the cool, brisk air. He'd lived in Las Vegas for the past five years, and even though the winters there could get cold, there was nothing like the smell and briskness of fresh mountain air.

The moon had set by this early hour, yet the stars at this altitude still shined brightly, casting the surrounding forest in a soft glow that set his mind at ease. He took in the moment, knowing it wouldn't last. The new day would bring more turmoil and more tragedy, even though *his* plans were still unfocused.

He stepped out into the snow and crunched his way to

the aircraft. He checked the power reading and saw that it was below half. The attached extension cord would charge the battery in less than an hour using normal 110-current, so he pulled the cord inside the cabin and plugged it into a socket.

Next, he went to the kitchen and lit a small propane burner on the stove, placing the tea kettle over the flame. He wasn't much of a tea drinker, and after a few moments of searching, he came upon a lone packet of Swiss Miss chocolate mix. Once his drink was fixed, he sat on the couch and stared at the red coals in the pot belly stove.

He had to come up with a plan, yet before he could, he had to have the answers to several critical questions, not the least of which: Who was behind the attack on the RDC?

He already had a solid suspicion, yet an operation this big was far beyond the capabilities of even Abdul-Shahid Almasi. Then, there was the question of how the information was acquired to mount the operation. That could only have come from inside the Center. Who would have access to such information, along with the motivation to give it to the terrorists?

It had to be someone with the highest clearance, as well as someone who could be bought. Xander couldn't imagine someone doing all this just for the money, although that was a possibility. More than likely, it was someone who also harbored an intense hatred for the organization, even though people like that seldom let their true feelings be known—

Xander nearly spilled his hot chocolate when a name flashed in his head. He trembled at the thought. *Could it be? Could he really be behind all the death and destruction from yesterday and all that's to come?*

It would explain a lot, like the apparent singular mission at the hovercopter hangar to find and kill *him*.

Jonas Lemon.

"Jonas Lemon," Xander repeated aloud, "you rotten son-of-a-bitch."

Jonas Lemon had spent nearly seven years in southern Nevada, so he knew how cold the desert could get in winter. Yet here in Dubai, it was nearing eighty and dipping only into the high fifties at night. He stood before the large plate glass window on the thirty-fourth floor of the *Burj Khalifa* building, looking out at the Persian Gulf and the huge artificial island community resembling a giant palm tree—*The Palm Jumeirah*—that had been built in the shallows. The construction project was impressive, as were most things in Dubai, and it was no secret that Lemon was glad to be out of Las Vegas.

Even though his former hometown ranked among the world's most popular tourist destinations, it held a pale candle next to what Dubai had to offer—if you could afford it. The government of the United Arab Emirates was rich beyond compare, and it showcased that fact in amazing ways within its showcase city. For the *nouveau riche*—such as Jonas Lemon—the opulence of Dubai was just the reward he deserved after all the years spent serving his previous master—the government of the United States of America.

Yet even now, his time here was coming to an end.

The last two weeks had been spent in an orgy for the senses as Jonas took in all the luxury Dubai had to offer, made possible by the second installment his benefactor wired into his Swiss bank account a month before. He mentally applied a pat on his back, congratulations for how well his plan was working. By not providing all the information he had at once, he not only guaranteed future payments but his safety as well. If he had revealed all to Almasi in the beginning, then the terrorist would have had no further use for him. This way, the madman actually provided security to make sure Lemon survived … at least until the last installment was delivered.

Yes, Jonas Lemon was no fool. He knew the score, and he had no illusions about the people he was doing business with. He had spent nearly ten years of his life fighting against such men, so he knew the threat they posed. And with one last installment soon due, he was even tempted to put into action the next phase in his plan, even before the payment was made.

Jonas smiled. *That would catch Almasi off guard and allow me to disappear to my Polynesian paradise before he knows what's happening.* Lemon already had enough money to last the rest of his life, yet who would suspect him of leaving before the other seven million was placed in his account?

It was important to always stay at least one step ahead of people like Abdul-Shahid Almasi. If he waited for the final deposit, then he would become expendable. So now, with each passing day, the thought of leaving early grew stronger until it was essentially a *fait accompli* in his mind.

He turned away from the window and back to the TV that dominated almost an entire wall of the suite. The device was a 72-inch Sony 5G OLED, and the images it displayed made his heart leap with joy. The RDC was in shambles, and with the lifespan of the surviving pilots now measured in days, if not hours. The country he once defended was now in an elevated state of fear, just as was expected, just as was needed….

The only regret he had so far was that Xander Moore was still alive. Although Jonas was not directly involved in the operation, he had specifically requested—indeed demanded—that Moore be personally targeted with units assigned to him exclusively. Almasi protested at first, complaining about the additional pilots—and other specialists—that would be required for the mission. But Lemon insisted. Reluctantly, Almasi agreed, and the *Xander Moore Hit Team* was assembled.

When it was reported that Moore was not present at

the time his home was destroyed—as he should have been according to the rotation roster Lemon had—the question then became: Where was he? Fortunately, the facial recognition program within the Maverick UAVs at the RDC had located him escaping into the open desert in the company of a woman identified as a Fox News correspondent named Tiffany Collins. Other units were dispatched yet were unable to stop him before he escaped in an experimental hovercopter.

Lemon had confidence that Moore would be located eventually, if not by Almasi's men and machines, then by the ones Lemon himself had hired to do the job. Xander Moore would die … and on his death certificate, it would read: Cause of Death: *Jonas Lemon*.

The seventeen-inch screen of the open laptop computer on the dining table suddenly flashed to life. Jonas walked over to the device and pressed the return key to authorize the connection. The dark face of Abdul-Shahid Almasi stared back at him; coal-black pupils surrounded by pure white made him appear wide-eyed and manic at all times.

"Have you been watching the news?" Almasi asked in perfect English, with just a hint of the British accent that revealed his formal education in that island nation.

"Of course, as has the entire world."

"I must congratulate you on the success of your plan. The information you provided has proved to be genuine."

"The mission has not been a complete success, not yet."

"Your nemesis, Xander Moore, *will* be found, Mr. Lemon, and maybe then you can accept the compliment. I do not give them out often."

"I'm sure you don't."

After a brief pause, Almasi continued. "Seeing that the operation is now in full motion, would you not see fit to provide the last piece of the puzzle so we can conclude our business?"

"Patience, Mr. Almasi. You will get it. But first, let the fear simmer for a while. America must be at the breaking point before they take it to the next stage. With the RDC out of action, there will be plenty of open targets to keep your pilots busy. Have some fun, Abdul-Shahid; after all, isn't killing infidels your favorite pastime?"

"Please do not be flippant with me, Mr. Lemon. What I do is not a hobby. I do it with the utmost seriousness and purpose."

"Forgive me; I'm just a little giddy about what has taken place over the past twenty-four hours. No offense was intended."

"You feel *giddy*—as you say—over the demise of your homeland? Isn't that rather odd?"

"You forget, Abdul, I'm a traitor of the first degree, so I obviously don't have as much love for my country as you give me credit for. I'm enough of a realist to accept that fact. Sure, the money is good and much appreciated, but I, too, have the utmost seriousness and purpose for what I do —have done."

"Your hatred for this, Mr. Moore, must be all-consuming."

The smile vanished from Lemon's face. "Moore is just the catalyst for my hatred, Almasi. He's the face I put to it. But it was the system that destroyed me. Now, I will help destroy that system … and along with it, Xander Moore."

"Even though I find your reasoning to be confusing and complex, I still respect it," said the terrorist leader. "Our singular goal, although arrived at from opposite directions, will soon be achieved. How we reached this juncture is only for Allah to understand. I accept it for what it is."

"So, what is the latest on Xander Moore?"

"Since his home was destroyed, we have been researching this newscaster he has with him, Tiffany Collins. He may be using her to hide him. She lives in Los Angeles yet has not returned to her home. Her family owns another dwelling, and we are pursuing that location in case that is where they have fled. I will keep you informed as to our progress."

"Good. Now, although I don't mean to renegotiate the terms of our arrangement this late into the process, why don't we make the death of Xander Moore a condition for delivery of the final data drop? That's not too much to ask, is it?"

"Indeed it is!" Almasi barked. Jonas could see Almasi's eyes grow even wider ... if that was possible. "This Mr. Moore is a distraction to our true mission. Do not attempt to complicate things any further."

"Relax, it was worth a try," Lemon said with a smile. "All right, the drop will proceed as originally scheduled ... unless you can terminate Mr. Moore beforehand. If that happens, then I *will* consider releasing the information early. That way, we both get what we want."

Lemon could see the devious mind of Abdul-Shahid Almasi working behind the manic eyes. Jonas had touched a chord. "That would be acceptable," the terrorist leader said. "I will send word out to make the death of Xander Moore a priority. Please remain where you are. Confirmation should come within the day."

"As always, it's a pleasure doing business with you, Mr. Almasi."

Without a return acknowledgment, the screen on the computer went dark.

That went well, Lemon thought, *even though now I'll have to move up the timetable for my departure.*

He looked around at the luxurious suite he had in the Armani Hotel, ensconced within the lower floors of the tallest building in the world. He sighed. "It will be a shame to say goodbye," he said aloud to the inanimate room, "yet I value my life more than I do your spectacular view and excellent room service. It's a sacrifice I must make ... if I intend to outlive Xander Moore."

"So you think this Jonas Lemon guy is the one who sold out the RDC?"

Thirty minutes before, Tiffany Collins came out of the bedroom looking as fresh and put together as when they first met at the Center, although now she wore a man's long-sleeve flannel shirt and form-fitting jeans, along with a pair of white Reeboks. The two were seated at the cabin's small dining table, finishing servings of canned corn beef hash and hash browns which Tiffany fixed.

"It has to be him. He had the access and the motivation."

"But to kill thousands of people just because you got him fired? C'mon, that only happens in the movies."

"Jonas has always been a psycho case, and he should never have been allowed in the program in the first place."

"So why was he?"

"Because he was the best drone pilot we ever had, that's why."

"Even better than you?" Tiffany asked with a mischievous smile.

"Well, that's up for debate. But he was *one* of the best."

"So what makes him a psycho, as you call him?"

"Jonas had the most detached emotions I'd ever seen when it came to his job. He would kill any target put before him without question or remorse. A real psychopath."

"Isn't that the goal?"

Xander pursed his lips. He felt like he was being interviewed again. He couldn't blame Tiffany; this was her job, and it was hard to turn it off. "I've known Jonas since the days of the Drone Racing League and from other combat-based competitions. He eventually ended up working for the military, piloting the old MQ-1 Predators out of one of the Ground Control trailers at Creech Air Force Base. His condition—you might call it that—wasn't apparent at first since the brass didn't consider killing the enemy a mental disorder. It was only after so many of his colleagues started having morality problems—and he didn't—that people began to notice. Unfortunately, rather than worry about him, they made him their poster boy."

"I imagine finding people who could handle that line of work without going bonkers would be welcome. You acknowledge the necessity for the foreign drone program, yet then criticize the people who carry it out."

"You have me all wrong, Tiffany. I'm not knocking it; I do realize the necessity and how difficult a job it can be. I could never do it, and I admire those who can. It's just that Jonas Lemon was, well, different. When the military downsized and started using smaller drones, he was the first to volunteer since he'd cut his teeth on that class of UAV. But because these compact units were able to operate in more crowded venues, with more potential for collateral damage, Jonas was a time bomb waiting to go off.

"With today's twenty-four-hour news cycle, as well as armies of critics looking for any excuse to blame America first, Jonas soon became a liability rather than an asset. On several occasions, he leveled entire buildings just to get at one man. The collateral damage was horrific, and the PR problem he caused for the military was more than they could tolerate."

"I thought *you* fired him."

"Not the first time. In reality, he was forced to transfer to the RDC a few years after its creation. The brass figured he'd do less damage fighting other drones than he did against live targets."

"That didn't happen, did it?"

"Nope, he was still just as reckless and callous as before. He would still take out an entire city block just to neutralize one enemy drone, and he didn't give a damn if civilians got in the way. To him, it *was* just a video game, with nothing being real beyond the screen. Suffering collateral damage in some mountain village in Pakistan was nothing compared to the fallout when innocent Americans died in a football stadium as a result of his actions."

"So, what was the final straw?"

"Atlanta, '37."

"Oh, my god, he was involved in that?"

"That's right. Forty-three civilians were riddled with bullets after getting caught in the crossfire between two combat drones. Sure, the target was taken out, but the cost was too high. I was the lead pilot of the backup team on site that day, and I witnessed what he did. As a matter of fact, it was *my* drone that took out *his* before he could do even more damage. And as the senior pilot at the Center, I was also the one who recommended his firing."

"So, what happened to him? After such a tragedy, you didn't just let him walk out the door, did you?"

"Of course not. Charges of criminal intent were filed, and he faced up to twenty-five years to life for his actions. He fought the charges, however, bringing in some high-powered civilian attorneys to defend him. They turned the narrative around and accused the government of making him the scapegoat for their poor planning and misman-agement of the operation. In the end, Jonas was stripped of his retirement, had his clearance revoked and then sent packing, leaving him with a stack of attorney fees that could choke a horse. He was married at the time, and she left in the middle of all this, taking their six-year-old daughter with her. The last time I heard of him, he was facing foreclosure and trying to file bankruptcy, which his own attorneys were fighting. His life was pretty much a wreck after that."

"So, where's he now?"

"I don't know. He left Las Vegas and disappeared—that was six months ago—and now this. I can't think of anyone else who could have done this, at least the inside part of the operation."

Tiffany stopped her questioning and looked askew at Xander. "You know him, don't you? This goes beyond the RDC, doesn't it?"

Xander took a long gulp of lukewarm tea before answering. "You remember I told you about the Drone Olympics and how I got three gold and two silver medals? I got the golds in the team events but lost out twice in the individual competitions ... to Jonas Lemon."

"So he *is* better than you," Tiffany said, smiling.

"The man has an uncanny sense of tactics and spatial awareness, even when looking through a pair of 3-D FPV goggles. He could visualize the entire battlefield and place himself in the drone itself. He and the UAV became one, and his reactions were just a fraction of a second quicker than mine. In the seek-and-evade event, I thought I had his drone cornered when, in fact, he'd lured me into *his* killing field. It wasn't pretty. And in the head-to-head combat competition, he was firing before I could even detect his drone. And then his ability to lead the target with his shots was, well, freaky. I scored one point against him before he closed me out. The whole individual competition was rather humiliating. That's when Jonas was recruited by the military. He was better than me—at that time—and they saw more value in someone with his particular set of skills than mine. I was more of the cerebral kind of guy, so I fit in better at DARPA. My time with the RDC would come a couple of years later, and only because they needed my knowledge and not my skills as a pilot."

"And now you think he's hatched this grandiose plan to take out the RDC and get revenge on you at the same time?"

"Well, I hate to admit it, but the plan that was carried out against the RDC wasn't his … it was mine."

Tiffany recoiled from the unexpected admission. "What the hell does *that* mean?"

"It was just a scenario I worked up when I was at DARPA, a what-if plan to take out *enemy* control centers, not our own. Remember, I spent a couple of years in D.C. just thinking up the worst things that could be done with drones. Jonas must have read the report, and when the shit hit the fan over Atlanta, he saw the writing on the wall and began planning for the attack before he lost his clearance and access to the RDC."

"Okay, so you've narrowed down how the RDC computers were breached, and you've even said who came up with the plan for the attack. But you still haven't said who's partnering with Lemon. He couldn't do this by himself. I'm pretty sure it's not Al Qaida or ISIS, so I would put my money on The Arm of Allah."

"I see you've done your homework."

"Remember, I was preparing for an hour-long special

about drone warfare, and the A-of-A is the fastest growing terrorist organization around these days, and they use drones almost exclusively in their operations. But this is huge, even for them."

"Exactly." Xander finished off his cup of tea and went for another. "Contrary to popular belief, it does require boots on the ground to set up an effective drone attack, and this was the biggest ever staged." he continued. "As a rule, the receivers on the units are very weak, so the main transmitter needs to be within a ten-mile radius or so, if not closer. They do this with local relays, usually found in cargo trucks and hidden from the public. Technology is advancing, but as it is now, that's the only way to carry out remote operations like this."

"But can't these drones be operated by themselves?"

Xander returned to the table with his fresh cup of tea. He looked at his watch: six-forty-one. He knew he had to get moving soon, but the prospect of facing the uncertainty of the outside world made him reluctant to end the conversation. Besides, the scenery was pretty awesome inside the cabin, even if the smooth coating of virgin snow outside had its own appeal.

"That's right. You're thinking about the autonomous drones, the point-and-release units that fly by pre-programmed instructions. What I'm talking about is the Remotely-Piloted Aircraft, the RPAs that require a pilot. For these, you need heavy-duty receivers and transmitters, along with a solid link with the control center, which, by the way, can be located just about anywhere these days, thanks to satellites. It wouldn't do for the operators to lose contact with their RPAs right in the middle of an op, even using Random Frequency Generators. So, some of the larger organizations—with the help of Iran and North Korea primarily—have been placing their own satellites in orbit just so they can maintain these designated links."

"But you could take them out?"

"Off the record, we're working on that, but like so many other areas of dispute with these rogue nations, they claim the satellites are up there for peaceful purposes and not for terrorist activities. It wouldn't do for us to start shooting down satellites and then have all the cellphones in North Korea stop working—which they'd make happen even if the signals weren't being routed through that particular satellite. Everyone knows what's going on, but the game still has to be played."

"Even after this latest attack?"

"That remains to be seen. So far, most of the damage has been to a semi-secret government facility and a small military base. Yet, if the terrorists use this opportunity to increase their attacks on civilians, then public opinion may leave us no choice. Of course, after that, *our* satellites will start being shot down, which just sends the whole thing tumbling over the cliff. I have to be honest with you, Tiffany. We're on the edge of the cliff right now, and it won't take much to push us over."

Xander could see the worry in the reporter's crystal

blue eyes. For a time yesterday, he'd noticed a detachment in her from the consequences of the attack, even as she was experiencing it. Yet now, she realized everyone was at risk, along with everything she held dear. Yesterday, she was a reporter on the scene of a major news event. Today, she could see how that event could consume them all.

"Sorry to lay all this heavy stuff on you," Xander said to fill the tense silence in the room.

Tiffany flashed him a brilliant smile. "Hey, I'm a big girl. And my job *is* to seek out the most newsworthy and impactful events happening in the world. I actually go out of my way looking for heaping piles of shit to report on." Although her smile was forced, at least she tried. "So, what's your plan—beyond surviving another day, of course?"

He snorted. "Yeah, survival would be a priority. As I said, terrorists have long memories. I've also noticed your cabin doesn't have a phone, and neither one of us appears to have our cells on us. I need to get in contact with, well, anyone who may have survived. And like all government agencies, we have our bosses back in D.C. Bottom line: I need a phone."

"Landlines are so passé these days, but you're right. And I also need to let the network know that I'm still alive. But I was so exhausted last night that I didn't want to bother with it. I can go over to the Nash's house next door and use their phone. They're old and retired and home most of the time; however, next door around here is about a half-mile hike up the mountain and through the forest."

"No problem, I'll come with you. A walk in the morning air will do me good."

"I'll get us a couple of jackets; I'm sure one of my dad's will fit you."

14

Damien Winslow tried to hold the computer steady as the huge Chevy Suburban negotiated the narrow, two-lane mountain road. As an aide, he used his thumb and pointer finger to expand the picture so he could see it better.

It was a satellite image of a tiny log cabin nestled in the forest not too far from his present location. The three-vehicle caravan had left for the address before the image was available, anticipating that this was where the target had fled. The order had come through to expedite the operation, so they set off even before receiving confirmation. It was a risk … but calculated. Besides, the twenty-thousand-dollar bonus they'd been promised made it worth taking.

As it turned out, the satellite image confirmed that they'd made the right decision. The strange-looking helicopter was in plain sight, resting near the front of the small cabin. The image was only sixteen minutes old, and according to GPS, the team was six minutes from the destination. It would be an unfortunate stroke of bad luck if the helicopter took off within that narrow timeframe, leaving them empty-handed. To narrow the chances of that not happening, Jacques St. Claire, the driver, was pushing the huge SUV to its limits around the sharp curves, made even more treacherous by the recent snowfall and the failure of Caltrans to clear the roads by this early hour. The other two vehicles were falling behind, but they would soon catch up as St. Claire made an abrupt turn to the right and onto a street called Pine Crest within the small mountain community of Idyllwild.

Two minutes later, the caravan reached the steep dirt road that led to the cabin. The heavy lead SUV turned onto the mushy surface and immediately ran into trouble. Even though four-wheel drive was an option on this model, the L.A.-based owners of the vehicle had opted only for standard front-wheel drive. A quick radio check of the other two vehicles found that none of the other SUVs had four-wheel drive either.

Damien gnashed his teeth out of frustration with the enviable. There was no other option. The vehicles parked at the base of the road—looking conspicuous in the quiet, rural town—and the team set out on foot for the half-mile hike up the steep, snow-covered slope.

Even though the vehicle caravan and his eight-man

team stood out like a neon sign, fortunately, there were no buildings facing the sharp turn in the road where they parked, and soon, the men were obscured by the tall pine and cedar trees growing on the mountain. All of his men were ex-military, well-trained and armed with either Beretta ARX-160 assault rifles or the old standby Uzi submachine gun. They were each prime specimens of male physical conditioning, so even at an altitude of one mile, they scaled the slope with ease, if not with stealth. They were in two groups, trailing one after the other to either side of the snow-covered road, and even though they tried, it was impossible to cover their tracks in the snow and slush.

Damien had been provided with a brief file on each of the targets, so he wasn't worried. The man they were after was literally an armchair warrior—a video game expert at drone combat rather than the real thing. The other was a plastic-looking Barbie doll he'd seen on T.V. On paper, neither posed much of a threat, even though taking out the woman would be a shame, not because Damien had any qualms about killing a woman, but because she was so hot.

It wasn't long before they crested the slope and came upon the rustic cabin with the out-of-place futuristic hovercopter sitting out front. It was nearing seven a.m., and the late rising sun of mid-December was just now beginning to peek over the mountaintop to the east and touch the tallest of the pines. There was a light inside the cabin, and as the team approached and flanked the front entrance, Damien spotted tracks in the virgin snow, indicating that someone had already been outside this morning. That's when he noticed the orange extension cord running from the aircraft and into the cabin, with the front door slightly ajar to allow for the cable's entry.

The only reason he didn't order a full-on frontal assault on the cabin was the fact that its occupants knew they were targets and may be prepared for more attempts on their lives. In addition, most rural cabins like this one had a weapon of some sort lying around, and Damien wasn't about to get one of his men shot simply because he was impatient.

And that was when Damien Winslow produced his own miniature drone. It was a six-inch-in-diameter spy drone running on four almost-silent rotors and linked to the small screen of his cellphone. He handed the drone to his second-in-command, Jacques St. Claire, and then activated the controller.

The bird-like device spun off toward the cabin, coming in low under the solitary front window before slowly rising to look inside. St. Claire and Damien studied the tiny image on the phone. There were curtains on the window, yet with a small gap allowing for a restricted view of the interior. When this proved to be inconclusive, the drone moved to the front door. One of Damien's men crouched on the front porch and gently pushed the door open wide enough for the drone to enter. The device stayed low, using its wide-angle lens to do a quick survey of the interior. No one was seen, yet there was a doorway to the left. The drone moved in that direction, entering through the open doorway into what was the cabin's solitary bedroom.

Unless the two targets were in the bathroom together, the cabin was empty. With hand signals, Damien sent his men inside. He followed a moment later.

There was hot water on the stove, and the remaining tea in the two cups on the table was still warm. Could they have seen them coming and dashed out the back? That was a possibility. There was a rear door, and the two sets of tracks leading from the cabin were clearly visible.

The forest was still in the shadow of the mountain; even so, there were no dwellings seen through the trees in the direction of the tracks. Trained in the Army Special Forces, Damien noticed that the length of the steps left in the snow was narrow, indicating the people were walking and not running, so maybe his team was still undetected. But where were they going? Two people seeking refuge from killers seldom took leisurely morning strolls, especially in ankle-deep snow and sub-zero temperatures. There had to be a purpose for leaving the cabin.

He split his men into two groups once again, one on each side of the tracks, and they set off climbing higher up the slope. The snow was thicker here and crusty from the cold shadow of the mountain. Each of his men wore heavy combat boots, yet even then, several slipped and fell during the climb. After several minutes, Damien detected the sweet smell of pancakes wafting in the still air. As they climbed higher, the smell grew stronger. A dog began to bark, with the cadenced sound echoing through the trees. There was a house up ahead, and they were getting close.

"A phone, of course, sweetie," Doris Nash chuckled. "But watch the minutes. We only have so many before I have to go all the way into Hemet to get a refill card."

"Thank you so much. When I find my purse I'll be sure to give you enough for a whole other card with three hundred minutes." Tiffany introduced Xander to the old couple; Jack Nash sent him a wink when Tiffany wasn't looking, an acknowledgment of Xander's excellent taste in women.

The Nash home was much larger than Tiffany's log cabin. It was on a separate road leading up the mountain from Idyllwild, with three bedrooms, two baths and a two-car garage. The couple had built it over thirty years ago as a vacation home. Now, in their early seventies, it was their permanent residence.

Jack Nash was seated before the T.V., and when Tiffany came near, he quickly picked up the remote and switched the channel from CNN to Fox and Friends. The reporter chuckled. "That's okay, Jack. At least now I know who their *one* viewer is."

Embarrassed, the wiry, nearly bald man rushed to change the subject. "Isn't this something? I mean, what happened in Las Vegas?" Xander came to stand next to the old man's chair. The regular programming had been preempted for near-continuous coverage of the attack. The on-screen talent was detailing how the strike had occurred and how there had already been three attacks along the Eastern seaboard that morning. It was as if the media was on a terrorist attack watch, just waiting for the next event to happen. A military expert was being interviewed, discussing the potential impact of the attacks and the secrets that had been posted to the internet.

"I'm surprised you're not in the middle of all this," Jack said to Tiffany. She exchanged a quick glance with Xander before responding.

"Yeah, it is my kind of story. That's why I need the phone. I lost mine, and I need to call the network."

Doris handed her the cellphone.

"Xander needs to call his office, too, if that's all right?"

"Just watch the minutes."

Tiffany stepped outside on the front porch to make the call. Doris joined her briefly as she yelled at her dog, Ginger, to stop barking. The old yellow lab obliged, making it easier for Tiffany to hear.

Xander continued watching the news until Tiffany returned and handed him the phone. "They're relieved, as would be expected. They're sending a car up from Riverside to pick me up."

Xander nodded. "Good. I'll be right back."

He stepped out the front door and into the subzero air outside. It was refreshing, and he sat in a padded chair protected from the evening snowfall by the overhang above the porch. Ginger came up next to him, and after dialing the emergency response number for the RDC, he began to scratch the dog behind her ears.

The phone was answered immediately. "Code, please," the mechanical voice asked.

"Six-Four-One-Nine-Red," he answered.

Within seconds, a live person came on the line. "Xander Moore? Confirm secondary protocol."

"Oscar-Bravo … sunrise."

"What's your location?"

"I'm in Idyllwild, California. I'm secure at this time. I'm with a news reporter named Tiffany Collins, staying at her cabin. Can you fill me in? What was the damage?"

"Extensive, with over eight hundred dead. The facility has been reacquired; however, all systems are down or have been compromised."

"And the operators?"

There was a pause on the line before the speaker continued. "Nearly one hundred percent. The assault drones probed throughout the facility for two hours, killing everyone they could find, along with coordinated attacks on the homes of the pilots that happened simultaneously with that on the facility. A few stragglers who were off the grid at the time survived and have been brought in. There was a report of a secondary assault to the east of the facility, believed to be aimed at you. Can you confirm?"

"I believe so. Look into the whereabouts of a former RDC pilot named Jonas Lemon. I believe he's the one who compromised the Center, providing the information for the terrorists to take us out. Any claim of credit yet?"

"There's been over a dozen who have, but nothing credible. The traffic on this one from the major players is quiet, which is unusual for something this big."

"I'm sorry, but could you repeat that," Xander said. "There's a dog here that just started barking."

"I hear that. I said no one credible has claimed credit." There was a delay on the line before the person on the other end spoke again. "Is the dog yours?"

"No, we're at a neighbor's house using their phone. We left ours at the Center."

"Is the dog's barking unusual?"

Xander felt the line of questioning was strange until he answered the question. "I don't know, but she did bark when we came up to the house—"

"Are you armed?"

"No."

"Then vacate the location immediately. Do not return the way you came, and if possible, acquire a firearm. Take the phone with you and make contact again once you're clear. I'm sending back up, but it will not arrive in time."

Xander watched as Ginger stood in the backyard and continued to bark, staring into the woods in the direction of Tiffany's cabin. He snapped the small phone shut and put it in the pocket of his borrowed jacket before going back inside.

"I'm sorry to say this, but I believe we're all in danger." He saw Tiffany turn pale while the Nash's looked at him with quizzical frowns.

"I'm one of the people who worked at the facility in Las Vegas that was attacked yesterday," he said by way of explanation. And before waiting for a reaction, he continued. "And I believe there are people coming up the hill right now who want to kill me."

Tiffany ran to the window and pulled back the curtains. All she could see was Ginger frantically barking at the edge of the dark forest beyond the small yard.

Doris and Jack noticed the worried look on Tiffany's face and knew instinctively that what Xander was telling them was the truth.

"Are you one of the good guys or the bad guys?" Jack asked Xander.

Tiffany turned from the window. "He's one of the good guys, Jack, and they're out to kill me, too, I'm sure."

"Well, whoever they are, they won't leave us alone, either—at least that's what happens in the movies." Jack went into a back room and returned momentarily with two weapons, one a double-barrel shotgun, the other a bolt-action hunting rifle. "Grab the shells, Doris."

His wife obediently opened a drawer in the dining room hutch and pulled out two boxes of shotgun shells and another of thirty caliber bullets. And then, from another drawer, she produced a Glock-21 GEN6, .45 caliber handgun.

She noticed the startled looks on the faces of her two guests. "One can never be too careful living up here in the mountains."

Jack Nash handed the hunting rifle to Xander. He took the heavy weapon and looked at Tiffany. The woman saw the worry on his face. "You don't know how to use it, do you?" she said incredulously.

"This is a Weathersby Vanguard S2 Sporter bolt-action 30-06 sniper rifle with a Nikon Monarch 3-12X42 BDC scope."

"Damn, son, you know your weapons," Jack Nash commented with admiration.

Xander looked at him with that same nervous expression Tiffany had noticed. "So what's the problem?" she asked.

"I've never actually fired one … not really. They were part of the arsenal in *Havoc II*."

"What's Havoc II?" Doris asked.

"It's a damn video game," Tiffany answered with disgust. "You mean you know all about the weapon, but you've never fired the real thing? That's just great."

"I do know how to shoot a handgun, but not a rifle."

Tiffany took the Vanguard from him; it was a bolt-action, single shot. She opened the chamber and took the bullets Doris handed her. "You damn city folk," Tiffany said, addressing Xander. "You couldn't find your ass if it was on fire. Give him the Glock, Doris, but you might load it first."

The white-haired woman handed him the handgun. "There's already a magazine in it—fifteen rounds. And here's another. Just pull the slide back to cock it." After that, she went into the bedroom and returned with a small .22 caliber rifle. "More my size, anyway," she said. "Now, the two of you head out the front. We'll slow them down from here."

"I can't let you do that," Tiffany said. "These guys are trained killers. You might take out a couple of them, but then they'll just blast your house to pieces."

"That's covered in our homeowner's insurance," Jack said with a smile. His eyes were bright as if he was enjoying the moment—the look of an ancient combat veteran with one last battle left in him. "Now go."

Xander took Tiffany by the arm. "C'mon. The only way to save them is by leading the bad guys away from here."

Tiffany nodded before allowing Xander to drag her through the front door. "I'm sorry!" she cried out before the door slammed shut.

"They're going to get killed!"

"Not if we can draw the attackers away from the house."

They ran down the driveway until it met up with a narrow, single-lane paved road that wound down the mountain and into town. The road was slick with ice, still solid in the cold of the morning shadow. Xander slipped and slid a good twenty feet down the hill before coming to a rest. Tiffany helped him to his feet just as they heard the first loud staccato of gunfire, the first being several low-pitch booms, followed by the buzz of small-caliber automatic weapons fire. Then, more booms, along with the occasional pop-pop of the .22. Ginger was still barking, at least until a sharp yelp sounded, and the dog fell silent.

Tiffany leveled her rifle in the general direction of the Nash's backyard and let off several shots. The automatic weapon fire ceased, as did the sound of Jack's shotgun. A few seconds later, there was another boom-boom, but then there was nothing.

"They're coming this way!" Xander yelled out.

"That was the idea. I just hope it's not too late."

There were more homes on this street, and the gun battle brought many of the residents out on their porches to see what was happening. With the attacks from yesterday being broadcast on every channel, people were on edge, although none truly believed the violence could reach them. But now there was gunfire in their peaceful mountain retreat.

Xander caught the eye of an intense-looking couple just before they ducked back into their home and bolted the door shut. Without warning, Tiffany grabbed his arm and pulled, causing him to slip and fall on the slick surface again.

"What the hell, Tiffany?" he scolded.

"I have an idea. Follow me."

They ran toward a turn in the road next to a rustic, two-story cabin. She moved along the side of the home before snatching the large plastic lid off a trash can. "This will do," she said. "See, no handle, just side latches."

"Yeah, so what?"

"Just over, there is an area the kids use to sled down in the winter. I used to do it, too, when I was younger. It goes all the way down to Pine Crest."

"You want us to ride the lid down the hill?"

"Yep. It's either that or face off against those killers. In my opinion, sledding would be a lot more fun."

"I can't argue with that."

Tiffany ran to the crest of a small ridge and looked over. "There's not a lot of snow, but enough. You get on first, on your belly. I'll lie down on your back. Watch out for the rifle. I don't want to lose it."

Just then, the small pile of snow next to them began to erupt at spots like miniature geysers, followed by the distant echoes of gunfire from up the hill.

"Hurry!" Tiffany called out.

Xander fell on the plastic saucer just as Tiffany's full weight was added, pressing down on his back. His face was precariously close to the ground, and as the disk began to slide off the ridge, it dipped, and he took in a mouthful of dirty snow.

And then the slope suddenly fell off under them, and

in less than a second, the saucer was racing down the hill at breakneck speed. The path they followed was well-worn, having been used for years by neighborhood kids. Most of it was wide, even though in some areas, it narrowed to only twenty feet between trees and gray granite boulders. Xander did his best to steer the saucer by shifting his weight, yet it was Tiffany who had the most skill. She rode his back, with both of her hands gripping his shoulders as she leaned left and right.

They were really moving now, with trees a blur zipping by. And then Xander heard an "Uh oh" from Tiffany just before she rolled hard to her left, taking him with her. They rolled off the garbage can lid together and began tumbling in the thin layer of snow. Arms flailed, and jackets tore as they hit pockets of dirt mixed in with the patchwork of snow.

As he trundled, Xander noticed the blue plastic lid take flight off a sharp rise at the end of the run … and then he plowed headfirst into a two-foot-high snowbank at the base of a thick pine tree. He hit something hard that stopped him completely, and he found himself sitting in a pile of snow with his back pressed against the rough bark of the tree, his vision as wobbly as his other senses.

Then he heard a yell and turned just in time to see Tiffany Collins fly off the same small sharp rise in the run as had the trash can lid. Her cry trailed off as she disappeared over the ledge.

Xander climbed to his feet, a little groggy but otherwise unharmed, and slogged through the snow to the point where the woman and the trash lid disappeared. The sled run ended where it met Pine Crest, just before the dirt road that led to Tiffany's cabin. Kids had apparently built a launching ramp at this point, where the most daring would attempt to soar over the road before landing on another downhill slope, where the ride could continue. The lid didn't make it; it was half buried in snow at the far side of the road. Tiffany, however, was nowhere to be seen.

Xander scampered over the ledge and onto the wet asphalt of Pine Crest Road. He ran to the other side, where the trail continued, breathing a sigh of relief when he saw the newscaster hiking up the right side of the trail about thirty yards below. When she reached the road, Xander extended a hand and helped her over the last pile of snow.

"I forgot about that part," she said in her defense. "I do remember it being a lot more fun in the past. I nearly smacked into a tree."

"Are you okay?"

"Yeah, nothing's broken, but I did lose the rifle somewhere. I'd hate to have some kids find it."

She started to walk across the street before Xander stopped her. "We don't have time for this. The bad guys could slide down here, too."

"You're right, of course. But we don't have a car, and I doubt if we can reach your crazy helicopter before they catch up."

Xander looked to where the dirt road splintered off from the main road, where three dark blue Chevy Suburban SUVs were parked along the side of the street, looking out of place for the surroundings. "Do you know how to hotwire an SUV?" he said.

"No … do you?"

"We're going to find out."

The pair climbed up the road the short distance to the first SUV. Xander tried the handle, and the door opened. He looked at Tiffany and smiled before jumping into the driver's seat. He bent down so he could see the keyhole while reaching underneath for the edge of the plastic panel covering the ignition system. He'd seen plenty of people on T.V. do this: just yank off the panel and connect a few wires.

Just then, he heard a jingling near his left ear. He looked up and saw Tiffany holding a set of keys by her fingertips.

"You found them … where?" he asked as he righted himself.

"They were in the visor," she replied with a smug look on her face. "I guess this is how hit squads do it. It wouldn't pay for the guy with the keys to get shot or blown up. This way, anyone making it back to the car can get it started."

"Makes sense; now grab the keys from the other two, and let's get out of here."

Thirty seconds later, Xander whipped the huge sports

utility vehicle around and raced down Pine Crest Road. Tiffany rolled down the window, and as the truck turned south on SR 243, she tossed the keys out into a small snowbank.

"You know, that will only stop them for a minute. I'm sure guys like that *do* know how to hotwire a car."

"Perhaps we should have done something more permanent."

"Like what?"

"I don't know, like maybe puncture the tires. We'd have to do two each because they'd have one spare per car."

"That's a brilliant idea. Let's go back and do *that*." Xander began to slow the vehicle.

"No, don't!" Tiffany cried out.

Xander pressed on the gas again. "I'm just playing with you."

"You bastard, how can you joke at a time like this?"

"It was worth it just to see the look on your face. Now buckle up. We wouldn't want to get stopped for not wearing our seatbelts."

"Maybe that's exactly what we need—a cop. At least then, we'll have some protection."

"And while we're trying to convince some highway patrolman that we're being chased by terrorists, the real killers show up with a small army packing automatic weapons."

"So, where *are* we going, if not to the nearest police station?"

"I know some people in San Diego who might be able to help, at least help us track down Jonas Lemon."

"Why would you want to do that? It's a little late, isn't it?"

"Maybe, but he's the only link to the terrorist group—or groups—behind the attacks. Just as they did with us, the only way to stop these guys is to take out their version of the RDC. Lemon knows who and where they are. Besides, I wouldn't mind having a little face time with Jonas myself."

"San Diego's a two-hour drive from here. I hope we can stay ahead of the guys with the guns."

"I know some back roads. It'll take us longer, but it's not the normal route someone would expect us to take. They'll be looking for us along the main roads."

"I hope Jack and Doris are okay."

Xander took Tiffany's hand and squeezed it. "I'm sure they are. The bad guys didn't hang around their place very long, and with all the ruckus they caused, they'll be looking for a way out before the police arrive in force."

"I hope you're right."

Xander reached into the pocket of his jacket and pulled out Doris's cellphone. "Here, hold onto this ... just watch the minutes."

Tiffany smiled, even though her blue eyes glistened with tears of worry. "At some point, I'm going to have to file a story about what's going on. Maybe if I did, it would shine a light on what's really behind all this."

"That's a good idea; however, you might wait until we have some good news. All you can say at this point is that we're all in a deep pile of feces. Nothing like starting a nationwide panic right here at Christmas."

"I think that horse has already left the barn. If the terrorists want to, they can have a field day with their little drones, along with every other crazy fanatic out there."

"I hope people a lot smarter than us are working on a solution. If not, then we're really screwed."

15

Hours before the scheduled ten o'clock meeting, the President and his staff were at work sorting through all that had happened across the country throughout the night. It seemed that the public had not come to grips with the consequences of the attack on the Rapid Defense Center the day before, at least not initially, especially on the East Coast. The tragic event was something that happened on the other side of the country, so how could it possibly affect them?

And so, on Tuesday morning, Americans got in their cars, boarded trains or entered subway stations, beginning this day like all the rest. That situation was about to change very quickly.

President Ortega and his staff were right in their assessment; Abdul-Shahid Almasi had enlisted the assistance of several other terrorist organizations and placed them on standby, waiting for the time when the RDC was taken out before acting. Now, forty-two simultaneous operations had been initiated across America.

For months beforehand, small groups of operatives had been brought into the country to prepare for the attacks. Many came with nothing more than suitcases of clothing, as they were able to acquire just about everything they needed for their missions locally, either from sympathetic supporters or from the local Home Depot or hobby shop. They set up relay stations for the more long-distant guided events, while other RPA's would be piloted from on-site for attacks on strategic targets, with their operators escaping in the ensuing confusion. Tractor-trailer rigs were great for this, with stations and wireless setups in the trailers for the pilots. They could be stationed anywhere within a ten-mile radius of the target; even then, periodic booster stations could be placed in cars closer to the action while the operators were many miles away.

It was also expected that domestic militant groups would seize upon the opportunity and fly crude, bomb-laden drones into abortion clinics, mosques, churches and synagogues, only adding to the impact of the RDC raid. In rare occasions, even personal grudges would be settled between individuals and disgruntled neighbors, expecting that these assassinations would be blamed on terrorists or others of their ilk.

Although it was warned that America's initial response would be weak; eventually, the full might of the nation would be brought to bear against those responsible. Even with the RDC out of the mix, the United States still had plenty of weapons at her disposal, if not to prevent the attacks, then to surely track down those who carried them out. The NSA, the CIA, and the FBI, along with a dozen other heavily-financed acronyms, meant that the window of opportunity for striking at the heart of the nation would be short-lived. As a result, the surge of terrorist bombings, shootings—and just general mayhem—would be compressed into just a few tragic days in American history.

Once the attacks got underway, they produced a variety of mind-boggling consequences.

The New Stock Exchange closed over fifteen hundred points down in a shortened two-hour trading session—the largest single-day drop in history. Meanwhile, retailers across the country attempted to open that Tuesday morning in spite of deserted malls and no-show employees; however, by one that afternoon, many stores gave up and sent everyone home. In addition, the airlines saw an eighty-percent drop in passenger loads that Tuesday, as people refused to leave their homes for any reason.

The other odd event—that basically tipped the hand of the terrorists—was when drones began to attack several of Amazon's regional processing centers, as well as airports and sorting hubs for FedEx and UPS. Now, even online orders were being refused, as companies discovered that the means of delivering their products was under assault, as well. Workers streamed out of these facilities in a wholesale panic once the pattern became clear.

Thirty-five hours after the attack on the RDC—and at the economy's critical time of the year—commerce in America came to a sudden and catastrophic standstill.

President Hector Ortega and his staff met this time in the situation room under the White House. President-elect Owen Murphy was in attendance.

"So, what more do we know?" the President asked, addressing this question to his CIA chief, Morgan Donahue.

"We're pretty sure it was The Arm of Allah that carried out the main part of the attack. There was a conspicuous lack of electronic traffic circulating at that time, which is usually a giveaway. So far, we've been able to determine that around two hundred ninety drones took part in the operation, both in Las Vegas and against the various response bunkers and employee homes in the area. We've traced the bulk of them—the ones they call Lightnings—to a break-in and theft of a storage facility near San Diego six months ago. When restrictions were placed on the sale of this particular type of drone, a lot of the manufacturers warehoused their existing inventories in the event the restrictions were lifted sometime in the future.

Over six hundred drones of various makes and models were stolen from that single facility."

"And you didn't see that as a potential threat?" the President asked, dumbfounded.

"We did, sir, yet in the case of previous thefts, we expected many of these units to make their way overseas for resale in countries that don't have such restrictions. Black-market drones can go for four to five times their retail value here in the States."

"Or they can be used for terror attacks right here at home."

"Yes, sir. But there were also a fair number of larger drones—ones they call RPAs—that also took part in the raids. We've been checking the serial numbers—at least on those that have them—and we're finding most are of North Korean manufacture that were sold through various Russian and Chinese companies to a variety of nations, both friendly and not-so-friendly. Some of the units were bought with weapons packages already installed. Others were sold as toys or for aerial photography and the like, with the weapons added later. The majority of buyers are in Europe or the Middle East, with some even in the U.S. Most of the bulk purchases took place over the past six months and amounted to a three hundred percent increase in orders when compared year-to-year."

"You mean American companies also bought these drones?" asked Governor Murphy.

"There are still plenty of drones being sold for legitimate purposes, Governor. They're used extensively in movie production, aerial photography, surveying, mining, and search and rescue, just to mention a few. It's just a lot harder to pass the background checks and the continual monitoring that goes along with the purchases, yet there are still entities that go through the process. It's the weapons package that makes these drones deadly. Certain companies, even here in the U.S., build weapons packages specifically for drone operations."

"Is that legal?"

"Domestically, they only sell to the government for a variety of applications. For international sales, they need approval from the State Department plus a valid end-user certificate. But to answer your question more directly, yes, sir, it is legal."

Before Murphy could launch into his next diatribe, Ortega spoke up. "Jack, we need to put a lid on this. I want an executive order drawn up ceasing the sale of all drones in the country, as well as to outside entities."

Ortega's Chief of Staff nodded slowly. "That will help ... some, Mr. President, but most of the major drone manufacturers are now located overseas, in China and Central America mainly. And Russia has recently jumped on the bandwagon, as well. Without their cooperation, a localized ban would have little effect. Considering the tense relations we have with President Marko these days; I doubt if Russia will agree to voluntarily reduce shipments. We can ban sales in the States, but it will not prevent future attacks, at least not in the short term."

"I understand that Jack, but the people are going to demand action on this front. They have to realize by now how dangerous unfettered access and operation of these drones can be." The President turned to the Chairman of the Joint Chiefs of Staff, Admiral Gregory Hagar. "What's our threat level in light of the RDC being taken out, Greg?"

The Admiral shook his head. "Mr. President, there's been a phenomenal increase in comm traffic since yesterday detected by the NSA and others. The terrorists aren't hiding it any longer. They were silent up until the raid, but now there've been continuous calls for action from across the board." He looked to the CIA Director Morgan Donohue. "Do you concur, Morgan?"

The tall, impossibly thin spy chief nodded. "There's ample evidence of pre-planning, both for this attack and the internet info dump. Abdul-Shahid Almasi—who we agree is the prime suspect in the attack on the RDC—used the classified information to plan the attack before making it public, but he's undoubtedly shared it with others. We suspect that enemy assets have already been moved into place and are just waiting for the right time to act." He cast his gray eyes around the room. "That time is now, Mr. President. It's going to get a whole lot worse from here on out."

Ortega lowered his head and tried to clear the

cobwebs from his lack of sleep. It seemed that all the dire warnings and what-ifs from last night's meeting were coming true.

"We must take preemptive action—"

"Please, Owen," President Ortega said forcefully, cutting off the President-elect. "Let me think. This is still happening on my watch, so I'm going to be held responsible for what does or doesn't happen."

Murphy's face turned beet red. Ortega was sure it had been years since the Governor had been spoken to in such a harsh manner, but he didn't care.

He looked to Jack Monroe. "Martial law—is that an option as a way to head off what's coming."

Murphy opened his mouth again to speak, but a glance from Ortega stopped him in his tracks.

Monroe looked concerned. "Martial law is usually reserved for events that have already taken place or are underway, Mr. President. As a precaution against a potential threat, it would be unprecedented."

"But can I do it? Besides, I'm sure that by the end of the day, we'll be in a full-blown war with the terrorists."

"There's been a debate going on for years about the National Defense Authorization Act of 2012 regarding Presidential authorization for declaring martial law. Some readings of Section 1031 say you do have the authority … preemptively."

"If I may, Mr. President," said Admiral Hagar. "Simply deploying military assets within the United States does not necessarily invoke martial law. Only when the authority of other law enforcement and legal entities is suspended does that become the true definition of the statute."

"Is that true, Jack?"

"Technically, yes," Monroe replied. "However, it's a fine line you'd be walking when authorities conflict, such as within state's borders or with the National Guard."

"Does the National Guard have the capacity to accomplish what we need in this crisis?" the President asked.

Admiral Hagar shook his head. "Not even close, Mr. President." He looked to the CIA Director for support. "According to the scenarios we've worked out in the past, we would have to secure not only large public venues but nearly every crucial infrastructure asset, such as power plants, dams, overpasses, waterways, as well as symbolic targets such as the Statue of Liberty and the Golden Gate Bridge. Even using all our military personnel to accomplish that would stretch us thin. This is a national crisis, sir, covering the entire gambit. After all, what's classified as a *potential* target these days? It can be something as big as the White House or as small as a critical bridge over a canyon out West somewhere. The cost of such an operation to the terrorists is so small relatively that they could stage a dozen such smaller strikes rather than a single large event. The question is, how do we protect ourselves against *everything?* The answer is we can't."

Ortega felt weak—weak and impotent. He knew the

situation was serious, but as was the habit of military professionals, when put in the stark terms Hagar was describing, there would be ... Armageddon.

In the tense moments that followed Admiral Hagar's speech, even Owen Murphy remained quiet. All eyes were still on Hector Ortega, and no one was willing to offer a suggestion for something so expansive and overwhelming.

In the thick silence of the room, a crisp knock came on the door to the Oval Office, a dissonant sound that made several of the people in the room jump. Without waiting for permission, the door opened and an Air Force Colonel entered. He handed a sheet of paper to the President and then departed.

Ortega unfolded the paper, and if it was possible for his features to turn even more sallow, they did.

"It looks like the fallout has begun," he announced. "Besides everything else happening this morning, the St. Louis Arch has just been brought down by a drone strike. And worse than that, Times Square is currently under attack. Local police were anticipating something like this, so they were already on scene with defensive drones of their own. However, the locals don't appear to be as proficient at this kind of thing as the RDC. Casualties are estimated at a thousand already, and there are also reports of random drone bombings of the subway system. Governor Keller has just declared a state of emergency and is calling out the National Guard to protect the bridges and tunnels."

The President could see the nervous rustling of his guests, as all were anxious to get back to work rather than spend time in a strategy meeting. As the leader of the nation, Ortega was ready to act. "Jack, do what you have to. In light of these recent attacks, as well as those that are coming, I'm declaring Martial Law throughout the Union. Admiral Hagar, coordinate with whomever you need to and then deploy your troops. We have to get a substitute for the RDC up and running as soon as possible. The military—other than the RDC—must have talented operators and drones of their own capable of stepping in, don't you?"

"The best of the best were siphoned off over the years to the RDC, Mr. President," Admiral Hagar reported. "And then budget constraints have kept us from continuing with any extensive drone program within the main military branches, at least as far as domestic operations are concerned. Frankly, sir, the problem is not capacity, it's coordination. The thing that made the RDC so effective was its ability to provide a uniform response to drone attacks. Right now, we have literally thousands of drones being used for private security. In addition, each branch of the military still retains a skeleton drone program. And then there's the estimated seventeen-thousand combat drones currently sitting idle and disconnected from command authority in the RDC bunkers."

"Did you say seventeen-*thousand*?"

"Yes, sir. And they're all slaved to RDC command. So,

you see, Mr. President, America *does* have the resources necessary to repeal the attacks we're experiencing. What we don't have is a unified command structure capable of coordinating the responses or a way to gain control of the RDC drones."

"And add to that, Mr. President," said Alice Grimes, the acting SecDef, "nearly all the pilots at the RDC have been killed or targeted for assassination based on the internet information disclosed. Even if the Center was operational, they wouldn't have the personnel to mount an adequate defense."

Ortega looked over at his stunned-into-silence replacement. He cast Murphy a pleading look, one that asked, in essence, *do you really want to take my place? If so ... then buddy, it's all yours.*

"Admiral, last night I asked you to assign one person to coordinate the response. I know it's only been a few hours, but how's that coming?"

"I have identified the individual, and he's beginning to form his own staff."

"Greg, I need action, not more bureaucracy."

"I understand, sir, and so does he."

"And how do we get access to the RDC drones—all seventeen-*thousand* of them?"

"We have crews combing through the wreckage of the RDC at this moment, trying to piece together the comm links necessary to upload new codes. Once this is done, my guy will have to set up a new command center and bring in every combat drone pilot he can find. Even then, it could be several days before we're making an impact."

"I don't think we have several days, Admiral. This thing is spiraling out of control, not only domestically but around the world. We need to shut this down, and I mean now!"

At 10:45 that Tuesday morning, President Hector Ortega went on air to announce the implementation of Martial Law throughout the country. He tried to assure a terrified population that this was strictly a temporary action aimed at the foreign entities operating within the borders and not against any citizens of the country per se. Courts would still function, and local police would be available as they always have been. However, now, the military would be deployed to protect vital national interests and to guard against strikes on venues that attract large numbers of people, such as shopping malls and sporting events.

In reality, mass gatherings of Americans were already becoming a thing of the past by the time the President spoke. The National Football and Hockey Leagues had already canceled all their games until further notice, while schools and colleges did the same. And with drones buzzing the skies of New York City, all plays on Broadway were shut down pending a resolution to the national crisis.

Within minutes of his announcement, the American

Civil Liberties Union filed a lawsuit against the United States Government, claiming that a declaration of Martial Law was, in fact, unconstitutional in this instance.

Other civil libertarians began to organize protests against the declaration, with counter-protesters adding to an already tense situation.

A nine-p.m. curfew was announced in Washington, D.C., as well as in other major population centers across the country, left to the discretion of the states.

Unlike the relatively slow rollout of the Covid-19 lockdown, American businesses and society literally shut down overnight. Masks and vaccines couldn't mediate this crisis. This was a modified shooting war, but with the enemy hiding virtually in plain sight.

It soon became the common purpose of the nation to limit the death toll from these ongoing attacks by simply not allowing any sizeable civilian gatherings to take place. Still, that left plenty of static targets to strike, and as if anticipating a lack of live targets, bridges, dams, overpasses and national symbols began to attract the attention of the killer drones.

Civilian militias began to form to protect homes, businesses and landmarks. And as was expected, with police and military assets spread so thin—and with thousands of stores sitting vacant and vulnerable—the looters came out in force. By early that afternoon, seventeen of them had been killed by either police or military units as the first troops began to take up positions to protect lives and property. In some cases, clashes erupted between the militia groups and the authorities, which resulted in even more dead lying on the street. This only enraged an already angry population, and by early evening on the East Coast, full-scale riots were taking place in every major metropolitan city. Casualties stopped being counted and reported as the raw numbers soared past ten thousand in a single day.

The nation was in total meltdown, and without the full brunt of the terrorists' follow-up attacks having even taken place … at least not yet.

16

Xander Moore and Tiffany Collins sat in silent shock as they listened to the frantic news reports on the radio of the Chevy Suburban. They had plenty of time to grasp the full impact of the disaster taking place across the nation, as it took four hours to make a drive that would normally have only taken two. And it wasn't the traffic that slowed the journey, even though there was a fair amount of it moving away from the cities and into the mountains or the desert. In order to avoid detection, Xander navigated country roads and surface streets from the city of Hemet through Temecula and over the hills into San Diego County.

It was approaching two in the afternoon on the West Coast when they made the transition from I-15 to Highway 78 in Escondido, heading west. By then, the news from back east and across the nation was so grim that they turned off the radio and drove in silence along what was by now a nearly deserted freeway. Xander worried a little about how conspicuous they looked; however, being the typical government-issued transport, most people would assume the huge SUV was an official vehicle of some kind.

Everyone except the killers who were out looking for them....

Xander left Highway 78 at the South Rancho Santa Fe Road exit and crossed back over the freeway. Fifteen minutes later, they were winding through the quiet streets of an area of San Diego County known as *The Ranch*.

The Covenant at Rancho Santa Fe habitually ranked among the most exclusive and expensive neighborhoods in the country, often leading the nation with the most homes priced over five million dollars. Current and past residents of The Ranch included notables such as Bill Gates, Janet Jackson, Howard Hughes and Bing Crosby.

Xander had an address memorized, even though he'd never been to the house. He smiled as Tiffany strained to catch glimpses of the palatial estates hidden behind ivy-covered walls or towering cypress, eucalyptus and palm trees.

And here he thought his home in Henderson was—had been—impressive….

Xander turned off El Camino Norte and onto a short looping street called Cerros Redondos before eventually turning into a wide, brick-laid driveway blocked by a set of towering posts and a twenty-foot-high wrought-iron gate and concrete wall surrounding the property. Through the gate, he could see a sprawling single-story home off in the distance, appearing more modernistic when compared to many of the more grandiose and traditional mansions in the area. The gate was closed, and Xander was at a momentary loss as to what to do next.

"Your friend lives *here*?" Tiffany asked.

"It's the last address I have for him. Hell, he may have moved on by now. It's been over six years."

"There's a call box over there. Why don't you go see if anyone's home?"

Xander climbed out of the SUV and walked over to the metal box set on a post to the left side of the driveway. There was a small video screen on the box and a single button. He pressed it. "Hello, Billy. Billy Jenkins. This is Xander Moore. Is anyone home?"

After thirty seconds and no reply, he turned back to Tiffany. "Hell, he could be anywhere—"

"Que?" said a female's voice through the speaker.

Xander turned back to the box. "Hola, yo me llamo Xander Moore. Soy un amigo de Billy Jenkins. Es a casa?"

"Un minute, por favor."

He turned from the box again. "At least *someone's* home."

"You speak Spanish?"

"Just barely anymore, but it came in handy growing up around here."

"You grew up around *here?*"

"No, I meant San Diego. I'm from the slums just north of the Seventy-Eight."

"And this house belongs to one of your old drone buddies? Seems like he would have been a good one to stick close to throughout the years."

Xander sent her a wry smile. The sad truth: She was right, and to this day Xander still kicked himself for passing on the chance that Billy Jenkins had once offered him: Full partnership in the company that would later become JEN-Tech Industries.

"Why you stinkin' son-of-a-bitch!" a deep voice boomed out from the box. "It *is* you."

Xander turned back to the video screen, which by now had come to life and was displaying the smiling, tanned face of William Michael Jenkins, CEO of JEN-Tech, as well as Alpha-Three on the Drone Olympics Gold Medal winning team from nine years ago. Xander was Alpha-One.

The gate began to swing silently open.

"Seeing what's been going on over the past thirty hours, you better get your ass in here, pronto," Billy said.

"Follow the driveway around to the right. I'll open one of the garage doors so you can hide that tank you're driving. Is that her? You don't have her tired up, do you?"

Xander frowned. "No, of course not; why would I?"

"Dude, get in here. Sounds like you're a little behind in your current affairs."

Five minutes later, Xander and Tiffany climbed out of the Suburban, which now looked small and insignificant inside the vast expanse of the largest private garage Xander had ever seen. From the outside, there were only four doors, but on the inside, there had to be over three thousand square feet of parking and workshop space. Among the six cars already in the garage, Xander identified a vintage Jaguar F-type, a Ferrari, two Mercedes and a tricked-out Jeep Wrangler, along with the largest hoverbike he'd ever seen.

And not surprisingly, from the owner of one of the largest military drone contractors in the country, one whole side of the vast, two-story room was filled with a confusing array of UAVs of all shapes and sizes.

Billie Jenkins appeared from an interior doorway. He rushed up to Xander with a wide smile and embraced him in a macho man-hug. "Damn glad to see you, Number One!" he exclaimed with emotion. "Hell, I didn't even know you worked at the RDC until I saw it on the news." He broke his embrace the moment Tiffany approached, displaying a brilliant smile of her own. He quickly wrapped her up in his arms, as well.

After what was an exceedingly long hug, they separated, with Billy wearing a sly grin on his face. "Call me a perv, but I couldn't let *that* opportunity pass me by; that was sweet! And, babe, *what* is that perfume you're wearing? I may have to buy the company after this."

"I thought you were married?" Xander said.

Billy kept staring at Tiffany. "Ancient history, dude. Even if it wasn't, it would be now."

"Chill out, man, you're embarrassing the lady," Xander said with a wink in Tiffany's direction.

"Newsflash, Mr. Moore," Tiffany said with a smile. "Anytime a billionaire wants to go on about me, I let him. You are a billionaire, aren't you?"

"I am today."

With that cryptic answer, the trio moved into the main house.

Xander had to admit he was impressed. His old surfing and drone buddy had done quite well for himself. "So, how big is this place? Hell, your garage is larger than my whole house … or what had been my house." Tiffany cast him a melancholy look.

"Actually, I'm slumming in this zip code. I only have a little over twelve thousand square feet, not counting the garage and workshop. I did have my eye on a little twenty-three-thousand square foot shack farther up the hill, at least until all this shit started coming down." Jenkin's tone suddenly turned serious. "Let's go into the living room; there's something you have to see."

The living room was the size of a regulation basketball court, with cream-colored carpet that was the softest Xander had ever felt. And it was spotless, something he imagined would be a near-impossible feat to maintain given the color. He let out a soft chuckle. *Hell, Billy probably just replaces it every time it gets dirty, rather than have it cleaned. That's how the one percent of the one percent live.*

They sat on a similarly light-colored, horseshoe-shaped sectional sofa made of velvety leather while a slender Hispanic woman came into the room with a tray of beverages. "Still the Diet Pepsi drinker, Xan?"

"Hopelessly addicted."

The lady offered the tray to Tiffany. There were three kinds of soft drinks plus a container of bottled water. "If you want something stronger, just let her know," Jenkins said. "Maria can make just about anything you can think of."

Tiffany took the water. "This will do just fine—for now," she said. "However, the night is still young."

Indeed, a thick, overcast sky and the shortened days of mid-December had cast a premature pall over the area, yet even now, the backyard was bathed in sensor-controlled lighting. Looking through the fifty-foot-wide bank of eight-foot-high sliding glass doors, the scene outside reminded Xander of the splashy glitz and brilliance of Las Vegas. The glass-like surface of the pool, along with the soaring palm trees and white-washed Greek and Roman statues in the backyard, were all bathed in radiant cones of professionally placed spotlights. And even with the continual water shortage in the region, Billy's grass was so green, so perfectly manicured, that it looked artificial.

"Thanks for letting us in, Billy," Xander said. "I know it's been a long time, and with all that's going on, I wasn't sure what you'd do."

Jenkins buried his chin in his neck and frowned. "You're shitting me, aren't you? We're old running buddies, Xan. And if I remember correctly, you're the one who introduced me to the wonderful world of drones. I owe you a lot."

Xander nodded and looked around the room. "How about five million ... and we call it even?"

Jenkins patted his pockets. "Sure, just let me get my wallet. I believe I have that much on me." But then the smile suddenly vanished again. "It's not true, is it? I can't imagine that it is."

It was Xander's turn to frown. "What are you talking about? You mean about the bad guys out after all the pilots from the RDC? *That's* true." He looked over at Tiffany, who gave him a small nod.

"Not that," said Jenkins, "the other stuff."

"Now, you've got me; what other stuff?"

Jenkins wrinkled his lips. "That's what I was afraid of. Here, I recorded this so I could replay it since I couldn't believe it the first time." He took a small tablet computer from the end table and punched a button. Above the huge river-stone fireplace, double panels slid away to reveal a hundred-inch flat-screen TV. Billy noticed Xander's mouth drop open. "Hey, my eyesight's getting bad, and this is the only way I can watch my soaps."

He pressed another button, and the TV came to life. On it was a recorded news report from CNN. Xander's headshot was displayed in a box on the left. Billy turned up the volume.

"…was responsible for the release of classified information regarding the Rapid Defense Center and may have been working directly with the group—or groups—that carried out yesterday's attack. Documents found in the ruins of Moore's Henderson, Nevada, home have left the authorities with little doubt that he removed highly sensitive data that revealed the security set-up of the RDC, as well as the steps required to launch an attack on the facility."

"What the hell!" Xander said as he jumped to his feet.

"It has also been revealed that Xander Moore was the author of a report that detailed how such an attack could be carried out, even though it was disguised as plans for an assault on a foreign-based facility."

"This is bullshit!" Xander said. He looked to a silent Tiffany Collins. "You were there; you know they're lying."

Tiffany stared at him with unblinking eyes.

The newscast continued. "It is believed that Moore set fire to his own home to cover up his activities, as other personnel from the Center were being targeted in the area by drone attacks." Tiffany's headshot now appeared. "After making contact with her station this morning, the fate of Fox News reporter Tiffany Collins is still unknown at this time, with her last known sighting being in the company of Moore at a home she owns in the town of Idyllwild in Riverside County, California. Eyewitnesses report that a gun battle took place near the home earlier this morning between government agents and Moore. Authorities we spoke with said they have no reason to believe at this time that the news broadcaster is involved in any of Moore's activities, but they say they are still investigating Collins' background for any possible links. In the meantime, the manhunt for Xander Moore continues."

Billy pressed the pause button, with an image of both Xander and Tiffany now filling the entire screen.

Xander turned a pleading face to Billy Jenkins. "It wasn't me … in fact, I think it was Jonas."

"*Jonas Lemon?*" Billy said as his mouth fell open.

"Xander nodded. "He used to work at the Center … until I had him fired."

Billy pursed his lips. "Maria, I think I'm going to need my usual!" he called out into the other room. "Jonas *fucking* Lemon. This sounds like something he would do."

"You know him?" Tiffany asked, finally coming out of her stupor.

"You don't believe any of this, do you," Xander asked Tiffany before Billy could reply.

"Of course not, but now *I'm* being investigated!"

"You think Jonas did this to get back at you?" Jenkins asked Xander.

"There's been no love lost between us for years, Billy, and you know it."

"It wasn't your fault that he got kicked out of the League."

"Even so, he landed on his feet after that and went to work for the military in the Predator program before eventually being pawned off on the RDC."

Billy shook his head as Maria brought him a caramel-colored drink in a tumbler. "That was one crazy son-of-a-bitch. But now they're blaming you and with evidence planted at your house, obviously. What are you going to do?"

With desperate eyes, Xander looked towards the hovering Maria. "Bring him what I'm having," Billy said, reading Xander's mind. "He looks like he needs it."

"Yes, Mr. Billy, and for you, ma'am?"

Tiffany shrugged. "Sure, why not? This thing just got a whole lot more complicated … and personal."

Billy leaned over toward Tiffany and handed her his cellphone. "Here, call someone. Let them know you're not being held captive by some crazed terrorist. I've known this guy since he was eleven and I was fourteen. He ain't no saint, but he's no traitor, either. There's no way he could be involved in this like they say."

Tiffany took the phone and stood up. She looked down

at Xander. She went to say something but shook her head instead.

"It's cool," Xander said to Tiffany. "Go make your call. I'm sure your friends and family are worried sick about you. But don't let them know where you are, not yet." He looked over at Billy. "I'm sure my old friend here will let you borrow one of his clunkers so you can get back to your normal life. I just need a little time to work out what *I'm* going to do next."

Billy Jenkins smiled up at the news reporter. "Take your pick from the garage, sweetheart ... as long as you promise to return it to me in person."

Flashing a strained smile at the men, Tiffany left the room.

Billy now leaned in closer to Xander. "Seriously, bro, what *are* you going to do? I've been watching the news, and this is huge. The country's gone bat-shit crazy ... and you know, they declared Martial Law?"

"We heard it on the radio. But how can they honestly believe I had anything to do with this?"

"Jonas—if he really is behind all this—has been planning it for a while. He probably had you pegged to take the fall from the beginning. And if there's one thing to be said about that bastard, he had one scary talent for planning shit."

"They—or he—sent a hit squad after me this morning, and they weren't government agents. Government-trained, I'm sure of that, but not agents. I guess they want me dead, so I can't dispute any of this, leaving Jonas to run free. I was wondering why they were putting so much effort into trying to kill me?"

"Did they succeed?" Billy asked with a smile just as Maria entered the room with their drinks.

"I'll let you know in a day or so. But now, *you* could be in trouble, too."

Billy took his second tumbler and chugged it. "Don't worry about me, bro, I'm rich! While you continued to *play* with your little toys, I went off to *build* them. *And the gov'ment's been berra, berra good to me,*" Billy said in his best imitation of Chico Escuela's famous quote regarding the game of baseball—accent and all. "Let me make a few calls," he continued. "I'm sure I can get this straightened out, if not publicly, then at least with the powers-that-be."

"That would help. Thanks."

Tiffany reentered the room and made a beeline for her drink. She, too, downed it in a single gulp.

"Okay, that's done, and they're relieved. But they really want me to get the exclusive from you, Xander. It might help to set things straight. I could use Billy's phone to record a quick interview."

"You're kidding, aren't you?" Xander said, flabbergasted.

"That's a good idea, Xan!" Billy said. "Get everyone out looking for Jonas instead of you."

"And why would they believe me? And what if Jonas has an alibi? I'd look like an idiot."

"Right now, you look like a *terrorist*," Tiffany said. "Let's at least tell our side of the story. I'll back you up."

Xander looked into the three pairs of anxious eyes staring back at him—even Maria was waiting for his reply. "What the hell?" he said finally. "What could it hurt?"

17

"Our powerful friends have used their considerable technological prowess to record a cellphone conversation that just came into the Fox News station in Los Angeles," said Abdul-Shahid Almasi to Jonas Lemon through the computer link. "They should have a trace on the phone very soon. The phone is active once again."

"Probably in San Diego, right?" Jonas Lemon asked.

"Preliminary … yes."

"He has a lot of friends there. I'd check out Jeremy Fenton, Karen Pardo, Billy Jenkins, Curt Tharp and Hugh Barden."

"Who are they?"

"They're his old teammates, a bunch of drone nerds from the old days," Jonas explained. "And if he's looking for someone with influence and resources, I'd put my money on Jenkins."

"I know the name. He is a drone manufacturer. I believe even I have used some of his units."

"Yeah, he's pretty big-time with the government these days and owns one of the few companies authorized to weaponize UAVs."

"Can he be a threat to us?"

Lemon laughed. "Only if he lives! I assume when you take out Moore, there can also be some fortuitous collateral damage. But don't you think it a bit risky to bring in the Russians at this point?"

"They already have extensive surveillance taking place across America. Besides, if our operation is carried to fruition, they will have very little to worry about from your country as far as reprisals go." Almasi's image smiled—something that was rare in his case. "As will we all, Mr. Lemon."

Jonas looked at his watch. He had a side dial set for California time. "It's nine at night in San Diego and the start of a new day here in the Emirates. Hopefully, your people will have this wrapped up pretty soon. I would really like to celebrate Moore's death at dinner tonight."

"And the codes? Are you prepared for immediate delivery upon confirmation?"

"All set to go. Just bring me the head of Xander Moore."

Jonas saw a look of confusion cloud Almasi's face. "A

figure of speech," Jonas quickly explained. "Simple video confirmation will suffice."

Colleen Hoover was asleep at seven in the evening of Tuesday, December 17, the day after the attack on the Rapid Defense Center. This was unusual for her. She was one of those rare individuals who got by on only four hours of sleep, an attribute that came in handy during her thirty years as a stock and commodities broker. Operating from the West Coast, she was usually at her desk by two a.m., preparing for the coming day on Wall Street. But these days, she lived in the same time zone as New York, and even though she was no longer active in the markets, she maintained her habit of rising early to greet the new day.

As Secretary of the Treasury, Hoover oversaw the largest economy to ever have existed on the planet Earth, even if most of her job these days entailed heading off one disaster after another. With the financial markets as fickle as they were, even the slightest movement in an unexpected manner or a rumor unsubstantiated would send them roiling. These days, she was the PR face of the US economy, tasked with downplaying every negative story while smiling confidently when the occasional good news came out.

After Friday's attack on the Dolphin Mall, followed by

the total massacre at the RDC, there wasn't a lot of smiling going on, even for the cameras. She had been up all Monday night with her advisors and in conference calls with the President and his people, fielding impossible-to-answer hypotheticals about the impact of the attacks on the economy. Her frantic schedule continued well into Tuesday morning as report after report came in regarding escalating terrorist attacks sweeping the nation. About four in the afternoon, she fell back on the couch in her office just to rest her eyes; the buzzing of her office intercom woke her up three hours later.

Colleen stumbled to her desk and pressed the button. "Hoover here, what is it?"

"Sorry to disturb you, ma'am, but the Chinese Finance Minister is demanding to speak with you." Her secretary—actually one of two she employed to keep up with her frantic pace—sounded tired and upset.

"He *demands* to speak with me?"

"He said he's been trying to reach Mr. Monroe at the White House but had been unable to get through."

Colleen looked at the clock on the wall. "Shit—it's seven o'clock!"

"Yes, ma'am, I would have wakened you if something truly important happened. It's just hard to tell these days."

"That's all right, Tabby. Thanks. I imagine Minister Koa is fit to be tied. He's probably been up all night trying to get hold of someone over here."

"What should I tell him?"

"Put him through, Tabby. It's really me he wants to talk with more than Monroe."

"Yes, ma'am. Here he comes."

"Minister Jing Koa, I can't say I'm surprised to hear from you," Colleen said.

"Madam Secretary, I apologize for the tone of my call, yet you must realize China is very concerned about the recent events taking place within your country, and it appears no one is willing to speak with us regarding this crisis. Even though your markets closed early, the rest of the world has continued to trade—at least for now."

Hoover pressed a button on the remote control on her desk, and a large TV on the opposite wall came to life, already tuned to the Fox Business Channel. The scrolling banner at the bottom said it all.

"Is this correct, Jing? A three-hundred-point drop in the Nikkei and over a thousand in the Shanghai Composite?"

"Yes, it's true, and this is only the beginning. As a warning, we are planning on closing our markets within the hour to keep the decline from getting worse, but that will only send a bad message to traders and shareholders. Without some good news to calm the panic, when we do reopen, it will be so much worse. Please tell me you have some good news?"

"I have to be honest with you, Jing, but I fell asleep for a couple of hours, so I'm not up on the very latest. Throughout the night and all Tuesday our time, we've been working on projections, and they're not good. I don't know how else to phrase it."

"*Not good* can mean a lot, Madam Secretary. What we need to know is whether or not the United States has further capacity to stop these attacks and to get your people back in the stores. The global consensus is that you do not."

"What do you want me to say, Mr. Minister? You can see the reports of the latest attacks as well as I can. You can also see the video showing empty malls. And this afternoon, the FedEx hub in Nashville was hit by no fewer than fifty drones, grounding their entire fleet. Smaller, less effective attacks hit Amazon and Walmart distribution centers. There's been a wholesale exodus of workers from these sites, and I'd be surprised if anyone shows up for work tomorrow—anywhere."

"It would appear these latest attacks are aimed solely at stopping commerce within your country. That speaks to a more sinister motive rather than simple terrorism."

"This is both physical *and* economic terrorism, Jing. But you're right. I said as much to the President earlier today. It appears the motive behind the attacks is to ruin our economy."

"And what happens to the economy of China if America's collapses? That is what everyone is worried about over here ... and elsewhere."

"Again, Jing, I don't know what to say. Our priority at

this time is to secure *our* nation and *our* financial markets and commerce."

"I realize that, and you must understand that your goal is shared equally by the Chinese government."

Hoover's wry smile was conveyed in her tone of voice. "Our two governments have been inexorably entwined for decades, at least financially."

"Your debt to my nation now exceeds ten trillion dollars, Madam Secretary, so I would agree our interests are mutual. The debt service alone, although less than ten percent of our domestic GNP, is both a vital and a symbolic part of our economy. And now there are people around the world—and here as well—who see America defaulting on your obligations in light of these attacks. Are they wrong?"

Colleen Hoover hesitated before answering. This had been a hot topic throughout the day, with many of the politicians and non-financial types saying screw everyone else; we have our own problems to deal with. Worrying about what impact our actions would have on foreign entities wasn't a priority.

Hoover knew—better than most—that America *did* have to worry about what others would think and how they would react. With America temporarily handicapped, it would be up to the rest of the world to help find solutions and pick up the slack. The United States was going to need a lot of money to repair the damage caused on just the first day of the crisis—let alone for the duration—and that money would have to come from someplace other than the homeland, and mainly through the sale of government bonds to foreign governments. If anyone will buy them after the actions the U.S. government was about to take…

"The thing about economics, Mr. Minister, is that so much of it is out in the open for all to see. Without a prosperous holiday shopping season, the United States will truly suffer economically. And this is so much worse than a periodic slowdown due to a weak economy. This is profound, and it will have a ripple effect across all sectors. But to answer your complex question. Number one, I don't know if we have the capacity to fight off these and future attacks. That's for others in the government to determine. Number two, as far as the U.S. economy and our obligations are concerned, we discussed this at length, and it was decided that we will not allow valuable financial assets to leave the country, either by the government or by individuals and corporations, not when we need that money to keep the nation from spiraling completely out of control. We have to put on a good show, Jing, and that will cost a lot of money."

"And our payments … are you saying they are in jeopardy?"

"Unfortunately, that is exactly what I'm saying."

"You would forego your payments to us?"

"Unless things change drastically within the next few days, the United States of America will not have a Christmas, and with seventy percent of our economy based on consumer commerce, it doesn't take a financial genius to see the writing on the wall."

"Then what are *we* to do? A default will spell the complete meltdown of our economy as well."

"Then I suggest that you make it clear to your bosses that what happens to America also happens to China. It's as simple as that. An attack on us is also an attack on you. Having said that, don't you think it's about time your incredibly large and powerful country began exerting influence over some of your more questionable affiliations? And I would start with North Korea and Iran. The attacks on my country affect you in kind. Only by stopping the terrorists can we—and I do mean *we*—persuade Americans to start shopping again." Colleen's frustration had grown by the minute, and now she let it all out.

"It's time for Chinese leadership to make a decision. Are you going to continue to assist and protect regimes that sponsor terrorism, or are you going to be against them? Considering how interdependent the world's economies have become, there is no way a superpower like yours can continue to ride the fence. If you want to save your economy, Mr. Minister, you will have to help America save ours."

There was silence on the line for almost an entire minute. "Are you still there, Jing?" Colleen asked.

"Yes, I am here. I will convey your thoughts and concerns to my government. They will not be happy."

"I'm sorry about that, Mr. Minister, but who *is* happy after the tragic events that have taken place in my country? None of us are happy, but *we* will do what we have to do to survive. Will China follow suit?"

"I will make a point of requesting that China reconsider some of our political ... accommodations. You know, I have always questioned the financial wisdom of my government's affiliations with certain groups and nations. However, that is politics, and I do not play politics. I am an economist, just as you, Madam Secretary. We have no time or tolerance for the games our leaders play, especially when such can affect our economic well-being. In light of the seriousness of the current situation, I am sure that my superiors will at least consider following the path that you —and I, to a less vocal degree—now advocate, especially after I relate the content of this conversation."

"I sincerely hope so, Jing. It's going to take all the civilized nations of the world to head off this disaster. There can be no middle ground, no vacillation and no ambiguity. Now, I will let you go. We both have a lot of work to do in a very short time."

"They say they'll look into it," Billy Jenkins told Xander after he spoke with his contacts in D.C., referring to Jonas Lemon. "But without any evidence, they're not lifting the all-points-bulletin that's out on you, at least not officially. It might be better if you turn yourself into the Feds. At least then, you'd have a significant layer of protection around you. You know you're innocent, and once they start looking into Jonas, it shouldn't be too hard to put two and two together."

"You could be right, but not until I see just how much trouble I'm really in. Knowing that bastard, there may be an air-tight case against me, no matter what I say."

"Okay, I'm ready," Tiffany said. She'd taken a few sheets of paper and jotted down a series of questions for her interview while Billy provided a small tripod with a cellphone holder for a steady cam shot. After the interview, it would only take seconds to email the raw footage to her station.

In typical interview fashion, two chairs were placed at a slight angle to each other, and Xander sat in one while Tiffany sat in the other. She borrowed a soft blue blouse from Maria's closet to replace the flannel shirt she'd been wearing and then spent twenty minutes in the bathroom preparing her hair and makeup—also from Maria's supply. It was a little past nine when all was ready.

With a nod from Tiffany, Billy pressed the record button on the phone.

"This is Tiffany Collins with an exclusive Fox News report shedding additional light on the terrorist attacks that took place yesterday afternoon in Las Vegas and elsewhere. With me is Xander Moore, the senior drone pilot for the Rapid Defense Center, and we're coming to you tonight from a secret location, which must remain secret, not only for the protection of Mr. Moore but for my safety as well.

"For the record, I was at the Rapid Defense Center yesterday conducting an interview with Mr. Moore when the attack took place, so I make this report as an active eyewitness to the tragedy that took place at the Center.

"First off, I would like to make a personal statement regarding the misinformation circulating in the media regarding Mr. Moore's involvement with the terrorists. I firmly believe all the accusations are false. In fact, I go so far as to say the information has been planted just to make him appear guilty. I was present when he discovered that his home had been destroyed, a tragic event that some reports say he did himself. It simply did not happen that way. In addition, I want to say here and now that I have never been mistreated or held against my will by Mr. Moore. Also, I was personally involved in a very serious attempt made on Mr. Moore's life that took place this morning at my cabin in Idyllwild, California, and not by agents of the United States as has been reported, but rather by men working for the terrorists behind these horrific acts of violence.

"I make these statements as fact since I was there and witnessed them with my own eyes.

"And now, let me turn to Xander Moore. As I mentioned, he is the senior drone pilot at the Rapid Defense Center, and he comes to us with a unique and expert perspective on the events taking place across the country. Thank you, Mr. Moore, for agreeing to this interview. I know the identity of RDC personnel is normally a closely held secret, simply from the belief that you could become targets for many of the terrorist groups operating around the world. That belief is undeniable now as we witness the wholesale assassinations of literally hundreds of your colleagues, along with their families. This must be particularly hard on you at this time."

"Thank you, Tiffany, but I also have to say to your viewers that you were right there in the thick of things, not only at the RDC but also during the gunfight at your cabin. Frankly, it's a miracle we're both still alive."

"I will—when the time is right—be expanding my report to include more of my personal experiences, but for now, let's focus on the RDC attack. You believe you know the motive for the attack, as well as the mastermind behind it."

Xander looked at the phone/camera and then back to Tiffany, not knowing which to focus on. He caught a slight nod from the reporter, and so he settled on her. "It's pretty obvious now that the motive behind all the attacks taking place is to prevent people from shopping and spending money during the Christmas season. The terrorists behind this want to see the collapse of the American economy. They knew that with the RDC still operating, most of their attacks would have very little impact. So they took out the Center first. Now, we're seeing a full-scale assault being made to bring the economy to a standstill."

"And who do you think is behind this operation?"

"I believe it to be the Arm of Allah terrorist organization and their leader Abdul-Shahid Almasi."

"Inside information had to be provided to Almasi for an attack on the RDC to succeed," Tiffany said. "You also have someone you suspect to be the traitor behind this release of classified information."

"I do. I believe it to be—"

A low-wailing alarm sprang out from Billy's cellphone.

"I thought you turned off the ringer?" said Tiffany, slapping her interview notes against her legs at the interruption.

Billy snatched the phone from the tripod and began to work the screen, his forehead revealing deep furrows.

"What's that?" Xander asked.

"It's what you think it is, buddy: a security alarm for the estate. It looks as if we have company."

"Are you still recording?" Tiffany asked.

Billy looked at the screen and then pressed a button. "Not anymore."

"Save it. This is some good stuff!"

Xander and Tiffany now joined Billy, huddled together in the center of the living room, looking at the screen on the phone. "I didn't hear an alarm go off outside," Xander said.

"Yeah, I prefer to hold my cards close to the vest;

otherwise, they may go for broke and just barge in. This way, I can control the situation. *Maria!*"

The house servant appeared immediately. "Get to the safe room."

"Si, Mr. Billy. Are you coming?"

"Not yet. I want to see what we can do to stop these guys before they mess up my carpets."

"You have a safe room?" Tiffany asked.

"Honestly, everyone in this neighborhood has safe rooms. It's like having a garbage disposal or a built-in microwave."

Xander looked around at the well-lit living room and glowing backyard. "Shouldn't we be doing something? If these are the same guys from Idyllwild, they mean business."

"Follow me," Billy said. He led them down one of the long hallways before entering a smallish room that looked to be his home office. He slipped behind the outward-facing desk and took a seat. Then smiled up at the other two. "I also have a command bunker," he said proudly.

"You've been expecting something like this to happen?" Tiffany asked.

"I'm in the weaponized drone business, sweetie. My babies attack anyone, anywhere, and I'm not naïve enough to think I'm immune to the repercussions. They kill thousands of people each year, on all sides." He noticed the look of disgust on Tiffany's face. "I don't intentionally sell to the bad guys, but I can't be responsible for what the government does with my toys or where they end up after the black market gets a hold of them. Hey, I get my share of death threats from people who blame me simply because I built the drones."

Jenkins activated a flat-screen monitor on the desk, and Xander and Tiffany moved around so they could see. "I also know what my units—and others—are capable of doing. However, in this case…" he zoomed in on the infrared signatures of half a dozen men scaling the walls surrounding his property, "…I only have *people* to deal with."

18

Damien Winslow was livid. This was not how he ran an operation, yet events were happening so fast and so unexpectedly that corners had to be cut.

It wasn't that he doubted the professionalism of his men. It was that they had no idea what they were going up against. Already, they had been taken by surprise at the mountain cabin, with two of his assault team waiting in the SUVs outside the estate with bullet wounds to tend to. The people in the Idyllwild house got lucky, catching the team by surprise. After his people were hit, Damien was tempted to seek revenge against those with the guns shooting at them. But then the real targets were on the move, and he had to leave the larger house and race down the hill in plain sight of a dozen gawking neighbors.

And then they stole one of his SUVs and took the keys

from the others. This was the result of poor intelligence and spur-of-the-moment planning. And now, as they scaled the wall surrounding the estate and dropped to the immaculate lawn below, they were engaging in the same reckless behavior that had already cost him time and manpower.

The home was located in an exclusive neighborhood where—undoubtedly—security was a prime concern, yet he had no knowledge of what the owner had in store for them. Did he have dogs on the premises or on-call security patrols? Were they on camera right now, with police being dispatched to an area where service would not be lacking because of the power and wealth associated with the area? He had to expect the worst, so time was of the essence.

Basically, all he knew of this location was the address and the name of the occupant. He wasn't even sure that his primary targets were here. If not, then the other four names in his phone would be located and checked; however, for some reason, *this* name and address were flagged as a priority.

He had eight men on scene—with the two wounded guarding the vehicles. Scaling the wall around the compound wasn't an issue, but now they were exposed in a sea of light, as it was obvious the owner of the property didn't have to worry about such mundane things as high electricity bills. And the house itself was still ablaze with light, which hopefully meant they hadn't been detected, not yet.

With his men in place, Damien had them spread out across a thirty-meter line. Two were sent scrambling for the side of the gigantic, modern-looking home while the others covered them. If dogs were present, they would have known by now, and to Damien's relief, his men reached the house without incident and without the sound of an external alarm.

Taking a pair of high-powered binoculars from his tac vest, Damien scanned the roofline of the house, looking for video surveillance. When none were seen, he grew more concerned. There *had* to be surveillance; one didn't own a home like this without it. And the fact that the cameras were so well-hidden spoke of a higher level of technology than most other sites.

He sent another two men to the front entrance before he and Jacques St. Claire ran for the few shadows that were present in the huge backyard. From here, he was able to look around a corner of the large lanai and into the fully illuminated living room. There was no one inside, yet there were several empty glasses sitting on end tables anchoring a horseshoe-shaped sofa.

Just then, he turned toward the backyard when the sounds of the night were interrupted by something new. He relaxed when he recognized it as the rat-tat-tat of sprinklers just coming on.

Damien was equipped with a tiny earpiece and throat microphone so he could communicate with his men. "Any activity out front?" he asked.

"Negative on the street," was the report from the waiting vehicles.

"Same at the front door; it's locked, and I can see around the row of garage doors. They're all closed."

"Maintain your positions," Winslow ordered. "We're moving to the rear patio doors—"

Just then, Damien heard a strange noise through the earpiece and a sudden groaning as if someone was in intense pain ... and then nothing.

"What was that? Report."

There was a momentary silence. "I heard it, too," said Nick Daniels at the front door. "Owens, Burke, come in."

When the two men sent to the side of the house didn't respond, Damien pulled back the slide on his Beretta ARX-160 assault rifle and fell back against the wall of the patio. "Daniels ... check on them. The rest of you, eyes open."

Five seconds later, Daniels reported his findings. "Two down ... Taser fire. They're out for the duration."

"Any sign of the attacker?"

"Negative. All's quiet ... except for that buzzing. Can you hear it?"

Damien couldn't. All he could hear was the rhythmic snapping of the sprinklers ... but then there was something. It was just a little off, an extra layer of sound lost in the mix.

"Listen up," Damien said. "We're dealing with drone people here, so be on alert for those little bastards. I believe we're under surveillance and have been since entry. We're going in, weapons hot. Take out anything that moves. On my count: Three, two, one ... go!"

Daniels had returned to the front of the house by then, and now he and his partner opened fire, shattering the ornately-carved wooden door before lowering their shoulders and crashing through into the foyer. They took up positions on each side of the room just before a brilliant flash temporarily blinded them. As fingers tightened on triggers, a pair of high-pitched pops sounded as sharp, double spikes struck both men on the skin of their unprotected necks. Fifty-thousand volts coursed through their bodies, stopping all voluntary movement and replacing it with spasms of excruciating pain.

Both men fell to the marble floor, writhing in pain as two box-shaped drones moved up and hovered above them, the wires to the spikes still attached to the UAVs. The units remained on station, although the voltage was reduced. It would be enough to keep the men incapacitated until living beings could come and take possession of the intruders.

Damien, with St. Claire on his back shoulder, slid open one of the wide glass door panels between the lanai and the living room. They came in low and with weapons glued to their cheeks, scanning all angles, looking for something to shoot. No targets were identified, not until four small UAVs entered from the direction of the garage, while another two zipped up from the backyard and flew in through the open patio door.

The two men lit off their weapons, spraying wild gunfire into the vast living room. Walls exploded, pictures fell, and the stone of the massive fireplace sent rock shrapnel cascading into the room and onto the cream-colored carpet. The drones scattered as automatic defensive programming took over.

When one of the hovering drones lined up on him, Damien dived for the leather sofa, just ahead of the pair of gold-colored darts that penetrated the back of the couch only six inches from his head. He fired, shattering the plastic and light-gauge metal drone to pieces.

Then he rolled to his left and rose up off the sofa, just as the twitching body of Jacques St. Claire flew over the couch and hit him in the back. Damien fell over the heavily lacquered burl coffee table and onto the carpet, where he instinctively rolled to his side several times so as to avoid becoming a stationary target. It wasn't enough. The Taser darts struck him in the buttocks.

The pain was excruciating, even if it was something he was vaguely familiar with. All Special Forces were required to experience a Taser hit as part of their training. But that was in a controlled environment while this was combat. Now, the fear factor was added to the equation, making the pain seem even worse.

With his face contorted in a mask of gruesome agony, tears escaped from his eyes, and through his restricted vision, all he could see was the ceiling of the mansion's living room. He had no control over his limbs; it was all he could do to gnash his teeth and issue guttural groans from burning lungs. It was as if his entire body was on fire....

Through whatever miracle of consciousness he still retained, Damien began to sense that the effects of the Taser were going on much too long, even if he did notice a slight lessening of the pain. He craned his neck in the direction of the crackling sound, only to see the blurred vision of an obedient and impersonal drone hovering above him. *The bastard's still feeding me voltage*, he thought. *This isn't good. Not good at all.*

Billy, Xander and Tiffany left the office with Jenkins holding an elaborate controller in his hands. When they entered the living room, Billy's mouth fell open in a display of unbridled shock. The place was a mess, with punctured walls and a shattered fireplace. The once-impressive T.V. was in pieces, and the rest of his furniture lay in ruins. The roar of the propellers from the four surviving UAVs was deafening, especially as they were in hover mode, with two of them still feeding a continual stream of crackling high voltage into the writhing bodies on the floor.

"Grab their weapons," Billy ordered. His tone was

tense, his eyes mere slits from the primal ferocity welling up inside.

Tiffany and Xander quickly moved throughout the room and then to the front door, collecting weapons before placing them in a pile near Billy's feet. They each retained one for themselves, with Tiffany giving Xander a quick lesson on how to fire an Uzi. When the intruders were disarmed, Billy cut the power to the Tasers. Even then, the men were still lost in the after-effects of electroshock.

Billy walked over to an intercom on the wall. "Maria, it's safe to come out. Open the front gate for the police, and then go in the garage and bring out a bale of wire." He shrugged, seeing the confused look on Tiffany's face. "Screw rope, we need to wrap these bastards up in wire."

Fifteen minutes later, all six men in the assault group were sitting on the littered carpet, backs against the sofa and wrapped nearly from head to neck in heavy gauge silver wire. Security cameras showed that the two men in the SUVs had departed the scene post haste when the ruckus started, leaving their companions to face the music inside the house without them, even as the wailing of approaching sirens signaled the end of a blown mission.

The captives were slowly regaining their senses, and after a brief inspection of their restraints, a silent consensus was reached; they weren't going anywhere, at least not of their own freewill.

Billy walked the line of hard, square-jawed men, scanning their faces, looking for the leader. They were all tough and determined, yet only one had the steely gaze of a leader. He stopped in front of Damien Winslow.

"You're the boss, aren't you?"

The man didn't speak, yet all the others sent furtive glances his way. "Good, now let's talk business—"

Before he could go further, Tiffany raced forward and shoved the barrel of an HK assault rifle into the man's chest. She had fire in her eyes. "You tell me right now what happened to the old couple in Idyllwild. Do it now … before I fill your chest with lead!"

Billy backed away—as did Xander—surprised by the intensity in the woman's voice, along with the absolute truth in her words.

"Back off," the man said. "They're fine. We left them alive as we chased the two of you down the mountain."

Tiffany glared at the man, searching his face for the truth. "But you did kill their *dog!*"

For a moment, Xander thought Tiffany was going to pull the trigger. But then she backed away. "You are one lucky son-of-a-bitch," she said. "If we were alone…"

"Me, lucky? I'd say the two of you are the lucky ones."

"Who do you work for?" Billy asked once Tiffany had retreated.

The man looked up at Billy. "Fucking nerd," he said. "Who do *you* think we work for?"

"Duh, let me guess: The bad guys?"

"Bingo. And they pay very well, so I'm sure we're not

the only team out looking for Moore … and now for you, as well, Mr. William Jenkins."

Xander had the man's cellphone and was scrolling through his recent text messages. He stopped when he reached one in particular.

"He knows the names of the entire team, Billy, all of us. That could only have come from Jonas."

Billy focused on the man again. "You work for Jonas Lemon?"

"I've heard the name, but he's not the main guy."

"Abdul-Shahid Almasi?" Xander asked.

"It's no secret," the leader of the assault team acknowledged. "And you should know that he has a lot more men available—and even drones—to get us out of any holding facility the police may put us in."

As if on cue, three San Diego black-and-white police squad cars entered the grounds through the now-open front gate and screeched to a halt at the shattered front door.

"Do you really think Almasi gives a rat's-ass about you?" Xander asked before the police entered the house. "Where are they, Almasi and Lemon?"

Just then, a pair of weapons-drawn and bewildered policemen entered the living room, aiming their handguns at Xander and Tiffany.

"Hell, if I know," the man on the floor continued, unfazed by the arrival of the policemen. "Everything is done long-distance these days. They could be in Timbuktu for all I know ... or right next door."

"Mr. Jenkins?" one of the policemen asked.

"That's right," Billy said, drawing the officer's attention. "I believe you're going to need a paddy wagon or two," he said with a smile. "And by the way, these guys are part of the group who attacked the Rapid Defense Center yesterday, so they aren't your typical, run-of-the-mill burglars. I'd call in whatever agencies you can think of to make sure they stay in custody and provide all the information they can ... through polite and humane interrogation, of course. No waterboarding." Billy winked at his captive. Then he scowled as he scanned his wrecked living room. "After all, we wouldn't want to hurt these gentlemen, now would we?"

The police officer took a moment to survey the room —including the line of captives wrapped in baling wire— taking in the complete scene before he nodded to his partner. The second policeman spoke into his shoulder comm. Two other policemen now entered the residence and rather rudely disarmed Tiffany and Xander. "Are there any other intruders around we need to know about?" one of them asked Billy.

"Two others got away in a pair of black Suburban SUVs. I captured the license plate numbers on video."

"Okay," said the lead police officer. He turned to the others. "Let's get this scene processed as soon as possible."

"Representatives from Homeland Security are en

route," one of the other officers reported. "They don't want anyone leaving until they get here."

Xander approached the policeman with the sergeant chevron on his sleeve and handed him Winslow's cellphone. "The people listed here are in danger as well. Can you locate them before anything bad happens to them? They should all be in the San Diego area."

The officer took the phone. He nodded as he fingered the button on his shoulder communicator. "Sergeant Espinosa to dispatch, I have a list of four names requiring their location and protective units to be assigned. This has something to do with the attack on the Rapid Defense Center, so give it priority status. The names are as follows...." The officer turned away as he read off the names.

Xander, Billy and Tiffany gathered near the dining table. "What now?" Tiffany asked. "You heard Homeland Security is on the way."

"I guess that depends on whether or not I end up behind bars," Xander replied.

"Don't sweat it, buddy," Billy said emphatically. "The story that's being spread is that you fought government agents in Idyllwild. Our guests here blow that narrative all to pieces. The rest will fall into place. I think you—and your gorgeous friend here—can relax now. I'll make sure the Feds take good care of you."

Billy then turned to glare at the men who had shot up

his house. "Do you guys have any idea what you've done to my resale value?"

"Boo, who, spoiled little rich kid," said Damien Winslow.

"Hey! Look over there!" Billy suddenly called out while pointing toward the front door. All heads turned in that direction ... and that's when Billy planted a heavy right cross to Damien's jaw.

The police turned back when they heard the hard clap. A tense moment passed ... until Sergeant Espinosa flashed a thin smile. "Okay, let's get these guys out of here. It's the least we can do for the homeowner and his guests after they did our job for us."

Billy was rubbing his hand when he leaned in close to Xander and whispered: "You know, I've never hit anyone before, but I may learn to like it."

An hour later, Billy's home was still a crowded mess, but this time with agents from Homeland Security and the FBI, along with a dozen military personnel dispatched from the nearby Miramar Marine Air Station.

"You want us to go where?" Xander asked, confused by what he'd just been told.

"Washington, D.C.," replied a stern, blond-haired man in a blue suit and striped tie. "A van's outside to take you to Miramar. From there, you'll take a corporate jet to the East Coast."

"What are we supposed to do when we get there?" Tiffany asked after having been informed that she was now part of the *'you'* the agent was referencing.

"That's above my paygrade, Ms. Collins. I'm just following orders. And by the way, I'm a big fan. I watch you all the time on TV."

"Thank you, mister…."

"Cain. Special Agent Adam Cain, ma'am. Now, if all of you will follow me, the plane's waiting."

"What about a change of underwear?" Billy asked.

Cain smiled. "Everything will be provided for you, and all at government expense."

Billy laughed and waved a hand at his over-sized living room. "Hell, Special Agent Cain. All of *this* was provided at *government expense*. Even so, lead on. Let's go for a plane ride."

Two hours later, they were aboard a military Lear jet, crossing over the Grand Canyon and heading east at over six hundred miles per hour. The plush executive aircraft offered wide, leather seats that folded out into full-length beds, and it wasn't long before all three of the passengers were sound asleep.

19

It was already ten in the morning East Coast time on December 18 when the jet arrived at Andrews Joint Air Force Base in the southeastern part of Washington D.C. Surprisingly refreshed by their four-hour naps and food that was provided, the trio boarded a gray military van for the short ride into the city.

Although the back of the van was windowless, Xander was able to see through the front windshield and noticed they were skirting along the length of the Washington Mall and passing the buildings that made up the Smithsonian Institution. He'd spent three years in the D.C. area working for DARPA before moving to the RDC and the dry desert of southern Nevada. The resurrected memories of his time here brought a chuckle to his lips.

He was in his early twenties at the time, handsome and well-paid, which gave him access to all the prurient pleasures the nation's capital had to offer. He shared an apartment in Georgetown with another of the DARPA studs, and the two men made a habit of tearing up the city nearly every Friday night until early Monday morning, spending money and breaking hearts like there was no tomorrow. By the time the duo broke up, they had become minor legends within the District's Under-Thirty social crowd.

He chuckled again, thinking how David Charlton ended up falling in love with a waitress from Applebee's and, as of five years ago, was living in Manassas with Janis and their *four* children. He left DARPA and now manages a Best Buy not far from his modest suburban home.

Xander's nostalgic reverie was broken when the van hit a dip as it entered a dark, underground parking garage. He couldn't see very well through the front window anymore, but it seemed that the van spent an inordinate amount of time driving deeper into the structure than was necessary. When the vehicle finally came to a stop, the rear doors were opened from the outside, and two Navy MPs stepped aside to let them exit.

Xander had no idea where they were since this part of D.C. was home to countless government entities, some of which most Americans didn't even know existed. In light of the crisis taking place across the country, this building could house any one of a dozen national security agencies. What this no-name organization wanted from the three of them was anyone's guess.

They were photographed and then immediately handed temporary ID badges that hung around their necks on silver chains before being shuffled into a guarded elevator for a ride to an unmarked floor. While in the elevator, Xander couldn't tell whether they were going up or down.

When the door slid open, more guards greeted them, along with an expressionless man in a grey suit and glasses. "Welcome, Mr. Jenkins," he said, extending a hand to Billy. The suit then turned to Xander and Tiffany. "And you, too, Mr. Moore and Ms. Collins." The *'afterthought'* pair exchanged hurt looks. Obviously, billionaire government contractors got more respect than a drone jockey and a T.V. reporter. "If you will follow me, I have some papers for you to sign before we can go any further."

"Papers?" Tiffany inquired.

"NDAs—non-disclosure affidavits, Privacy Act and other national security disclosures—you know, the usual."

"Usual for some people." Tiffany pointed out. "Where are we?"

The man stopped and turned to the reporter, locking a laser-like glare on her blue eyes. "I have been authorized to inform you—all of you—that if you do not wish to continue beyond this point, you are free to leave. You will be escorted out of the building and moved to a hotel until a return flight to California can be arranged."

Billy squeezed Tiffany's arm. "Relax, sweetheart. I

have a pretty good idea where we are. This is just their S.O.P."

The man continued to stare at Tiffany, waiting for her reaction. When she didn't move toward the elevator, the man turned on his heel and led them down a short hallway to a large, wood-paneled conference room.

The next ten minutes were spent signing forms without letterhead, and when it was done, no copies were provided. And then, as if on cue, the door opened, and an older, balding man in a short-sleeve, button-down shirt strode in.

"Welcome, all of you … to DARPA."

"Why all the secrecy, Nathan?" Billy asked as he shook the man's hand. "DARPA isn't exactly unknown, and I can look up your current projects roster online."

"Those are the projects we *want* you to know about, Billy. They're the ones we hope our adversaries will try and emulate, just so they'll throw millions, even billions of dollars, at high-cost, low-yield projects. What we do *here* are the projects we don't want anyone to know about."

'Nathan' turned to Tiffany. "Ms. Collins, I understand you feel a responsibility to your profession to reveal all, but I assure you that by doing so, you will cause the deaths of hundreds, if not thousands, of innocent people. Some things need to be kept secret, and that's not out of some sinister purpose to do evil. It's to keep others from either learning what we know or building effective defenses against our advances. I hope you understand."

"After the past few days *I've* had, it's my sincere hope that you have some answers to all the crap that's been happening. Having gotten a glimpse behind the curtain, I'm feeling pretty damn helpless and discouraged right about now."

The man Billy called Nathan shook his head. "I can't say we have all the answers, but we're getting close." Nathan turned to Xander and shook his hand. "I was with DARPA when you worked here, Mr. Moore, yet we never crossed paths. I am, however, very familiar with your work, both here and at the RDC. Welcome."

"I should have known," Xander said with a smile. "But I must admit, I'm relieved. I have more confidence in DARPA running things than I do the military."

"Oh, we're not running things, Mr. Moore. As a matter of fact, I don't think anyone is at this time. We're still trying to gather our wits about us and devise a plan. Now, if you come with me, I'd like to take all of you on a little tour, at least of the departments pertinent to your areas of expertise."

As they entered the outer hallway and a second elevator, Nathan turned to Xander. "I'm terribly sorry for what happened to the RDC. I'm sure you lost quite a few friends in the attack."

"I appreciate that, Nathan, but even after the flight out here, I'm still pretty much in the dark about the full extent of the damage."

"Your people are back in control—you probably knew

they would be since the lifespan of a UAV is so limited. Yet, as you may suspect, the damage to your capabilities is extensive. Some command-and-control activities are being switched to the old stations at Nellis and Creech, although they're going to require weeks of upgrading just to get basic communications going again with your remaining bunkers. Tindall Air Force Base in Florida has assumed some other control, as well as the NSA and the CIA."

"The NSA?" Tiffany asked. "What do they have to do with drone operations?"

"Nothing, really, Ms. Collins; it's just that they have some of the most-advanced communication equipment on the planet. What's needed at this time is a way to access the RDC's surviving drones and deploy them in defensive roles."

"What about the pilots?" Xander asked. "How many survived? I was under the impression it was a near-total wipeout."

The elevator stopped, and the four passengers exited into another hallway. A four-seater golf cart was waiting, and they climbed in, with Nathan driving, Billy in the passenger seat and Xander and Tiffany in the back.

"Thirty-nine of your pilots survived, and you might be happy to learn that one of your team was among them, Charlie Fox. He was surfing at the time of the attack."

"And David Lane?"

"I'm afraid not. He was at home in Las Vegas."

"He has a wife and daughter."

"I'm sorry."

"You seem pretty-well informed, Nathan," Tiffany said. "What exactly is your association with the RDC?"

Nathan smiled and glanced over at Billy. "Oh, I have no affiliation with the RDC. It's just that since the attack, I've been drafted into providing advice and tentative control regarding our drone response and countermeasures. Some general at the Pentagon is the actual Supreme Commander of drone operations now, but he's apparently smart enough to know when experts are needed. I've been given tactical command over our recovery and response."

"And what about the drone attacks?" Xander asked. "Are they continuing?"

"Unabated, I'm afraid, although a pattern has appeared."

"What kind of pattern?" Billy asked.

"A possible motive for the attacks."

Billy looked over his shoulder at Xander in the seat behind Nathan. "I thought revenge was the motive?" Billy said.

"It's a little more complicated than that, although we understand the link between Jonas Lemon and the RDC. That's something we're pursuing, along with Abdul-Shahid Almasi and his own reasons for hating the United States."

"So what *is* the motive?" Tiffany prodded.

"Economic upheaval."

"That goes without saying, dude," Billy said.

"Even so, there've been an extraordinary number of attacks on malls and online delivery outlets. Someone is doing their best to make sure the U.S. economy screeches to a halt, essentially, *Merry Fucking Christmas*. But the question we need answered is who benefits from a collapsing U.S. economy?"

"With how interdependent the world's economies are these days, it doesn't appear *anyone* could benefit," Tiffany offered.

"What about the terrorist groups and their sponsors?" Xander asked.

It was Tiffany who answered. "Countries like Iran and Syria sell an awful lot of oil to first-world countries, including the U.S. If we go under, there would be such a glut of oil on the market that their economies would also collapse. And other countries are debtor nations, dependent on our ability to repay our loans or make good on bond interest payments. That's why it doesn't make sense for there to be any attacks against America. Without us, the whole planet goes under."

"And yet the terror organizations, under the sponsorship and protection of these legitimate nations, are hitting us left and right," Xander countered. "That seems to go against the argument you just made."

Tiffany nodded. "Most people don't actually believe America can be defeated, and especially not through terrorist activity. The sponsor nations believe this, too, so they use these organizations to advance a political agenda while at the same time enjoying the benefits of a prosperous United States. Something has changed, however, if the terrorists are being allowed to continue. Its common knowledge that Bin Laden was terrified when he saw the towers come down on 9/11. That was so far beyond what he'd been expecting, and a world united against Al Qaida was something he wasn't prepared for. The first few years after 9/11 were the worst for international terrorism, up until everyone saw that America was going to come out just fine after the attack. That's also when politics took over and once again began to dictate U.S. military operations."

"So you're saying the terrorists involved in these attacks are not under the control of their traditional masters, that someone else is pulling their strings?" Xander said.

The golf cart stopped in front of a steel, double swinging-door, but no one got out, not until this line of conversation was concluded.

Tiffany was thinking out loud for most of her dissertation, carrying events to their logical conclusion. "I guess I am," she said. "Even though Almasi and Lemon may have planned the attack on the RDC, that operation was limited in scope. What's happening now; that's what doesn't make sense." She looked at Nathan-No-Last-Name and saw him smiling, a slight squint in his eyes.

"It would have to be another entity that is more-or-less isolated from the world economy, yet still powerful enough to fill the void left by a weakened America." Her eyes grew wide as she saw Nathan give her a nod. "Russia!"

"Excellent, Ms. Collins," said Nathan. "That's our belief, as well. In recent years, following the tragic war in Ukraine and other Baltic states, Putin and his successor, Marko, have been hoarding oil and other natural resources. They've also increased their gold supplies and linked the value of the ruble to the commodity. In sort, they've created an almost independent economy apart from the rest of the world. By destroying the U.S. economy, they not only take us out of the game but also China, Japan and most of Europe. The only financial superpower left standing would be Russia, ready with assistance to whoever comes knocking."

"At a very high price," Tiffany added.

"The highest."

"Isn't that an act of war?" Billy asked. "The Russians may not have soldiers on the ground, but they're the puppet-masters for those controlling the drones."

"And what would you have us do, Billy?" Nathan asked. "The links to what's happening are tenuous at best. We have no hard evidence. And with the ripple effect the attacks are having, it's only a matter of days before we reach critical mass. The dominoes will fall as stock markets crash, loans default and panic sets in. This will be Greece twenty-five years ago all over again, only a thousand times worse."

"That's if the attacks continue and the people don't

regain confidence in the country again," Xander said. "I hope that's why you've brought us here, Nathan, to show us that DARPA has found the solution to our drone problem."

Nathan slid out of the driver's seat. "Why don't we go take a look? As I said earlier, we're getting close."

"*'Close'* would imply you need more time," Xander pointed out. "And that is something we don't have."

"That's it?" Disappointment was evident in Billy's voice. "And then you'd have to have scramblers set up within, what, five miles or so of an attack?"

Nathan seemed genuinely hurt by Billy's reaction. "I said it wasn't perfect, but it's a start."

Xander picked up the small plug-in module known as a killbox. "Over ninety percent of attack drones have these attached to their flight controllers. If they can be neutralized, that *does* put us ahead of the game."

"I realized that, but if what you're saying is true, we don't have time to deploy scramblers all across the country in time to save Christmas."

Xander turned to the scientist. "How far along are you on this technology?"

Nathan nodded, sending a scowl in Billy's direction. "This isn't something we just started working on a couple of days ago. This has been an on-going project for several years, ever since the killboxes first showed up. Fortunately, there are only three facilities that make the little bastards, so we're not dealing with a lot of component variety."

"So, take out the factories," Tiffany offered. "I'm sure no one is going to squawk much, considering what's happening now."

"That's already underway," Nathan said. "But that won't stop the UAVs already equipped with the modules. And to answer your question, Xander, we have a way to tap into cell tower transmissions and blanket just about any area in the country within seconds with our suppressor signal. However, when we do, certain frequencies are disrupted, if not completely jammed."

"This defeats the Random Frequency Generators?" Billy asked.

"That it does not. It only affects the basic operation of the killbox, and then it only tends to confuse the programming, not completely override it. Test drones remain on station, but they're infected with a form of computer Alzheimer's. They can't remember what they're supposed to do when they get to where they're going."

"That still leaves the RPA's."

Nathan turned to Xander. "Countering the Remotely-Controlled Aircraft is where live pilots come in. You, and others like you, are still vital; however, now you'll only have the RPA's to contend with."

"Only if we have the combat drones available and the pilots to operate them."

"So, Nathan, are you ready to put your scramblers to work?" Tiffany asked.

"Forty-eight hours, maybe a little longer. We first have to gain access to the major cell carriers' transmission servers and satellites. Teams of Feds are out right now doing just that. We're not giving the companies much choice, seeing that this is a national security emergency, and we are operating under the authority of Martial Law."

Nathan looked at Xander and smiled. "Now, Mr. Moore, I'd like to show you something you may find interesting."

The DARPA rep took them to another room where a solitary object rested under a canvass tarp. Nathan pulled away the cover.

Both Billy and Xander gasped when they saw—or more correctly, thought they saw—what was revealed under the tarp.

It was a combat drone, yet like nothing they'd ever seen. First of all, it was long and flat, measuring nearly ten feet in length, with six two-foot-diameter rotor rings on each side and angled slightly to the inside. The thrust would be aimed toward the bottom of the UAV while allowing for a free flow of air from the top of the rings. But what made this unit truly unique was the odd shimmering effect of the finish, something that made it hard for the eye to focus on any individual part. At a quick glance, the craft would appear as a blur, just a figment of the imagination.

"Teflon, isn't it?" Billy asked.

"That's right," Nathan confirmed. "It's something that's been in the works for a decade, starting at UC San Diego, your old stomping grounds, Mr. Moore."

"What am I looking at?" Tiffany Collins asked.

"It's an invisibility cloak," Xander answered. "A micro-thin coating of light-absorbing Teflon with microscopic ceramic disks embedded."

"But I can still see it—sort of—so it's not really invisible."

"Of course not, Ms. Collins," Nathan said. "It only serves to cut down on some of the visible aspects of the UAV, as well as the radar signature. It's not truly invisible—just like all stealth technology isn't completely stealthy—but it is a step forward."

"I should say it is," Billy exclaimed. "We've been working on this technology at JEN-Tech for years, and all we've been able to come up with is a heavier, shinier drone."

"Even if you did come up with the proper formula, it would be cost-prohibitive in civilian applications," Nathan said.

"And I can still see the weapons—even though they're covered in the same stuff," Tiffany commented as the four of them moved closer to the drone and began to run their hands and fingers over the smooth, reflective surface.

Tiffany was right. The unit itself was not more than a foot thick, with a four-foot by eight-foot platform forming the top panel. And on this platform was about every weapon imaginable.

"These are 60-cals," Xander pointed out, "and full-metal jacket?"

"Exactly," said Nathan. "This unit can operate with over a ton of armament and at speeds of up to two hundred miles per hour. The flight controller is hardened and with our best RFG, so there'll be no jamming of this baby. Made of titanium and reinforced composite, it can take a direct hit from an 88mm canon shell and just bounce away. You may lose some of the add-ons on the platform, but they're a sixty-second change-out package. Operational altitude is up to ten thousand feet, maybe higher. Complete telemetry and target tracking to cut down on collateral damage."

"Where's the power box?" Billy asked.

"The most-advance fuel cells made," Nathan said, "and integrated into the support structure under the weapons platform. Operating time at full power is six hours, and then a thirty-second change out for a new battery pack will have you up and running again. And one other thing...."

Nathan walked over to a self-contained pilot's station that resembled a huge sit-inside video game pod. He reached in and pressed a button on the control pad. The UAV came to life, filling the large room with a torrent of swirling wind. Everyone covered their eyes for a moment before all the minute dust in the room was swept away. And that's when Billy and Xander looked at each other in utter amazement.

"Except for the wind in the room, the damn thing's silent!" Xander exclaimed.

He moved as close as he dared to the spinning propellers, each enclosed in its own rotor ring. The motors were actually part of the ring and of such a low profile and fully integrated into the design that it was hard to spot them. There was a sound, yet it was such a low-pitched hum that it reminded Xander of a running refrigerator; it was that quiet.

"Please step away, Mr. Moore. There's one more feature I'd like to show you."

Xander obeyed. When nothing happened, he turned to look at Nathan. "Sorry," the scientist said. "Just trying to build a little suspense." He then pressed another button on the console.

The huge drone stayed airborne momentarily as four of the propeller rings—two on each side of the vehicle—rotated to the vertical. In a matter of seconds, the drone now had four wheels resting on the floor, with the two center rings helping to provide modest lift and added maneuverability. The two small pusher propeller rings at the rear would add forward thrust.

"Now it's a ground unit, capable of maneuvering within tight quarters or all-out sprints at over one hundred miles per hour over land. Each ring is operated independently of the others, enabling the Goliath—that's what we call this model—to spin on its axis in place. And with the props engaged, the craft can hop over obstacles or even transition to full flight mode in seconds flat."

There were several other drone models that were both ground and air units in production these days, but nothing with the capabilities of the Goliath. Xander and Billy were speechless, even when Nathan powered down the drone and then leaned against the control pod with a satisfied grin on his face.

Eventually, Billy was able to shake himself from his stupor.

"Who builds these things?" Billy asked with suspicion. His company was the leading domestic producer of advanced military drones, and he'd never seen anything like this before.

"Actually, we built this one … and fifty-nine others."

"Sixty!" Xander cried out. "You have sixty of these things? Where are they? Are they operational? Do you have a command center set up?"

"Relax, Mr. Moore, you'll get your chance to play with our new toy—"

"Screw that, *Nathan!*" Xander said, moving closer to the scientist. "I don't want to play with the damn things. I want to use them to stop the killing that's taking place. With sixty of these units and your killbox override system, we could make a real difference."

Nathan was taken aback by Xander's sudden display of passion. "I'm sorry if I implied something other than your complete devotion to your duty as an RDC pilot. And yes, we do have a command center set up. It's over at Andrews."

"And where do you have these units deployed?"

"Most are in the D.C. area, with a few in Texas for testing, and five in the Middle East, aboard the aircraft carrier *Gerald Ford*. They're the next generation of CIA attack drones, scheduled for operational release by the end of next year."

"Next year, screw that! We need them in the next hour."

"I know that, and since Monday, we've been scrambling to get the domestic units out to where they're needed the most. With their high cruising speed, most are being released to fly to their stations autonomously, taking only a few hours to get there at the most. The limiting factor is getting the relatively few power packs out to these sites and, of course, our lack of skilled pilots."

Xander looked at the now inert drone. "I doubt if I could fly that thing without a pretty intensive training course."

"Not so. All the flight controls are compatible with those of the Viper-class, and the control stations are fully integrated and intuitive. Simply flying the Goliath isn't the problem; it's the combat skill with a drone that's lacking. Tactics, spatial awareness and coordination are the qualities that make a great drone pilot." Nathan hesitated as his face grew deadly serious. It was his turn to take a step closer to Xander. "And that, Mr. Moore, is why *you're* here."

Xander blinked several times as he felt all eyes fall on him. "I'm just one guy. I can't do it all."

"No, you can't, but we also have Billy." Then he looked at his watch. "And in about two hours, you'll have your entire Alpha Team at Andrews and manning control pods."

"No shit! Still, that's only six of us."

"We're also bringing in Charlie Fox and another dozen of the surviving pilots from the RDC. And we do have a few of our own skilled operators, the ones who helped with the design and testing of the Goliaths. You may have to give them a crash course in killer drone operation, but they do know the equipment. By the end of the day, there should be over forty pilots manning the fifty drones we have available stateside."

"Hey, Nathan," Billy called out. "I'll pilot your fancy drones, but on one condition."

Everyone was shocked by Billy's statement. How could he attach a condition on saving the lives of innocent Americans, as well as protecting the nation's vital infrastructure and most treasured landmarks?

"And what would *that* be, Mr. Jenkins?"

"That I get the contract to build these things when they go into full production."

Relieved, Nathan smiled. "That's another reason why *you're* here, Billy. The papers are already drawn up and just awaiting your signature."

"I have something to say," Tiffany interrupted. All eyes now turned to the reporter.

"We're in the middle of a pitched battle with a bunch of unmanned killer robots, and now you're introducing the most deadly drone ever made into the mix. At what point do you stop adding fuel to the fire? You know, all the bad guys will do is copy the technology from your Goliath, and soon, the sky will be filled with even more lethal weapons. At some point, this has to stop."

No one spoke for a moment; it was Xander who broke the silence.

"Until we can change the hearts and minds of people, there will always be the next new weapon system being created. The Goliath drone isn't a deterrent against other Goliaths, but it is a defense against the evil that men *will* do. I wish it wasn't like this, but I'm a realist. It's not the weapons themselves that have to change, but the nature of the people who use them. That's the real enemy we face. Until we can change people, there will always be the need for Goliaths in the world."

20

Abdul-Shahid Almasi had all the scheduled attacks on the American homeland listed on his computer, and as he received reports of their implementation, he would check them off with a satisfied grin. The Westerners were vulnerable and fully exposed, and Almasi's associates were carrying out raid after successful raid with very little resistance.

This was the start of the third day after the destruction of the Rapid Defense Center, and he could see from the list that this was to be *the* decisive moment in the history of the United States. Sixty-four separate attacks were to take place: on highway overpasses, bridges, power plants, landmark buildings and national monuments. As had been predicted, the shopping malls now sat empty, as did all the sporting venues across the country. There were no substantial human targets to be found, so the emphasis for today would be on the long-term crippling of the nation's infrastructure, which will result in limited future travel and delivery of vital resources—such as electricity—to an already shell-shocked America. Long after the raids subside, the infidels will still be suffering from these glaring reminders of how helpless and impotent they are within this new world order.

Timetables were listed on his computer screen and keyed to local time in Pakistan. Over the last hour, nineteen raids were scheduled to get underway, and now Almasi sat at his desk in the living quarters of his underground bunker in the heart of Karachi, anxiously awaiting the stream of incoming data to lift his already ebullient spirits even more.

As with the past scheduled assaults, he had newsfeed banners set to run along the bottom of his screen, letting him know when an attack commenced. In another part of the bunker, men watched various TV screens and would update the banners as information became available.

After a few minutes—and only three confirmations—Almasi began to get mad. What were his people doing in the viewing room, watching a soccer match rather than the news? He pressed the intercom button.

"Farouk, why am I not getting all my feeds!" he yelled into the box.

The response was immediate. "But you are, Abdul-Shahid. We are closely monitoring all the news channels."

"There are nineteen attacks underway and yet I have

only received confirmation of three. Check on this and get back to me."

Thirty minutes later, the pattern had become clear, and Almasi was furious at its implications. Only one other attack had been reported, and his own channel surfing had produced similar results as did his monitors. Fifteen of the attacks had not commenced. He checked the files before taking his cellphone and dialing a number.

The first call didn't go through. The next two were picked up by voicemail. The fourth was answered.

"Kareem, this is Abdul-Shahid."

"I can see who is calling."

The rudeness of the reply made Almasi hesitate before continuing. "I am inquiring as to the attack on the Florida nuclear power plant. I have not received confirmation. Have you run into difficulty?"

There was a long pause on the phone before Kareem Sarkis answered. "I have called off the attack, Abdul."

"You have … why?"

"I have been instructed to."

"By whom?"

"By Tehran."

Almasi was stunned by the completely unexpected reply. "I do not understand. You're saying Tehran does not want you to complete your mission?"

"That is correct."

"Again, I ask why. The Iranians have been amongst our biggest supporters. And now we have America reeling.

There must be a motive for their actions. Are they seeking a delay or a full termination?"

"They want me to stop all activities in America, and Abdul, I too asked them why."

"What did they say?"

"They said the situation has become more complicated. That was it. I pressed them for more, but the order was unequivocal. However, shortly after the call from the Minister, I received another from a source within the Council of Ministers. He told me that China is applying pressure on them to have all attacks brought to an end."

"*China!* Why would they interfere?"

"Economics, my friend; the Americans have bought the Chinese, and the communists are now fearful of what a bankrupt America would do to their own finances."

Almasi's eyes appeared to vibrate in their sockets as he fought desperately for the words that would salvage the conversation. "I understand what you say, Kareem, and I also know you receive much of your support from Iran. But I can assure you of a new benefactor if you do proceed and one even more powerful than Iran."

"You speak of Russia. Yes, I am aware of your collusion with President Marko and his supporters."

"Then you know they are willing to finance your operations well into the future."

There was another long pause on the phone before Kareem responded. "We both know how the Russians operate. They would support us as long as it remains socially and politically acceptable to do so. However, Iran supports us out of ideology, not by political whim. I cannot afford to alienate my longest and most loyal supporters for something that could only be temporary and with too many conditions attached. The Iranians are aware of your ties to Marko and have warned me against taking such action. I am sorry, Abdul, but my part of this operation is over."

"But we are so close! Only a few more days and America will no longer be a force in the world. We will be free of her threats and her interference. Kareem, you have always desired your own country, along with permission to deal with the Israeli situation as you see fit. With America gone, you can do that."

"I have also been told to cease our aggression against the Zionists, at least in the interim."

Now, it was Almasi's turn to grow silent. He was stunned—and scared—scared that others would fall sway to the same pressure from their handlers. "We must not succumb to outside influences, Kareem. Our cause is just; it is Allah's will. We fight for Allah, not for politicians, no matter where they may be located."

"It is over, Almasi. Our organizations can only exist with help from others, and when presented with alternatives, I *must* obey. I *will* obey. Goodbye, Abdul. Please do not contact me again."

The connection went dead.

Out of panic and desperation, Almasi checked again

to see if any of the other scheduled attacks had commenced, but none had. So, it wasn't only Kareem; it was all the others within his coalition who had succumbed to the backdoor pressure and threats from their host nations. The Zionist pigs running America had used their financial influence to pressure China and, in turn, North Korea, Iran, Syria, and possibly even Pakistan to make calls and issue their own threats and warnings.

His plan was collapsing right before his manic eyes—at least that part of the plan.

He dialed another number. The phone rang several times before a strange voice answered.

"Who is this?" Almasi demanded.

"Who is *this*? The deep voice echoed.

"Almasi."

"Forgive me, Abdul-Shahid; it is Faisal Haddad with the surveillance team on Jonas Lemon."

"Why are *you* answering the phone?"

"We received instructions to watch Lemon closely; we assumed it came from you."

"It did. I believed he was planning something."

"Your suspicions were correct. We caught him leaving the Burj Khalifa through a service entrance and in disguise."

"Was he harmed?" Almasi's heart skipped a beat as he awaited the answer.

"No, he is fine. He is here with me if you wish to speak with him."

"Give him the phone."

"Yo, Abdul!" Jonas Lemon said a few seconds later. "I guess there's no outfoxing the fox."

"I have dealt with merchants of information before. You have done nothing that has surprised me."

"So, no hard feelings? I was just looking to cover my ass—"

"Shut up! We have a problem."

"*We?*"

"Yes, we. Our plan is falling apart."

When Jonas spoke next, his voice was serious and lacked his normal flippant attitude.

"Moore is still alive?"

"This is much worse than your obsession with Xander Moore. The other groups are abandoning their missions and withdrawing from the operation."

"Why in the hell would they do that?"

"Pressure brought forth from China has forced their host nations to threaten the coalition with loss of support if the assaults on America continue."

"Because China fears for their precious investments in the United States," Jonas said, finishing the line of thought. "And they're going along with the demands, of course."

"Most are, and others will follow once they see the operation failing."

"Dammit!" Jonas yelled through the phone. "I gave

you America on a silver platter—all of you—and now none of you bastards have the balls to see it through."

"I am still committed," Almasi said between clenched teeth.

"You're just one small organization, and you weren't planning on having to pick up the slack. I told you we only have a narrow timeframe to win this war. Without America brought *all* the way to her knees, we've gained nothing."

"There's still one operation that *can* be carried out."

The long silence on the phone told Almasi that Lemon knew what he was talking about.

"But you'll need the transponder codes for that," Lemon pointed out.

"That's right, Jonas, and I am through playing games with you. Give me the codes so we can salvage what we can from all our efforts."

"But Moore is still alive."

"Fuck Moore! He does not matter at this point. Your revenge can come later, yet mine is still possible. Now, give me the damn codes … or do I order my men there to bring *your* head to *me* on a silver platter?"

"Don't threaten me, Almasi," Jonas growled.

"Give me the fucking codes!"

"Transfer the money, and then call off your men."

"Give me the codes first. I will keep my word. What happens to you after this? I do not care. Your death will provide me with no satisfaction, no redemption, yet along my other path, I will find both. I will give you your money. Now give me the codes."

A few tense heartbeats passed. "All right, but transfer the money now and have your goons get me a computer with internet access."

"Return the phone to Faisal."

Ten minutes later, Jonas Lemon confirmed the funds' transfer and emailed Abdul-Shahid Almasi a file containing an algorithmic series of numbers.

"These will work?"

"They should. The modified master frequency generator you have will be able to reverse the process and broadcast a blast once the channel is open. After the new bounce-back codes are accepted, the rest will fall into place. You'll have no problem gaining access, and at that point, you won't need any of the others from your cowardly coalition of the unwilling."

"With how this day has progressed, I cannot share in your confidence that the codes will work. And you should know, if this information is found to be false or unworkable, I will seek you out—even on your South Pacific island hideaway. You see, Jonas, there are no secrets you can keep from me."

"Only the transponder codes, and trust me, they *are* good. Just make sure you have at least forty-five seconds for the initial upload. Once started, the signal will lock and begin to filter throughout the entire grid. It's the ultimate computer virus—"

"You never said anything about needing time to upload the codes! What if we do not have forty-five seconds?"

"All programs take time to upload; I thought you knew that. But relax, Abdul. Use the broken link back at the RDC to gain entry. The techs who open the source won't be expecting someone else to be waiting to slip in."

"You had better hope we are given the time because if this mission fails—whether by your fault or mine—I *will* gain satisfaction and redemption in your death."

"Do what you have to do, Almasi … and I will do the same."

"Goodbye, Jonas Lemon. Let us both pray that this is the last time we speak with one another." Almasi pressed the red 'end' button on the phone.

Next, he quickly dialed another number. After thirty seconds, the phone began to ring, and it was answered immediately.

"I am sending you the transponder codes now."

"Now?" said the American voice on the other end of the line. "I thought we weren't going for another two days, at the soonest?"

"Everything is in place, is it not?"

"Sure, it has been for weeks."

"Then what is your problem?"

"I don't have a problem," the man's voice conveyed frustration and insult. "Just send the damn codes. I assume you'll be controlling the master feed from there?"

"I will. When can you be ready?"

There was a pause on the line, and then, "One p.m. tomorrow, at the soonest. That's a little over twenty-four hours. I need to round up the last members of my team. They weren't expecting to be needed so soon."

"That is not acceptable. We go with or without them," Almasi said. "I will be back in contact with you in forty-five minutes. Have your team ready to move at that time."

"Forty-five minutes! That's not—"

Almasi cut the connection, and then, in the deathly quiet of his underground bunker, he gnashed his teeth and firmed his resolve. He could still salvage the events of the past few days with something so huge that it would impact the United States of America for generations to come.

Within the day, Abdul-Shahid Almasi would make history … by destroying it.

21

The reunion that afternoon at Andrews Air Force Base between Xander and the other Alphas was both touching and emotional. These were people he'd known since his pre-teens in most cases. Together, they'd discovered the joy of building and flying drones, and when the time came to test their skills against the best of the best, they rose to the occasion in gold medal-winning fashion.

"I should have known the two of you would be right in the thick of things," said the only woman on the Alpha Team, Karen Prado.

"Hey, don't blame me," Billy Jenkins protested. "Xan showed up at my door yesterday—a door that's been shattered to pieces from about a thousand bullet holes, I might add—and now I'm in Washington, D.C., trying to figure out how to save the country from a deadly horde of ravenous drones."

Karen smiled. "Yeah, he does have that effect on people." She had been Xander's first, even if he suspected Billy was hers. When adolescents spend so much time together while sharing a common passion, things are bound to happen. The affair didn't last; they seldom do at that age.

"So, Karen, you got married … and divorced?"

She snorted. "I got the first one out of the way early, so I could make way for Mr. Right." She looked at Billy and winked. "And now someone with shitloads of money would be just the ticket."

Billy wrinkled his nose at her. "When will I find a woman who loves me for me and not my money?"

Hugh Barden slapped him on the shoulder. "Don't knock it. Once they get to know the real Billy Jenkins, money's about the only thing you have going for you."

Hugh was the true lady's man of the group. Crowding six-foot-five, the slender, mixed Hispanic and Caucasian man had a perpetual tan, curly black hair and a brilliant white smile. He was the least technically proficient of the group, yet he was a ruthless bastard when it came to drone piloting. Given a small nudge, he would have turned into a taller and better-looking version of Jonas Lemon.

Xander hugged the other two members of the team in turn. Jeremy Fenton was short, plump, and had the stereotypical look of a tech geek. He and Xander were the first to discover UAVs, and it was through the obvious joy they both displayed when at the controls of their small quadcopters that the others thought they'd give it a try. And the rest is history.

"Curt, they let you out?" Xander asked the last member of the team—the tallish and stocky Curt Tharp.

"Not really, but your friends here obviously have some clout. They said if I play nice, they could even make it permanent."

"Dude, I was only kidding!" Xander said with shock and embarrassment.

"I wish I was, but that's what you get for running with the wrong crowd. Wouldn't you know it that with all the drugs being legalized these days, I would get caught dealing in the one that wasn't."

"How long have you been in?"

"Six months." Curt noticed the concerned looks on the faces of the other Team members. "Don't worry. I understand they want us to fly some drones. Up until the day I reported to Lompoc, I had a controller in my hand. It's like riding a bike, right?"

"A quarter-of-a-million-dollar bike, Mr. Tharp," Nathan commented. By now, Xander had pried a last name out of him—if it truly was his last name. It was Hall. Nathan Hall.

"No shit?" Curt said, looking with anticipation at Xander and Billy. "They're going to let us play with quarter-mill toys?"

Xander nodded with a smile. "That's what you get when you spend other people's money. You kinda lose perspective about the true value of things."

"That may be so, Mr. Moore," Nathan said. "Still, try not to break anything. And if you do, you'll be billed for it."

Curt threw up his hands. "Then I'm outta here. Take me back to prison, boys. At least there, if I break something, it's just a couple of skulls that needed it in the first place."

Xander now stepped up and assumed command of Team Alpha, just as he had so many times in the past. "Okay, fun and games are over; this is some serious shit we're facing. I'm sure you've all been keeping up on recent events—"

"Hard not to; it's all that's on these days," Karen said.

"Unfortunately, you're only seeing the tip of the iceberg. This is more than just a series of random terrorist attacks against the evil Western Empire. We believe there are people who want to ruin America economically, and they mean to do it by destroying Christmas."

"Are the people you speak of green-skinned with pointed ears and a mangy dog as a companion?" Hugh asked.

"I'd take the Grinch any day over these bastards, but here's what we have: The RDC has been taken out, and even though there may be a fair number of combat-rated drones sitting idle in the rapid-response bunkers across the country, we don't have time to reprogram them to respond to secondary control. Thanks to Mr. Hall and DARPA—"

"DARPA?" Karen asked.

"The Defense Advanced Research Projects Agency," Xander said.

"A bunch of super-smart guys and gals who get to play with the most advanced toys imaginable, and with all the money the government can provide," Billy finished for him.

"Where do I sign up for *that* gig?" Jeremy Fenton asked. "I'm a super-smart guy who likes to play with toys."

"Just for the record, Mr. Fenton," Nathan Hall said, "I've looked at your resume, and if we survive—or more precisely if *you* survive—you have a spot here with us."

Jeremy's mouth fell open for a moment. "I wonder if it's too soon to talk about my salary requirements. You know, I don't come cheap?"

"We'll certainly take into consideration your current pay scale at *Best Buy* when determining our offer, Mr. Fenton. We might be able to do a *little* better."

"Excuse me, but can we get on with the task of saving the country from a horde of blood-thirsty extremists?" Xander asked. When no one else interrupted, he continued. "Thanks to Mr. Hall and the people at DARPA, we have a small fleet of highly-advanced prototype drones to send up against the attacking units. Also, his people have found a way to neutralize killboxes, so we'll only have to go up against RPA's. Since it appears most of the major, coordinated attacks have been carried out mainly using killbox-equipped drones, the terrorists may be unprepared for the loss of such a substantial amount of their force. Also, many of the opportunists jumping on the bandwagon are using remotely-controlled UAVs, yet they aren't that sophisticated. These units can be easily jammed since few are equipped with RFGs. The bottom line: Once we deploy, the number of units we'll have to engage should be drastically reduced. Now, the drones you'll be flying are called *Goliaths*. They are the largest, most-advanced combat drones ever built—"

"Is anyone else here getting a hard-on?" Hugh asked.

Karen raised her hand. "I'm not."

Xander shook his head and looked over at Billy and a silent Tiffany Collins. "You can dress 'em up… You just can't take 'em anywhere."

"We get the idea, Number One," Curt Tharp said. "This is serious, and we're the team of superheroes brought in to save the day. So, where are these super drones that we superheroes get to play with?"

"Follow me," Nathan Hall said. "And don't touch anything that says, 'Don't Touch.' It might explode."

22

The man in the yellow vest looked up from the pile of debris and frowned when he noticed the letters emblazoned across the breast pockets of the black jackets the six newcomers wore.

Derrick Howard could almost hear the man thinking, *What the hell is the EPA doing here?*

Howard flashed his ID at the man. "How's it going? We're here to help."

"Help? How is the EPA going to help sort through this mess?"

Derrick smiled. "Well, help might not be the right word. We're here to monitor the release of toxic gases within the ruins, specifically mercury and asbestos. Is this the communications building—or what remains of it? We need to get down to the equipment bays."

"Yeah, it is. There's another group of techs down

below. There's an access over by the yellow tape. Good luck, though not much survived. Those fucking drones…."

"Yeah, I hear ya. Everyone last one of them should be banned."

"You got that right. Watch your step going down. Most of the overhead is unstable."

"Thanks for the heads-up."

Derrick nodded to his team, and they set off along a cleared path within the massive pile of rubble where a five-story building once stood. They found the yellow tape and the surviving metal steps that led underground. Before descending, each man placed a white surgical mask over his face.

Below ground, the damage wasn't as bad as on the surface, but it was still a mess. The shattered remains of dozens of plastic drones lay everywhere along the wide corridor. Once the batteries had drained on the attacking drones, the survivors of the RDC emerged from hiding and systematically bashed the inert UAVs to pieces. The process was cathartic to a point, yet it did pose a problem for the forensic teams that came in afterward, looking for serial numbers and other identifying markings.

Three floors down, the damage was even less, although it was apparent the killer drones had reached the main communication rooms for the Center. Here, strategically placed missiles, bullets and bombs had ripped the huge banks of sophisticated equipment to shreds. Add to this the complete destruction of the topside communication dishes, and the RDC was effectively cut off from the outside world.

Yet this was just the exposed part of the comm center. Embedded within walls and floors, before running far below ground in fortified concrete tunnels, the main feed lines still survived. Some ran to power sources outside the Center, while others led to the graveyard of shattered satellite antennas and dishes on the surface.

Air Force techs had set up portable relay equipment outside, with a new arrangement of nine interlocking dishes pointing into the sky. Once-severed comm lines had already been reconnected to this temporary set up, and now all that remained was for the team below to finish their work before the array could be lit up.

In the underground comm room, eight Air Force techs were in the process of tracing broken coaxial cables, ethernet lines and thick fiber-optic bundles, looking to make contact with the equipment on the surface. To help with the task, they'd brought in their own version of miniature mainframe computers, towers of server-holders rolled in on six-foot-long metal carts.

Two other airmen stood around the huge room holding M27 rifles and looking bored. They perked up momentarily when Derrick Howard and his group entered.

"Damn, the EPA," said an airmen whose name patch read *G. Garner*. "That's a new one. We've had FEMA, the CIA, FBI, even the NTSB down here, but not the EPA."

Derrick smiled at the young man. "The Environmental Protection Agency is *everywhere*," he said menacingly.

"So it seems. Just stay out of the way of the techs. They're a touchy bunch when it comes to their equipment."

"Don't worry; we brought our own: air sniffers and such."

"Dang, you mean you'll be able to detect the bean burrito I had for lunch?"

Derrick frowned and wrinkled his nose under the white mask. "Man, that's disgusting. Let's hope not."

With a nod, his men retired to a vacant corner of the room and began opening their heavy black cases. All the equipment was battery-powered and contained within the boxes. Switches were flicked as lights and screens came to life.

A few of the Air Force techs looked over at them and frowned but soon returned to the tedious work of tracing orphan wires for their source and purpose.

Derrick approached a group of techs who were on their hands and knees at what looked like a small crop of thin wires growing out of the floor. "How's it going? You guys making progress?"

"Fuck it!" said one of the men without looking up. "This is like looking for a needle in a pile of elephant shit."

The man next to him looked over his shoulder at

Derrick and took in the EPA label on his jacket. His breast tag read *D. Grissom*. "Don't mind him; we're doing fine. We should have a preliminary link-up in a few minutes. Should we be wearing masks or something?"

"That wouldn't be a bad idea, at least until we're done with our air samples. We brought a supply of N95s just in case."

One of Derrick's men passed out the masks to the other people in the room, and then the team huddled together, having pulled up broken equipment supports to use as chairs.

Derrick sat next to Steve Vasquez. "Are we syncing?" he whispered.

"Piece of cake," Vasquez answered. "Still, this is a lot of data to upload in only forty-five seconds. I think they're being optimistic. And then the carrying capacity of the connections may not be all that high."

"What are you trying to tell me?"

"That we may need a lot more time for the upload than forty-five seconds."

Derrick pursed his lips in frustration. He knew Almasi was waiting halfway around the world for the moment the upload was complete; he would know at the same time as Derrick and his team. The link between Las Vegas and Karachi was already solid and verified; just waiting for this new connection.

He carefully watched the techs across the room. Derrick was sure there would be some indication from the workers when connections were established, even though the equipment in the cases would know as well. Originally, the plan called for the team to access the room after the link was reestablished. Even if all the RDC drones were accessed at that point, the operation called for the existing codes to be overridden by the ones Almasi would provide. That would have involved a hard tap on the lines, yet without so many people in the room.

But now the crazy terrorist wanted the override to happen sooner, basically in conjunction with contact being initially regained with the bunkers. It was estimated that even if the military was able to reestablish contact, this would only be the first step in changing out the transponder codes to correspond with those linked to new command centers. The old codes would have to be expunged so no conflicts would exist, and then new ones would be loaded.

The codes Derrick carried in his equipment were ghosts of the existing RDC codes already in the flight controllers of the drones. The thousands of UAVs hidden away in hundreds of locations across the country would instantly accept the command authority of these transponder codes, even before they would allow their current codes to be dumped.

Two days from now, Derrick and his team would have had no problem overriding any new codes installed in the drones. But now the job was trickier. The techs in the room would surely notice the presence of a second signal once the link was established. Derrick had to think of some way to keep them from noticing the ghost signal for what could amount to a minute or more.

He called over two of his men, the two of whom were classified as muscle on the team and not vital to the upload operation. He briefed them on his plan.

And then they waited.

A full hour later, the tech who had complained about the difficulty of the job lifted off his knees and leaned back against a side wall. "Damn, Sarge, that was a bitch."

Tech Sergeant Grissom also climbed to his feet, along with his entire eight-person team. He and two other men moved to a table that held its own array of sophisticated electronic equipment. He began to type on a keyboard. "Let's see what we've got," Grissom said. He reached under the white surgical mask and scratched his nose.

They all watched the computer readouts with rapt attention until one of them pointed at the screen.

"Yeah, looks good, doesn't it? Check the alignment."

A moment later, he stood back from the table and stretched his back. "Looks like we have it, strong and steady. Let the brass know, Zach."

Suddenly, a soft chirping sound arose from the other side of the room, and all eyes turned toward the source.

The EPA guys seemed agitated, and Derrick and two others rushed up to the tech team holding small readers resembling microphones.

"What's going on?" the tech sergeant asked.

"High levels of radon have been detected, in fact, off the chart."

"Seriously? What could cause that?"

"Is it dangerous?" another of the airmen asked.

"Dangerous? Hell, yeah!" Derrick exclaimed. "It's radioactive." He looked at his other two men.

"It's concentrated on this side of the room," reported one of them.

"Please, sergeant, can I get your men to move over by the doorway while we bring in fans and investigate the source?"

"Now? How long will it take?"

"Not more than five minutes or so, that's all."

"C'mon, Sarge," said the complainer. "I could use a break anyway."

"We have to monitor the link."

"Every second?" Derrick asked.

"Well, no," relied the tech sergeant. "But we just got it back up."

"Five minutes, and it'll be clear. Better than killing yourselves just so you can watch a damn computer screen."

"This shit can kill us?"

"In the right concentration."

"What about you guys?" the sergeant asked.

"We're trained for this stuff. Now, please, sergeant, let us do our job so you can do yours."

"Yeah, sure, just let me know when it's safe."

"Roger that."

Fifteen minutes later, Derrick Howard and his team had left the underground comm room, having certified that the air was now safe to breathe.

In fact, they were already in a green EPA van and heading down the hill from the ruins of the Rapid Defense Center by the time Sergeant Grissom noticed something was wrong. Moments before, they had a solid link with the bunkers, and now, in rapid succession, the links were being lost. This was unusual since the original link was a blanket broadcast to all the RDC bunkers and did not single out any individual location. Now, the progression was obvious, and the sheer number of bunkers they were losing became evident.

By the time Grissom made contact with his superiors at Nellis, the word had already reached Washington D.C. that something wasn't right. Contact *had* been established with the bunkers, and now they were losing it.

Nathan Hall, as the tacit head of the newly-designated Rapid Defense Center East, saw the spread of broken contacts in a graphic display on a huge monitor on the wall of his temporary command center at Andrews Air

Force Base. At first, he cursed the technicians; the original link wasn't as solid as they'd reported. But then, once all the bunkers were dark again, sporadic reports began to come in saying that some of the bunkers—mainly those in the D.C. area—were opening. Tech crews were inside all of them, and they backed away as dozens of combat drones suddenly sprang to life and lifted out of the bunkers within five seconds of activation, giving the people in the bunkers no time to react.

Nathan grew weak-kneed when he realized what was happening.

He picked up a microphone and set it to broadcast Center-wide, which in reality consisted of only two converted aircraft hangars on the base, one housing the command center and the other the control pods for the Goliaths.

"Attention all pilots and techs, man your stations! The RDC bunkers have been activated, and the drones inside are going mobile, but they are not—I repeat—*not* under friendly control."

He set the microphone down on the table and watched on another monitor as thirty military and civilian drone pilots in the neighboring hangar ran to stations and lit up their screens. Then his cellphone rang.

"Hall here."

"This is Xander. What the hell are you talking about—*not under friendly control?*"

"It means the transponder codes in the bunker drones have been hijacked. Need I say by whom?"

"How many bunkers have been compromised?"

"All of them, Xander, every last friggin one of them."

There was silence on the phone for several seconds before Xander spoke again. "There are over seventeen-thousand combat-rated drones in those bunkers, and you're saying Almasi has control of all of them?"

"'Fraid so. I'm expediting the activation of the cell towers with the killbox neutralizing signal. It'll have the added benefit of confusing the RDC auto drones as well since it acts on the flight controller itself. But that still leaves the RPA's. How many are in the inventory? I haven't had time to research everything the RDC had going."

"Over three thousand."

Nathan let out a whistle. "Well, I would hazard a guess that Almasi doesn't have three thousand pilots sitting around somewhere, ready to take control of all those units. That's one way to look at it."

"Probably not, but he has enough to cluster attack just about anywhere he pleases and then transfer his people to other locations once those raids are done. He won't be able to recharge any of the units, so these are all use-and-discard."

"But three thousand combat drones, that's ten times more than what's been used in any of the attacks so far. And just when the attacks were beginning to taper off."

"We should be able to tell which bunkers have been activated, right?"

"That we can, at least visually, or by the techs on site."

"That will give us target zones. What do we have so far?"

Nathan scanned the information on the large monitor while a Navy petty officer handed him a sheet of paper. "You're not going to like this, but sixteen bunkers have been activated in the D.C., Alexandria, and Arlington regions. The auto drones should be dead in the water by now, especially in this area where we have the most assets. But that still leaves over a hundred and twenty-five RPA's from the report I've just been handed."

"What better target than D.C., Nathan? I'll get the pilots ready, but we only have nine Goliaths in the area. The rest have already been sent out to other locations."

"If I recall some from the surrounding zones, they could be here in under an hour. That might get another six or so on station."

"An hour, hell, Washington could be in ruins in an hour. I'll get my people up and prowling immediately. Maybe we can delay some of the major damage until re-enforcements arrive. You recall the other drones; we'll do what we can from the air."

"Good luck, Xander. I'll continue to get the killbox signal disseminated while monitoring things from here. We'll feed your pilots coordinates as they become available."

23

Abdul Almasi surveyed the rows of flight control stations in the large room fifty feet below the surface of his unassuming residential compound in the suburbs of Karachi, Pakistan. He knew eventually he'd acquire the transponder codes from Jonas Lemon, just not so soon. He only had forty-two pilots at the compound, far fewer than he had originally planned for at this stage of the operation. They would have to do. Before the desertion of his allies in the drone war against the United States, he planned on transferring control to another two hundred pilots located across the Middle East, Europe and even in America. Now, his former allies would regret their decisions as they saw the incredible firepower that the Arm of Allah now had under its control. They could have shared in the ultimate battle against the infidels and been a part of the legend that would be spoken of for centuries.

Now, it would be his legend alone.

Yes, his task was now more difficult, and it would take longer to accomplish. In addition, he would have to utilize the same forty-two pilots for countless operations. The pilots would not be able to maintain the pace for long, which would also slow his progress. But now that couldn't be avoided.

Eventually, the Americans would seal off the remaining bunkers, possibly by parking tanks over their exits. He would then destroy the trapped drones inside, making sure they couldn't be turned against him in the future.

He would have to act fast, hitting the most high-value targets first. And fortunately for Abdul-Shahid Almasi, most of America's symbolic high-value targets where located in or around the Washington, D.C. area.

As a precaution, he sent out commands to activate a hundred additional bunkers across the country, placing the freed drones into standby mode once outside and superficially hidden from detection. Battery charges had to be preserved until the drones were called upon, which hopefully would be soon, and before the authorities could track them down.

There was a loud murmur permeating the flight control stations.

"What's wrong?" he called out over the rising din.

A senior pilot, Vladimir Krensky, turned from his station. "The auto drones are not responding, at least the ones in the D.C. area. Some of the others are—the ones you've asked to be dispersed into the countryside—but none in Washington."

The transponder link he had with the bunkers gave him access to the video monitors within the bunkers. He activated the feed from two of the bunkers near the White House.

Sure enough, the auto drones—mainly the smaller, sacrificial lambs of the arsenal—had their propellers spinning away in the launch area as they hovered ten feet in the air. But they weren't *going* anywhere. Frantic technicians and military personnel in the bunkers were trying desperately to knock the drones out of the air. The soldiers used the hovering UAVs for target practice while the techs swung metal rods and even folding chairs at the drones.

Almasi fingered the detonation codes for the two bunkers he had on the screen and was only mildly surprised when nothing happened. Somehow, the Americans had figured out a way to override the embedded commands in the flight control programs, leaving just the basic take-off-and-hover instructions.

"What about the RPA's? I do not see them."

"They have launched successfully," the Russian drone pilot replied.

"How many do we have in the area?"

"One hundred twenty-eight; however, only forty are

currently under our control. We're hiding as many of the others as we can on the ground to preserve battery life."

"Proceed with your attacks, Krensky. Use the hidden units as backups. I will monitor defense actions, if any."

The Secret Service operated its own fleet of protective drones. These were specifically assigned for duty in and around the White House or when the president was on the move. The pilots of these drones were highly-skilled, if rarely tested; however, with the increasing number of amateurish attempts on the President's life over the past few years, they were gaining a lot of real-world experience to go along with their constant drills.

The drone fleet was held in four underground bunkers at each corner of the White House property, with command-and-control responsibilities shared between an external building to the right of Lafayette Park and also deep under the residence near the Situation Room.

Fourteen pilots were on duty at all times, along with an equal number of technicians tasked with computer and video monitoring. The bulk of these pilots were tasked with countering external threats to the building, with four manned defensive drones within the building itself.

Since the recent crisis began, there had already been five lone-wolf attacks on the White House, launched primarily by single-issue groups such as anti-abortion advocates and the resurrected Occupy-Whatever movement. None of these assaults managed to breach the outer perimeter before being taken out through a combination of the responding defensive drones, as well as targeted lasers and drone Tasers now being employed for building security.

When the remote detectors picked up the tale-tell BuzzKill of approaching drones, the techs at the stations at first thought it was a glitch in their system. There seemed to be a whole cloud of contacts that suddenly appeared out of nowhere. Fortunately, it was only a matter of seconds before confirmation came in from Andrews that this was indeed a drone attack in the making consisting of units from the previously inaccessible RDC inventory. The bunkers housing these units were scattered throughout the monument section of the city, placed there to afford near-instant reaction time to impending threats. No one had ever envisioned that the drones originally placed there for defense could be used as offensive weapons. It was only a matter of seconds before the air above the Washington Mall was swarming with killer robots, and all painted in ironic red, white and blue of the RDC.

"Mr. President, you must evacuate now!" said the Secret Service agent assigned to *Caballero*—the code name for Hector Ortega.

Ortega was caught off guard, yet when three more agents rushed into the room and almost carried him out of the Oval Office, he knew this was serious. A bewildered Owen Murphy was left sitting at the President's desk for only a moment before his own Secret Service detail entered the room. Soon, both President and President-elect were shoved into adjoining security elevators and carried far below the White House. The tunnel was long and fortified and ended at a fallout bunker complete with communications, living quarters, food stocks and an advanced medical facility.

Ortega entered first, followed moments later by Murphy. Most of the President's senior staff were there by now, although Admiral Hagar was at the Pentagon.

Once inside, the massive vault door was closed, and only to be reopened from the inside.

"What's happening?" Ortega asked as he entered a glass-walled conference room lined with video monitors and filled with grave-looking people. Jack Monroe, Ortega's Chief of Staff, spoke first.

"Someone's been able to activate the combat drones in the RDC bunkers in the downtown D.C. area. These units are in the air and preparing to attack."

"By someone, I assume you mean Almasi?"

"I would assume, Mr. President."

"But I thought the attacks had essentially ended. That's the word we got from Beijing and by our own count. The volume of attacks is down ninety percent over the last six hours."

"Obviously, the pressure Colleen Hoover suggested the

Chinese exert on their puppet states had the desired trickle-down effect; that's the reason for the sudden drop off in drone strikes. But now it looks as if Almasi has found another way to carry on without his coalition."

"By using our own drones against us."

"Not all of them, sir. Nathan Hall at DARPA is reporting they can neutralize the autonomous drones with a new jamming signal they've developed. But that still leaves the piloted drones to contend with."

"How many of those does that madman have access to?"

Monroe looked to Alice Grimes for the answer. "Nationwide, there are over three thousand RPA's—remotely-piloted aircraft—"

"Three thousand!"

"But he doesn't have access to all of those anymore."

"Why not?" asked Owen Murphy, speaking for the first time.

"Since we've lost control of the RDC bunkers, we've been systematically barricading the exits to hundreds of rapid-response bunkers. Even then, Almasi—we assume it's Almasi at the controls—is blowing up the inventory of drones in these bunkers using the bombs on the RPAs. If he can't use them, well, neither can we."

"So, what's about to hit D.C.?" the President asked.

"These are the RPA units that got out of the local bunkers before we could do anything about it."

"How many are we talking about?"

"A couple of hundred were activated. We're not quite sure how many he has under his direct control."

"Would two hundred RPA drones require two hundred operators?" Jack Monroe asked Alice Grimes.

"Exactly, and we don't have any idea how many pilots he has available to know how many are being sent against us."

"What about other defenses, the White House drone force, for example?" Ortega asked.

"Already deploying, but we only have fourteen pilots on duty at this time."

"Countermeasures?"

"Basic, but sir, the incoming drones are the top-of-the-line RDC drones. They're every bit the match—if not more—for the UAVs in the Secret Service arsenal."

Ortega was already seated; otherwise, he would have fallen when the implications of what he was being told suddenly dawned on him. He had trouble collecting his breath but finally managed to mutter, "The drones are going to hit the very heart of the nation's capital, and there's nothing we can do to stop them."

The relatively weak defensive force provided by the Secret Service drones rose up into the cold December air just as the sun was setting on the fourth day of the national crisis. They didn't last long, overwhelmed by the sheer number of combat drones sent against them. And now the attackers spread out, with over one hundred independently-controlled killer drones hitting at will the seemingly inexhaustible supply of national monuments, symbols and buildings in this part of the city.

Some saturated with missiles and bullets the large glass facades of the nine museums of the Smithsonian Institution that lined the Mall, while another group sent tiny, yet powerful, rockets into the base of the Washington Monument. Seconds later, the iconic obelisk toppled over and crashed to the ground in a thunderous cloud of concrete dust, with the debris field scattered across the Ellipse and pointed directly at the south lawn of the White House.

With no viable defense protecting the White House, even the lasers and drone Tasers were overwhelmed by the number of attackers and the entire south face of the White House was soon saturated with missiles and gunfire. In the meantime, other drones concentrated on the huge dome of the Capitol Building, with some hovering near the structure while triggering the ubiquitous explosive charges contained in all RDC drones. The vast dome broke apart in places and crashed inward, leaving ragged cavities in the once majestic structure.

Now, the remote operators steered their deadly charges west over the Reflecting Pool, with gunfire shattering the black granite surface of the Vietnam Memorial, before proceeding above the long series of steps to hover near the seated statue of Abraham Lincoln. Moments later, the most recognized symbol of American civil rights and unity was nothing more than a dusty pile of crumbled masonry.

By then, six minutes had passed since the drones lifted from their hidden bunkers.

"Damn you, Nathan!" Xander yelled into his comm. "I thought you said these things are easy to pilot?"

"Just relax and feel the controls. You're jerking them all over the place."

"It would have been nice to have even a minute of training before heading out on our first mission."

Xander and the other five members of Team Alpha were struggling with an impossibly short learning curve as they guided the nearly-invisible Goliath drones towards the battlefield. To the monitors in Hangar One at Andrews, the flight paths of the drones tracked like that of drunken hummingbirds, zigging and zagging from side to side while doing their best to maintain a somewhat forward heading.

Flight time from Andrews to the Capitol Mall was only three minutes, yet by the time Xander got his team into the pods and their birds in the air, the attack was already well underway. Now, as they arrived on-site, the scene revealed in the dim December sunlight was one to bring a tear to any proud American.

The entire area was a crumbled and burning inferno. From the Capitol to the White House to the fallen Washington Monument, nothing was as the postcards portrayed, not anymore. The image of the falling buildings of the World Trade Center was a tragedy, Xander thought, but this was so much worse. This was the capital of the nation, and now it lay in ruin.

"Incoming!" he heard the voice of Karen Prado cry out, both in his headset and in her proximity in the control pod to his right.

"Where?"

"Everywhere!"

Even with the low radar and visual signature of the Goliaths, a few of the RDC octocopters zipping about had nearly collided with a couple of the stealth drones. Reports were made, and a swarm of red, white and blue-painted JEN-Tech Viper IIIs began scouring the skies for the elusive defenders.

"Attack at will," Xander ordered. Then, he gathered his strength and willpower. "Alphas … *let's clear the air!*"

Fully ensconced in the off-site perspective provided by their FPV goggles, the members of Team Alpha broke into individual attack units, with each pilot now having gained a decent feel for their aircraft. Brilliant flashes of light erupted out of thin air as the 60s cut loose, rippling into the hardened plastic and fiberglass frames of Vipers. Designed by Billy's own company to withstand hits from the standard 5mm nylon-jacketed armament, the Vipers—before today Xander's preferred combat drone—were no match for the supercharged shells issued forth from the Goliaths. A dozen of the attackers evaporated in the air above the Mall.

Xander and Billy then set off toward the White House while the others tracked raiders near the Capitol and the Library of Congress. The White House was just a shell of its former self by now, with half of its structure lying in ruins and lost in a cloud of smoke and lit by lapping fire. There were a dozen or more enemy drones buzzing over the property, firing into the surviving front façade of the once-iconic building.

The two Goliaths whipped around the building unseen and unleashed a barrage of killer fire into the hovering drones. The DARPA drones had laser-guided targeting, and it only took a split second to lock onto a dozen hostiles at once, followed by a single press of the firing trigger to take them all out in rapid succession.

"There are still over thirty targets surviving," Nathan's voice said over the comm. "They appear to have backup units at their disposal, so the final assault tally is unknown. Units now crossing the Potomac, heading for the Pentagon."

"I'm on it," Hugh Barden called out.

"Be careful," Nathan warned. "They have a couple hundred defensive drones of their own covering the building, and they'll shoot at anything that comes their way."

"Can they defend themselves?" Xander asked.

"Nine Vipers just slammed into the building and detonated," Nathan reported, "So, I guess not, at least not against suicide drones."

"Be on alert, everyone," Xander ordered. "If they're

willing to sacrifice active units, that means they may have a lot more in reserve. There could be a second wave coming. Nathan, any word on the President?"

"He's safe, somewhere below the White House."

"Good. Billy and I will head over toward the Smithsonian. What's the count now?"

"Thirty or so still remaining, even though it's now confirmed; we're picking up sporadic late entries to the party; probably been hiding on the ground somewhere."

Xander caught sight of six enemy drones soaring over the Air and Space Museum, releasing a line of missile fire as they flew by. Xander lined up on them and pressed the firing trigger. Half of the drones shattered, and it was almost comical to watch the survivors pull up and begin spinning around, looking for the source of the incoming. Two of them were looking straight in Xander's direction when he opened fire on them again.

Xander could imagine that in a secret and secluded control room located somewhere halfway around the world, a group of bewildered drone pilots were scratching their heads, wondering what the hell just happened.

Unfortunately, their confusion didn't last long, as each of the enemy pilots linked with another six reserve drones and rejoined the battle.

"Team Bravo now on station," a deep, masculine voice boomed over the comm. Xander didn't recognize the voice.

"Team *Bravo?*" he questioned.

"Well, you guys have Team Alpha copyrighted. Major Jim Lyle, USAF, reporting for duty."

Xander lifted the goggles from his head and looked around the huge hangar. Four more of the pods were now occupied by men in uniform. One of them sent him a crisp salute.

"Four more Goliaths just came in from Hampton Roads," the Major reported. "We're some of the test pilots for the G's. We've been sitting around in the back, just twiddling our thumbs with nothing to do—until now. So, is there a uniform defense strategy, or are we free-balling it?"

"Welcome to the party, Major. Free-balling, the enemy forces are spread all over the place, hitting whatever targets of opportunity they can find. Feel free to chalk up as many kills as you like."

"Roger that. Engaging."

In less than five minutes, Xander was soaring high above the battlefield, looking for the stray target to strike. There didn't seem to be any left.

"The air is clear, at least above D.C.," Nathan Hall reported. "Return to base for recharging and reassignment. We're getting reports of RDC drones hitting New York. We have half a dozen Goliaths in the area, so it looks like it could be a long night."

It was always a strange sensation for Xander when he removed the FPV goggles after a particularly intense battle. From being completely absorbed in combat at the site to suddenly sitting in a comfortable leather chair in a modestly quiet and relatively peaceful command center, it was always a jarring experience. The Goliaths were programmed with a return-to-home function, so he and the other members of Team Alpha didn't even have to wait for their Goliaths to return to Andrews before they were suddenly linked with Goliaths in New York, without so much as a second of rest between battle theaters. Now, Xander and his friends were ripping through the glass and steel canyons of New York City, chasing yet another swarm of enemy drones.

Although it wasn't completely dark, power was cut to the city to reduce the chance of electrical fires and to make the forest of buildings that much harder to navigate, especially for pilots located on the other side of the planet.

Immediately, the Alphas were fed targeting information, and the battle was joined.

The city had already been hard hit over the past couple of days, with most of its residents evacuated or hidden away within the thousands of massive structures. This new fight soon escalated into a high-speed game of cat and mouse, as the RDC Vipers, under the control of Almasi's pilots—many of which had just been laying waste to Washington, D.C.—had learned that there was a stealth presence stalking them. And when a number of their sister units began to be blown apart from unseen machinegun and missile fire, the pilots elected to run rather than stand and fight.

Unfortunately, Xander realized too late what most of them were running toward.

"Can anyone get there first?" he shouted into the comm.

"I'm out of position, up near Central Park," Curt Tharp reported.

"I'm close, near the Tunnel, but they're thirty seconds ahead."

"Dammit, we can't let this happen."

Xander gunned his Goliath and soared out toward South Manhattan. As he shot out over the water, the iconic Statue of Liberty erupted in a halo of tiny explosions. The copper and steel figure began to bend forward at the waist, even as the long arm holding the perpetual flame of freedom broke away and fell to the ground of Liberty Island.

By the time Xander arrived, there were no enemy drones to shoot. They had all plowed into the statue while simultaneously exploding. He felt weak and impotent as he hovered near the deformed, green-tinted statue. She hadn't fallen, but she was badly damaged, just another entry on the long list of shattered symbols of America that had suffered at the hands of Abdul-Shahid Almasi … and Jonas Lemon.

Soon, the other five members of Team Alpha were also in the air above the Statue of Liberty. No one said a word for a full minute.

"Sorry to interrupt," Nathan's voice said softly. "I just

thought you'd like to know that we're getting only a few reports of escaping RDC drones leaving the other bunkers, but nothing large-scale. We've been able to shutter most of them. So, Almasi has started detonating the explosives on the trapped RPAs in the bunkers. I'm commanding the New York Goliaths to return to their local base. The rest of you can take a well-deserved break. I'll use Major Lyle's pilots for any of the mop-up work. Great job … all of you."

"Great job?" Karen's voice protested over the comm. "Just about everything that identifies with American greatness has been destroyed, and we did very little to stop it."

"It could've been worse," Nathan offered.

"That's what they always say," Xander whispered, yet loud enough so everyone could hear. "And the sad part about it, they're right."

24

After the attacks on Washington and New York, Almasi returned to his combination office and living quarters to analyze what just happened; however, he didn't have much time alone before the obnoxious Russian general, Nikolay Burkov, entered without knocking or invitation.

"There are some disturbing occurrences taking place in America, Abdul-Shahid. Would you care to share with me what you know of these?"

Almasi watched with wide, manic eyes as the fat Russian officer took a seat in front of his desk and returned the unblinking stare with one of his own.

"Seeing that you enter here without invitation and then make a statement without details, you will have to be a little more specific as to what *occurrences* you speak of."

"First of all, I have been monitoring the frequency of

the attacks, and they appeared to have ceased completely, except for the botched activities I just witnessed."

"Botched? You call that botched?" In a violent fit, Almasi picked up the remote control on the desk and turned on the T.V. that sat on a credenza to his right. Even with the sound on mute, it was clear from the shots of burning iconic buildings and ruined national monuments that something tragic had just taken place in America's capital. "Look, the White House is in ruins, the Washington Monument has fallen, and the Statue of Liberty is a twisted and armless relic. And you call that *botched*? I call it victory!"

"Even in the presence of stealth drones you knew nothing about?" the general asked. "We have invested a lot in you, Abdul-Shahid, including your ability to keep your coalition together. That appears not to be the case."

"Don't blame me for that. China is the reason North Korea and Iran have forced my allies to abandon us. Even so, the damage caused to the infidels up to this point should be adequate to meet your goals. And now, with the images of a shattered White House and Capitol Building to haunt the Americans, I cannot see them returning to their normal lives any time soon, if ever. You will have your economic collapse, just as I promised."

The obese Russian grunted. "Perception is everything to the Americans; you should know this, Almasi. It is clear now that future attacks will subside and that there is a new secret weapon to be deployed against the ones that do take place. Now that we are aware of their existence, we have tracked the returning stealth drones to Andrews Air Force Base, where they will surely be revealed to the public as the ultimate safeguard against future attacks. And whether right or wrong, the government will offer up as proof the inevitable decline in your drone attacks. Ortega and his people will put all their efforts into advertising this fact, and with time still left for the population to regain confidence and a feeling of security—even in light of the damage you have caused over the past few days."

"Bullshit! The Americans are traumatized and scared. It will be a long time before they recover."

Burkov shook his head. "Have you not learned anything from the past? All you have to do is look to the attacks of September eleven to see that the Americans are more resilient—and resistant—than you give them credit for. And when the motive behind the recent crisis is revealed, do not be surprised to see the American people rise up in protest to our goals, just to spite us. I will grant you that the economy of the Western world has been hurt, but not fatally."

Almasi was growing angrier by the minute. He had done all—even more—than the Russians had asked of him. And even after his coalition had fallen apart, he was still able to launch the most devastating attack on American soil ever—even worse than 9/11. Far worse.

"You forget that the media will fill the airwaves with these images non-stop for months, even years to come.

The American people will not be allowed to forget what I —we—have done this week."

"Let us hope they never learn the full involvement of my government, Abdul-Shahid. Your small, diverse organization is impossible to declare war against and have it mean anything; however, my country is a legitimate member of the world community. And you *are* right. These images will be broadcast, and just as with 9/11, world sentiment will side with the United States. We—meaning my country—could be in for a very difficult time if the truth is ever revealed."

There was something in the Russian's tone that made Almasi take the last statement as a threat. "It will not be me who reveals the truth, Nikolay. I have no interest in deflecting attention or responsibility. Whatever befalls The Arm of Allah, I will welcome it, even if I am to become a martyr to the cause."

"That is very noble of you ... and reassuring."

"You seem not to understand *my* motivations, Nikolay. I *want* America to know who did this to them, and by doing so, my name will live forever in the nightmares of America, right alongside Bin Laden—*even before Bin Laden's*. And you speak of the Americans regaining confidence in their security, yet you also seem to overlook the fact that I have destroyed nearly all their combat drones, even those hidden in the RDC bunkers. Of course, the auto drones would not detonate, yet I still had control over the RPAs. Except for a relatively few stealth drones, they do not have anything available to put before the country as a viable deterrent to future attacks."

"By our estimates, you managed to destroy only a third of the RDC's capacity, and even now, they have discovered your link into the bunkers and are in the process of using it themselves to gain quicker access to the remaining drones."

Almasi's stomach tightened. He had not heard this before. "That cannot be correct—only a third? I personally sent out the detonate command to all the drones we controlled."

"Their scientists were in the process of negating your control at the time your order was sent. With hundreds of bunkers involved, you did not have the opportunity—or the desire—to verify every detonation. You assumed it was more. Within days, thousands of their obnoxiously painted drones will be on display as a show of force against the non-existent future attacks you speak of. Once out in the open—and with a dramatic drop off in attacks—the Americans will be convinced that the crisis is over."

"Then we must not let up! I still have over a hundred RPA's available that escaped the bunkers before they were resealed."

"And what would you strike at, Almasi? Your remaining force is of limited power and range. It will do us no good for the batteries to fail mid-operation and have your mighty drones fall from the sky. That would be embarrassing."

"Then we must make this attack both effective and symbolic."

"Again ... at what target?"

"At the stealth drones!"

"They are housed at a powerful military base, Almasi. It would be foolish to attempt such an attack."

"No ... it will be *bold* ... and unexpected! By showing I can strike at their military facilities while also eliminating their prized propaganda toys, the uncertainty and paranoia may last a while longer, at least through the season. Once December twenty-fifth has passed, there will be nothing to salvage. The Americans will move on, passing over this season in anticipation of the next. The negative effect on their economy at that point should be enough to push them over the edge, do you not agree?"

The Russian was silent for a moment as his eyes stared back at Almasi under bushy, unkempt eyebrows. "I agree they're close to a total collapse, and another week or so without a major surge in commerce could be enough."

"Yes! We just need to keep the Americans in their homes for a few days more. And what better way to do that than to show that we still have the capability to take out their most effective weapon against us."

This time, the Russian snorted rather than grunted. "That is assuming you truly can. As I said, your assets are few and their battery-life limited. Where are these drones you say you can use in the attack?"

"They are in the D.C. area, drawn from local bunkers.

The only reason they weren't used in the first attack was the lack of pilots to control them. Now, my crews are free to take on this new mission, and I have reserve pilots I can now call on with a little time to prepare."

"Very little time, Abdul-Shahi. What you suggest cannot be delayed." He paused while considering the plan. "Very well," the fat Russian general finally spoke. "I will have target information on the stealth drones to you within twelve hours. I must send in assets to make sure we have the precise location. You will only get one opportunity at this."

Almasi smiled—something he rarely did. "That will be acceptable, Nikolay. Give the Americans a little breathing room and let them think the worst is over. And then I'll hit them again. It will be the final nail in their coffin."

"Or in ours, my radical friend. Soon, we will know which."

25

"Are you sure of this?" Xander said, staring agape at the sheet of paper that had just been handed to him.

"It came from the tap Almasi placed on the bunkers back at the Center. It's faint and was hard to trace, but the NSA gives it a ninety-percent credibility rating."

"Karachi ... not Islamabad?"

"It's about as far from the capital as he could go. Still, the location appears to be right in the heart of the city."

"You even know which building?" Xander was in a mild state of shock. He tried his best to keep his expectations under control, but he was fighting a losing battle. And seeing the ecstatic expressions on the faces of his team members, as well as on Tiffany Collins, didn't help.

"We've got the son-of-a-bitch," Hugh Barden exclaimed.

"And Jonas may be there, too," Billy threw in.

"If only," said Karen.

Xander looked at the even expression on the face of Nathan Hall. "But you said he's in the city. Is it possible to drop a huge-ass bomb on his head and get this over with?"

Hall shook his head. Xander was anticipating what came next. "He picked the best—or worst—possible location, depending on which side you're on. First of all, he's in the middle of the second most-populous city in the world, and sending in a massive bunker-buster to blow out a crater a quarter-mile in diameter will probably not go over very well with the locals."

"They started this!" Jeremy Fenton pointed out.

"Almasi did, not the people of Karachi," Nathan pointed out. "Even then, there are other considerations. His compound is sandwiched between a hospital and a school. The inevitable collateral damage is something the brass won't accept."

"Then *we* go in," said Jeremy Fenton. "I'm sure you have RPAs in the region or ones that can be placed there in a reasonable time."

"The military—not DARPA—has units over there," Nathan said just before a wicked smile stretched his lips. "And we also have five Goliaths aboard the *Gerald Ford*."

Hugh slapped the older man on the back … a little too forcefully. "So, there you have it! We go in all stealthy and shit and take them out before they know what's happening."

"Karachi is located on the Arabian Sea," Tiffany offered. "Where's the aircraft carrier now, Nathan?"

The man tried to look calm but failed miserably. "About five hundred miles south, steaming north at thirty-five knots."

"You bastard!" Xander said. "You already have the op underway."

"It was worth keeping it under wraps just to see your expressions. Yes, we're a go. Five of you will pilot the G's, and an additional twenty-five JEN-Tech Panther Fours will provide support and backup guided by the military pilots."

"I'm glad to see my babies are on our side this time," Billy said. "You know how hard it was to fire on them yesterday?"

"They're great machines," Nathan said.

"Yeah, but we made mince-meat out of them with the Goliaths. You know how humbling that is?"

"Let's hope the Goliaths can do the same to Almasi's drones. You know he'll have defensive cover," Karen said. "And to another point: You said you have *five* Goliaths. There are six of us. So, who gets left out in the cold? As the only woman on the team, I sincerely hope it ain't me. You guys wouldn't survive the sexual discrimination lawsuit I'd slap on ... well, everyone!"

Nathan came to the rescue, much to Xander's relief. "Since Mr. Moore has the most combat experience from his tenure at the RDC, I suggest he take the lead and the rest of you draw straws. That way, we can avoid any potential lawsuits, and the remaining team member can lead the Panther squadron."

When no one protested—for real or in jest—Nathan's face turned deadly serious. "The *Ford* will be on station in twelve hours. We launch shortly thereafter. We're getting close to shutting this thing down, yet there's no telling what that bastard Almasi has planned next. Whatever it is, we can't let him carry it out. This has to be the decisive battle. America can't take very much more of this."

26

"Ready up! We drop in five minutes." Xander's voice echoed off the cold steel walls of the aircraft hangar, which by that time had grown deathly quiet. He walked along the rows of pilot pods, nodding at the young men and women at their stations, offering quick words of encouragement.

On the screens were thirty different views from inside the C-130 Hercules cargo transport. The drones were still hooked to chargers, yet their cameras were active. In an amazing feat of courage and daring, the huge cargo plane had managed to lift off the deck of the aircraft carrier—the largest plane capable of a carrier-launch. Now, within minutes, the tail of the Hercules would open, and the contents of its cargo bay would be unceremoniously dumped out the back.

Xander's team was ready, as were the twenty-four military drone pilots manning the JEN-Tech Panthers—with Billy Jenkins in command. As it turned out, Billy volunteered to lead the Panther squadron since it was made up entirely of UAVs his company manufactured. Karen Prado thanked him by laying a wet kiss on his lips.

As the transport plane dropped to twenty-thousand feet over the glistening blue waters of the Arabian Sea, Xander slipped into his pilot pod and flexed his fingers. They were about to do something that had never been done before but, in theory, should work. The drone cargo was to be literally dumped out the back, powered off and left to freefall. At five thousand feet, the motors would switch on, and the fourth-generation Qualcomm Snapdragon 801 SoC flight controllers within the Panthers would take over, providing gyroscopic stabilization within microseconds of activation. The Goliaths were much larger units and would be affected more by wind drag. They also operated using a different flight control board, yet the results *should* be the same.

If the drones weren't able to stabilize within the narrow altitude window, they would unceremoniously splash into the water below, bringing a quick end to the ambitious operation. Yet this was the only way the Panthers could reach the target with enough battery charge to last an hour on station. The Goliaths had more than enough power to have flown from the carrier all the way to the mainland, but there were only five of them, and with such a spur-of-the-moment operation as this one, no one was fully aware what they might encounter, either on the way to or once they reached Almasi's compound.

Another UAV—this one a sixty-foot-wingspan spy drone—was aloft at over forty thousand feet and would provide the command links with the NSA satellite tasked to the mission.

Satellite imaging also provided the pilots with a fairly detailed layout of Almasi's compound. Like most residences of the wealthy in the Middle East, this one was isolated from the poor masses by a twenty-foot high, white-washed concrete wall, with one main entrance for motor vehicles and two smaller doors for pedestrian traffic.

Six structures dotted the grounds, with three large buildings serving apparently as living quarters. There were two other buildings that had a fair number of women and children going in and out, and then a long, single-story garage with four, twenty-foot-wide raise-up doors. Somewhere in the complex, there had to be access to the underground command post used by Almasi and his pilots. At the time, no one had a clue which building it was in or how complex the maze of tunnels and chambers would be.

Xander was assured that the huge Goliaths were nimble enough to navigate tight quarters, especially when transitioned to ground-mode. The much smaller Panthers wouldn't have any trouble—they were designed for close-quarters-combat. Reality would depend on the widths of the corridors in the underground labyrinth.

Without a doubt, Almasi would also have a hidden cache of defensive drones somewhere nearby. These didn't necessarily have to be on the property and could be in one of the surrounding houses or shops. So, besides having to seek out and gain entrance to the true heart of the compound, Xander knew they'd also be fighting off a whole horde of rabid defenders.

In addition, Nathan Hall was correct when he pointed out the strategic location of the compound. The hospital next door wasn't big, but it did have a steady stream of patients and workers entering and exiting at all hours. And the school to the west of the property was a kindergarten-to-high school equivalent, with hundreds of children present during the day. The timing of the attack was set for early morning, just at sunrise in Pakistan, so there shouldn't be too many school children on the grounds at the time.

Xander had no illusions that the team could get in and out without at least some collateral damage, either caused by his people or by Almasi's. Yet the stakes were too high not to take the risk. Let the chips fall where they may, but this was the head of the snake, and it desperately had to be severed.

The press of humanity in the underground command chamber was incredible and had a smell to match. Over the past half-day, Almasi had additional control stations moved in and hooked up, and now he had over eighty pilots crammed into the room, which included a mixture of Arabs, Persians and Russians, along with a few Koreans thrown in for good measure.

With access to ninety-two RPAs scattered throughout the bushes, fields and culverts of Northern Virginia, it was imperative that he get as many of these units into the battle as soon as possible. Overwhelming firepower would be the key. With battery levels already below optimum, he was operating under a severe time constraint. Even though the drones were disposable after the battle, they still had to maintain charge throughout. Therefore, the raid had to be quick and decisive.

The outcome of this battle—which now encapsulated Almasi's entire war against America—would be known in less than half an hour. His legacy now rested on the efficiency of his strange mix of drone pilots. He also had the element of surprise on his side. After all, who would expect him to launch a major attack on a force of advanced drones that only a day before he didn't even know existed?

He felt his lips stretch out into a weak smile. His face wasn't used to the expression, and he didn't do it out of joy. It was a grin of inevitability. He knew that if this mission failed, the Russians would not allow him to live. He was too much of a liability, as was his entire organization.

So, not only did his legacy rest on the events of the next thirty minutes. His very existence on the planet Earth was at stake, as well.

The cargo plane descended to ten thousand feet when the cargo chief opened the rear door. The three-man crew was bundled in thick coats to protect against the cold, while the attack force sat stoic and unaffected by the temperature. These drones were rated down to minus twenty below zero Fahrenheit; in fact, the colder it was, the faster their circuits fired.

The thirty combat drones rested on a wide conveyor belt, and when activated, the belt began to rotate towards the rear of the plane. The first row of drones awkwardly fell out the back, tumbling in the crisp, clear air without the aid of parachutes. Row after row fell out the back until seven seconds later, the cargo bay was empty.

The UAVs were now tiny dots in the sky, dispersed over a wide area and falling at a rate of one hundred twenty-two miles per hour. And then, the first of the automatic stabilizers kicked in. Rotors spun up, and within a second, the internal gyroscopic controls took over. The drones stopped tumbling, even though they still fell freely toward the ground. Slowly, so as to not over-stress the props, the drones began to break their descent. As the seconds passed, the rate of fall declined until the units were now in controlled flight and gathering into a large, bird-like formation.

Xander and his pilots debated whether or not they would use the FPV goggles during the freefall. It was finally decided they wouldn't. The tumbling, dizzying effect would be disorienting and possibly interfere with their effectiveness at the controls. However, when the units stabilized and gained right-up flight postures, goggles slipped on, and suddenly, Xander and the others were halfway around the world and falling fast toward the blue water of the Arabian Sea. No less than a few deep gasps were heard in the hangar as the pilots adjusted to their new perspective.

There was a thin cloud layer below, and the turbulence within caused some of the drones to wobble and break formation. But as they broke into the clear again, the skill of the pilots corrected the flight paths with perfection.

At two thousand feet, the pilots—seated in an aircraft hangar seven thousand miles away—steered their charges toward the shore and the looming mass of structures ahead. Karachi was a huge city that dominated the coastline of southwest Pakistan. A mostly Muslim population of over thirty-million called the city home, and its ports were the lifeblood of the region, including not only Pakistan but Iran and India as well.

It would take thirty seconds to reach the shore, and by that time, the Panthers would be radar visible, even as the Goliaths remained hidden.

Xander was counting on confusion to give them time to enter the city and get lost in the metropolis. The confusion would be on the part of radar operators and air traffic control personnel at the local international airport. The signal on their screens would be like nothing they'd seen before, a thin cloud of contacts with no strong, individual central point. It would be like a large flock of birds, yet all with light metallic coatings. Hopefully, this strange mix of data would be enough to create hesitation before reports were sent. By then, Xander and his force would be beyond the defensive perimeter and inside the city itself.

Tiffany Collins stepped outside the hangar for some fresh air as the hundred or so pilots and techs that occupied the huge single room were engrossed in their individual tasks. She wasn't one of them, and she felt conspicuously like the proverbial fifth-wheel.

It was a few minutes past nine in the evening when the operation got underway to take advantage of the time difference between Washington, D.C. and Karachi, and the mandatory curfew around Andrews AFB had just gone into effect. Now, as she stepped into the clear, cold air, Tiffany was briefly shocked and revived by the thirty-degree temperature of mid-December. She'd spent considerable time in the area reporting on various stories, yet her tenure in L.A. spoiled her to near-perfect year-round weather. Even then, this was just what she needed to get her mind refocused.

The two hangars which Nathan Hall had commandeered as his temporary operations center were located at the south end of the western runway at the Andrews Joint Military Base and about five miles southeast from the horrific scene of destruction along the Washington Mall. Tiffany walked to the edge of the building and looked in that direction. There was an abnormal glow over the area as repair and rescue crews worked long into the night under brilliant flood lights. The damage caused to the buildings would take years to repair … the damage to the American psyche much longer.

The night was not quiet, even with the curfew, as a chorus of sirens warbled in the distance. On the western side of the pilot's hangar, along Arnold Avenue, the parking lot was full of vehicles, but beyond that, over the rest of the base, only the headlights of the occasional security vehicle were seen. As for the rest of the city, its occupants now hunkered down for another night, unsure what the new day would bring.

Tiffany Collins knew more than most, yet even she was as uncertain as those locked behind their front doors. Even if Xander's mission succeeded, what did the future hold in store for America? Irreparable harm had been caused to the country, including physical, economic and emotional. Mentally, she began to work out the lead to her first broadcast once she was allowed to resume her duties. It wasn't coming easy; the subject was too vast to be condensed into a single sentence.

She struggled with the problem for a few minutes before she was distracted by a new sound rising up against the backdrop of the night. She focused on it, noticing the increasing volume. This new sound evoked a primal fear in her, as it did in most people. This was a potential threat, something that could cause pain. It was the sound of bees in the air. It was the sound of *BuzzKill*.

27

Almasi's compound was located in the Bizerta Town District of Karachi, which, fortunately for Xander's team, was only about ten miles inland, near a large soccer and badminton stadium. All the drones in his attack formation were locked into GPS, yet the pilots had the discretion to use whatever circuitous path they wanted to reach the compound if being pursued. So far, no credible defense had shown itself.

Xander was rushing in low through the already traffic-clogged streets at nearly twenty miles per hour and fully engrossed in his flight when someone grabbed him by the shoulder. The sensation was so incongruous that he jumped and nearly fell out of his seat. Upset, he slipped the right lens from over his eye while doing his best not to slam into the side of a building somewhere on the other side of the planet.

"What the hell?"

"Xander, there's something weird happening outside," Tiffany Collins whispered into his ear.

"I'm a little preoccupied at the moment. Go tell Nathan."

"He's in the other building somewhere. Do you have any drones operating in the area?"

"What area? Here or in Pakistan?"

"Here, smartass. Outside … here?"

"Not that I know of. Now let me get back to work—"

"Then there's a whole boatload of enemy drones heading this way!"

With one clear eye, Xander noticed several of the other nearby pilots looking in his direction. "What are you talking about?"

"I can hear them outside. It's getting louder. What you call *BuzzKill*."

Xander looked hard at Tiffany and could see the panic in her eyes. "Franklin, take over my unit until I get back."

"Yes, sir," said a voice from behind them. Nearly all the thirty active pilots had backups assigned to them. Lt. John Franklin was his.

Xander now pulled off the goggles and climbed out of the pod. "Are you sure about this?"

"I know the sound of drones by now. Can't they be picked up on radar?"

"Depends on how low they are. Duty officer!"

"Over here, Mr. Moore."

Xander and Tiffany ran up to an Air Force lieutenant-colonel. "There's a good chance the base is about to come under attack. Are there any defensive units available?"

"Against drones? Not many, just the Goliaths in the other building."

He looked at the crowd of trained pilots filling the room. There were plenty of extras, just not a lot of drones for them to man. "Charlie, give up your seat to your back up and get over here."

Five seconds later, Charlie Fox was at Xander's side. "What the hell, boss, we're about to engage."

"The base is coming under attack. I need you to take command of the Goliaths they have here and coordinate a defense."

Charlie looked at the stunned Air Force officer and then back to Xander.

"Colonel, give Mr. Fox all the pilots with the most experience flying the Goliaths. Get them into control pods, even if you have to boot out some of the Panther pilots. We need to get the G's into the air ... and I mean now!"

"Yes, sir. Captain Slater, you and Blue Squad ... into seats! I'll get the transponder codes to the Goliaths. We have incoming. Scramble on the orders of Mr. Fox!"

Charlie Fox looked askew at Xander. "Thanks a lot, boss. Nothing like a little pressure to make a guy's day."

"You'll be fine. Just do what comes naturally."

"What, surfing?"

There was a loud, concerned murmur filtering

through the huge hangar by now, just as Nathan Hall and a cadre of officers representing various branches of the military rushed into the building.

"Yeah, we know," Xander said to him before he could speak.

Nathan's jaw fell open. "How?"

"Tiffany heard the *BuzzKill*. Fox and Colonel Rogers are in charge of our defense. They need the transponder codes for the Goliaths."

Nathan nodded to an officer, and a small flash drive passed to Charlie Fox. Without another word, he and Col. Rogers ran off into the mix of control pods.

"Almasi must have learned our location," Xander said to Nathan.

"But where did he get the drones for the attack?"

"He must have released more yesterday than we thought, but they can't be fully charged, so we just need to keep them away for a few minutes. Can you take over here? I have to get back to Karachi."

"Of course. Now, take that bastard out. That's another way of stopping this attack."

"Roger that. Good luck."

Xander then pulled Tiffany Collins to him and kissed her hard on the lips. And then he was gone, leaving Tiffany wide-eyed and weak-kneed while Nathan Hall exhibited a shocked look of his own.

"Some guys have all the luck," was all he said before walking away.

"Approaching target," Muhammad Bin-Osei reported over his shoulder. "No resistance as yet. We are coming in along the streets from the south."

"Good. Stay low to avoid radar."

If there was one advantage of having the Russians on your side, it was that they had an ample supply of satellites orbiting over America at any given time. Almasi had a real-time aerial view of the two target hangars displayed on the main screen across the room. They were the last two along the western runway of the air base, with a wide tarmac surface leading up to the north side of the buildings and then continuing out the south side before curving back toward the main runway. Aircraft could taxi directly into the maintenance hangars and then pull straight out once released for duty. There was a two-lane parking lot on the road running along the western side of the first building, and it was jammed with cars, even at this late hour.

Almasi frowned at the image. General Nikolay Burkov was standing next to him. "Is it unusual to have so many cars in the parking lot at this time of night?" he asked the experienced military officer.

"Not really. This is where the stealth drones are stored. They may require an inordinate amount of maintenance and upkeep."

Just then, in the live image on the screen, the large

doors to the eastern building began to open, sending brilliant yellow light flooding over the white concrete surface outside. Almasi and Burkov tensed. Something unexpected was happening on the other side of the world.

Just then, several objects streaked out of the building. They sparkled in the illumination before disappearing into the darkness beyond the reach of the lights.

"They've launched their stealth drones!" Almasi cried out. "All pilots, be on alert!"

"Did you notice?" the Russian general remarked. "The stealth feature is designed mainly for daylight deception," he continued. "At night, they are still dark yet appear to flicker in the sky. Shoot at anything that sparkles!"

The mood in the room suddenly grew tense as Almasi's pilots guided their RPAs out from the confines of the streets leading to the air base and began to scatter. Some jumped the fence bordering the base, while others took to the sky to begin a systematic search for the elusive enemy drones. The objective of this operation was to destroy these relatively few stealth units, and it was supposed to have been easy with them sitting unprepared in lightly shielded hangars. Now, they were mobile, and nearly all the pilots in the room had experienced their deadly efficiency the day before.

However, now they knew what to look for … and what to expect. This time, the outcome would be different.

And that was when the first of Almasi's attack drones blew up.

"I got one of the bastards!" Charlie Fox announced over his comm.

"There's about a hundred more to go, Charlie," Xander reported. "Be careful. We don't have any spare Goliaths."

Xander was back in Karachi now, having resumed control of the Goliath once again. The five G's were about ninety seconds out from the compound and a minute ahead of the slower Panthers. Xander and his team would initiate the assault and hopefully draw out the defenders from their hiding places just as the Panthers arrive and engage them.

With units attacking the hangars from outside, Xander wondered how many pilots Almasi would have available for defensive duties back in Karachi. Every pilot pulled from the attack on the hangars to man a defensive drone would increase their chances of living throughout the night.

This was such an unusual situation for Xander Moore. Never before had *his* life been in danger during a drone event. Now, he—and all the other people in the two hangars—were both targets and attackers. The fastest trigger, with the most accuracy, would win the day.

Through his headset, Xander heard the ping of an incoming video call. Comm channels for the headsets were highly classified especially the video links. He was upset. Already, his mission had been interrupted too many times. And now someone was calling in. He checked the time to target: a little over a minute. He reached forward and pressed F3 on his keyboard.

"Make it quick! We're about to—"

"Engage? Yeah, I know."

The image in the tiny box at the top left corner of his heads-up display made Xander gasp.

"Surprised to see me?" said Jonas Lemon. "I can tell from the look on your goggled face that you are."

Xander gathered himself. "It's just that I told my secretary to screen my calls."

"Flippant as always, I see."

"Well, seeing how long it's been, you have caught me at an inconvenient time. Do you mind if I call you back?"

"I'm hurt, Xander … and we used to be such good friends. I suppose you're too busy to chat with me because of your impending attack on Almasi's command center?"

Xander guided his Goliath drone around a particularly sharp curve in the road and then over a single-story house before dropping down to near street level again and stirring up prodigious amounts of red sand.

"Sorry, but I don't have a clue what you're talking about, Jonas."

"Who are you talking to?" Hugh Barden asked, leaning over from the pod next to him.

"No one important … just Jonas Lemon."

"No shit? Well, tell the son-of-a-bitch to stop hiding and face us like a man."

"I heard that, and you can tell baby Hughie that if he'd just let me know which one of the Goliath drones is his, I'll certainly oblige. I don't think any of you have gone up against a Ninja Five before, have you? It's so much better than the Ninja Two I used at the mall in Miami."

"So, that was you."

"Yeah, and it was fun, like the old days. It would have resulted in a no-score back on the circuit."

"Listen, Jonas, obviously you're pretty well wired into things, so if you don't mind, I really have to get back to work before the boss dings me for taking personal calls on company time."

"Oh, but this isn't a social call, dude. I just thought you'd like to know who you're going up against at the compound. And unfortunately, I can't be in two places at the same time, or else I'd be with the group attacking your hangars right now. Still, we have a lot of game left ahead of us, so bye for now. But I'll still be dropping in from time to time throughout the battle."

The image of Jonas Lemon disappeared from the screen.

"Heads up, everyone, Jonas Lemon is on site in

Karachi and manning something called a Ninja Five. Has anyone ever heard of one?"

"Nathan Hall here, Xander. I have. They're not stealth, but all down the checklist, they're superior to the Goliaths."

"Now you tell me. I thought we had the baddest bots on the block."

"Stealth makes you the best ... with the exception of the Ninja. Hopefully, there's only one on station."

"Count on it, Nathan. Jonas is the type to insist on having only the best and only for himself. That could be our saving grace."

"Compound dead ahead," Karen Prado reported. "Here we go. Game on."

The five Goliaths soared over the twenty-foot-high wall and dropped down to near ground level. Huge swirling torrents of red sand curled up into mini-tornados, filling the grounds in a blinding dust storm.

"All this dust is making us stand out like neon signs," Jeremy Fenton announced over his comm. "I'm taking some heavy gunfire from the tall building on the west side."

"Well, we didn't come here for an exhibition match," Xander growled. "Weapons hot; let's level the place!"

The concrete block building Fenton had mentioned suddenly lit up with hundreds of pin-point explosions as 7.56mm rounds perforated the structure. Even before Xander and his team could take aim at the shooters on the roof, a good half of the building fell inwards, collapsing the snipers' firing platform.

As was expected, Xander now saw bearded men shoving women and children out the doorways and into the center of the compound while they retreated for cover. With bullets and pencil-missiles filling the air, several of the women and children fell to the ground, covered in blood. Xander was sure he'd seen some of the men inside the doorways aiming their AKs at the backs of the victims.

In response, Xander spun the Goliath around and sent four accurately-aimed missiles screaming through the doorway. An instant later, a billowing cloud of white smoke blew out the bottom of the building. Small balconies on the three stories above gave way and crumbled to the ground.

"Be careful, Xander," Karen called out. "We don't want to block any entrances to the underground complex."

"I hear ya; it's just that I couldn't let those bastards get away with shooting women and children in the back."

"Here come the defenders," another voice announced over the comm, a radar tech who was not part of the Goliath team. "Forty-two at first count, could be more deploying."

"Forty-two? Damn, that's a lot," Curt Tharp said. "Where are the Panthers?"

"We're staying back a little," declared Billy Jenkins.

"Let the bad guys commit, then we'll sneak up on their six."

Just then, a rocket-propelled grenade streaked from a corner of the long garage-like structure and struck one of the Goliaths. The craft was thrown backward and tumbled to the ground, a trail of broken armament littering the ground.

"Who's hit?" Xander asked.

"That would be me," Curt Tharp said sourly.

"Status?"

"Looks like I lost my upper weapons package. I can still fly, but I only have the five-mils on the sides and a single block of twenty missiles."

"Circle around the building and find that asshole with the RPG."

"With pleasure, just watch out. It's obvious these super drones *can* be hurt."

And then the air above the compound was suddenly thick with smaller UAVs. With his trained eye, Xander could tell that a good two-thirds of them were auto drones tasked with defending the compound using attached bombs and bullets, striking anything that didn't fit their pre-programmed profiles. Whether the sensors could pick up the Goliaths with enough confidence to make a determination was anyone's guess. But the Panthers would be targeted. This also told Xander that Almasi didn't have a lot of extra pilots to assign to the RPAs. He kept them manning the drones whizzing around outside the hangars.

Charlie Fox and the pilots of the nine Goliaths placed their craft in the space between the perimeter of the base and the hangars. If the Goliaths were the targets, the attacking drones would have a hard time taking them all out, even with over ninety approaching units. Yet the other way to neutralize the DARPA drones—and frankly, the easiest—would be to take out the pilots first. After that, the units would be sitting ducks. So, as Charlie and the others watched the first wave of former RDC combat drones close on them, they knew they were both an assault force as well as a defensive line. And for Fox, he had exactly forty-eight seconds of flying experience on the quarter-million-dollar UAV.

Fortunately, he didn't have time to worry about his predicament before the two forces joined, and instinct took over.

For piloting a supposedly stealth combat drone, Fox was startled at how accurate the fire was from the attackers. The first few seconds of the engagement were spent dodging incoming fire rather than singling out targets to strike.

He aimed his camera at a point where he knew other Goliaths were in the air, and that's when he noticed an obvious glowing and flickering in the dark sky to his right. "Damn it, they can see us!" he announced. "We glow in the dark. Break off and pursue. Stealth is not going to cut it this time."

In his first strafing run on the incoming hijacked RDC drones, Fox was able to shred six of them before he detected buffering from his tail end. He scanned his aft camera and saw at least ten of the red, white and blue-painted UAVs coming up behind him, filling the air with missiles and gunfire.

Suddenly, the rear-view camera went black, and he noticed a slight pitch to the left as something went flying off the Goliath. Now, with a full minute of experience under his belt, Charlie Fox decided to go for broke. He aimed the craft straight up and gunned the motors. The drone shot off into the dark sky, leaving his adversaries far behind. He watched his heads-up display as his speed jumped past one hundred seventy miles per hour, which was faster than any drone he'd ever piloted. He let out a soft whistle just as he began to pull the drone over in a large looping maneuver.

Now, he sent the drone screaming toward the surface, passing two hundred miles per hour in a flash. Below, he saw a cluster of enemy units streaking after a faint object that glistened in the night. Charlie locked his guns on ten targets simultaneously and, with a press of the trigger, unleashed a torrent of hot lead. The Goliath slowed noticeably from the recoil of the guns but soon regained forward momentum again. All the targets splintered into a thousand pieces.

"Anyone keeping count?" he asked into the comm.

"Still over sixty active signals," an unknown voice stated. "Concentrations to the north, circling back in and headed your way."

"Much thanks, Mr. Wizard. Keep us informed."

Just then, a series of bright flashes to his right assailed his night-adjusted eyes. He glanced down and saw a line of missile flame headed for the eastern hangar.

"Command hangar, missiles incoming, impact eastern side! Take cover!"

It was only two seconds between warning and impact before the entire side of the metal hangar exploded. Flames lashed out, and half the roof bent over toward the main runway. A series of even brighter explosions appeared farther off to his right, over the vast open expanse of the flight line. But this time, it was from exploding drones and not from missile fire.

"Mr. Wizard, you still with us?"

"Yep, I'm in the control tower. Looks like another eight hostiles just bought the farm."

"Thanks for the update."

Fox guided his drone down toward the crumpled east side of the hangar. He zoomed in the focus of the forward camera to get a better look inside the building. There were people running about, helping the injured and dragging away the dead, but as far as he could tell, a good half of the interior was still intact. Huge tractors used in towing aircraft had been lined up near the east wall of the hangar and had absorbed much of the explosive force. Even then, that entire side of the building stood open and vulnerable to a second attack.

"Calling all Goliaths, this is Fox. It looks like the strategy has changed, and they're going for the hangars now. Form a shield around them. If they take out the pilot hangar, the mission in Pakistan will fail, and all of this will have been for nothing. Oh, and by the way, we'll be dead, too. Let's not let that happen."

There was a chorus of acknowledgments from the other Goliaths, which now numbered seven in total, with two having been destroyed or rendered inoperable from enemy fire.

"A new wave is coming up from the west and south," reported Mr. Wizard.

"I see them. Nothing gets past, okay? Now let's do some engagin'!"

"We must take out their command hangar," Abdul-Shahid Almasi was saying. "Once we do that, the drones outside will fall from the sky."

"Unless they take us out first," said General Burkov.

"Our center is underground and fortified, while theirs is out in the open and unshielded. And our defenders here are now on site. We should prevail."

"Yet you did not anticipate being under attack yourself."

"What is your problem, General? Since when have the Russians been the smartest military minds on the planet? I did not hear you voice any concerns about such an attack until you employed your incredible powers of hindsight. Not every event can be predicted, and your second-guessing and snarky criticisms are getting tiresome. I would welcome some constructive suggestions for a change, although I doubt you are capable of formulating any."

The fat Russian officer flared with anger and took a step in Almasi's direction. In a blurred motion, the slender, wiry terrorist produced an eight-inch-long curved knife called a *scimitar* and placed it against the pale, flabby skin of the General's neck. He pressed the Russian against the back wall of the huge chamber and into the shadows where they couldn't be seen.

"I have personally beheaded no fewer than five men in my time, Nikolay, and eight of my bombs have taken the lives of invading infidels—just like you. Do not push me further. I have real blood on my hands, while you only have reports and paperwork as proof of your warrior fire. You are in my world now, and it is so much more savage and primitive than you can ever imagine."

Almasi withdrew the blade and backed away. The Russian general, having never experienced his potential death so intimately, was stunned into silence, with sweat forming on his forehead.

After a moment, he took a deep breath and tugged at the bottom of his green service jacket to pull it down tight over a protruding belly. "I will allow you this one indiscretion, Almasi, but be assured, I do not favor threats or physical assault."

"Then you are in the wrong business, General. This is what the real face of war looks like. And if you cross *me* one more time, I will hack at your fat neck until your head rolls at my feet. Do not doubt me."

Almasi turned his back on the Russian and walked away to resume direct command of not only a battle raging above their heads but another taking place on the opposite side of the planet.

28

"Incoming, we're launching countermeasures!" The voice was that of a military pilot whom Charlie Fox had never met, even as the man sat in a command pod twenty feet away.

"We have countermeasures?" Fox queried.

"Look on your board. Four buttons on the left side: flares and ball bearings. I'm sending them all."

The barrage of four tight missile trails came down from high above, closing on the western hangar—the building housing the drone pilots. Suddenly, the sky between the hangar and the incoming streaks of yellow fire filled with a cloud of brilliant light, as well as the reflections of thousands of tiny balls of metal. The missiles fired by the RDC drones were launch-and-forget, so they continued along the same trajectory even though the path was blocked by the countermeasures. They entered the bright cloud a split second later and disintegrated.

"Great job!" Fox cried out.

"Yeah, but that's all I have. These units were not designed to go up against this many advanced UAVs."

"Now that I know about the countermeasures, I can pick up some of the slack."

From far below, another missile trail sprang into existence. "Where the hell did that one come from?" Fox called out.

"I see him. He'll be toast in about two seconds."

In the meantime, the missile fired from the doomed drone was still on its way toward the pilot's hangar, and there was nothing any of them could do to stop it.

"Xander, get ready; we're about to take a hit."

The missile struck the middle of the huge south-facing roll-away door, puncturing the lightweight metal with ease before passing through to the interior of the building. Half a heartbeat later, it exploded.

Charlie Fox, ensconced in a control pod three rows in and facing away from the hangar door, felt the blast of heat even as it spared his pod from serious damage; however, the row closest to the door didn't fare as well. Nine control stations took the brunt of the blast, deforming the compact metal and plastic pods into unrecognizable chunks of debris. No one could have survived the crushing impact of the blast.

Fox looked around at the surviving pods. He only

knew one other person in the room intimately, and that was Xander Moore. He didn't see him, but he did recognize three other members of Xander's Karachi Goliath team.

"Xander, are you okay? Xander…"

"Yeah, I'm fine. But we lost a Goliath in Karachi. Who was hit, can anyone tell?"

There was an awkward silence on the comm. 'C'mon, someone take a look."

"Jeremy's Goliath just crashed into the garage building." It was Hugh Barden's trembling voice.

"Jeremy, come in. Answer me."

Silence.

"Dammit!" Xander shouted.

Jeremy Fenton was one of the pilots killed in the Andrews hangar….

"Xander, take a look at the side of the garage where Jeremy crashed." It was Karen Prado on the comm.

"What?"

"I said take a look at the building. I think there's a ramp leading down."

Xander shook his head. He had known Jeremy longer than any of the others, since second grade, as a matter of fact, and long before they discovered drones. "A ramp?"

"Yeah, I'm blasting open the front doors. This may be our ticket to the big leagues."

The area in and above Almasi's compound was now filled with nearly a hundred buzzing drones, all performing an elaborate ballet of sorts. Billy and his Panthers were now on site and blasting through the auto drones without too much trouble, even as the RPA's controlled from underground did a number on his squadron. The smaller drones seemed content with fighting amongst themselves, so when Karen sent two missiles into the wooden doors of the long garage, the remaining four Goliaths, under Xander's command, darted inside the building without resistance.

Curt's drone was badly damaged, more than he'd first suspected. Half of the propellers were idle, and he was down to only a handful of munitions.

"I'm not going to do much good down below. I'll stay up here and warn of any hostiles coming your way."

"That'll work. Okay, the rest of you, this can get tricky. I've had my share of battles within office buildings and shopping malls, but never with a unit this big. Switching to ground-mode, I think we'll be able to maneuver better. When we get below, spread out, and the first one finding the pilot's rooms, give a shout-out. And then fuck 'em up good. Most of those pilots will be controlling the drones outside the hangar, the same ones who killed Jeremy. Let's return the favor."

The ramp leading underground started off wide and with a high ceiling to accommodate the construction equipment used to dig the tunnels. There were four main corridors leading from the ramp, and three of them were covered by the remaining Goliaths. Xander took the corridor on the far right, with Karen disappearing into the one next to him, while Hugh shot down the one on the left.

To his relief, Xander found that the main corridors remained relatively spacious; in fact, a pair of golf carts could pass easily by one another in the passageways. He now had the Goliath riding on the four rotor rings. The controls for ground travel were a little touchier—at least his lack of experience with them made it appear so—and he scraped the walls of the corridors more than once before getting the hang of it.

The labyrinth was huge and included living quarters, equipment rooms and dining facilities, plus a major control room packed full of bulky pilot's stations. To build and supply such a vast underground complex, adequately sized passageways were needed. This made the journey fairly easy for the huge drones, even though there would be no sneaking up on an unsuspecting terrorist, not with a Goliath.

Although virtually invisible and silent in their mechanical operation, the Goliaths nonetheless stirred up vast quantities of dust and sand, even in ground mode. The wind from the two horizontal rings, plus the smaller pusher blades at the rear, produced a dull swishing sound that echoed down the unfinished drywall and mottled concrete floor of the passageways. All along the way, the team was met with waiting gunfire. Occasionally, an armed man would appear from a side room and fire at the drone. The gunshots caused no damage to the UAV, so Xander ignored such attacks, choosing instead to save his ammo for when it really counted.

"I just entered a larger room down corridor number four," Hugh Barden reported. "No sign of the pilots yet—holy crap! Now, there's something you don't see every day."

"What are you talking about?" Xander asked.

"Just the largest, meanest drone I've ever seen."

"It is active?"

"Active? Oh yeah. It just came out of a side room and caught me from behind."

"What are you trying to say, Hugh?" Xander pulled up a side of his goggles and looked to his left and Barden's control pod. The man was leaning back in the seat and shaking his head.

"Nothing really, Number One, except that I'm dead. I assume that was Jonas's Ninja. The bastard just plastered my Goliath against the far wall. I'm out for the duration."

Xander slipped the goggles back on and was instantly halfway around the world again. He hadn't heard any sounds of a battle taking place, so Jonas must have fired without warning and took out Hugh with a single shot. Now, his force was down to just two Goliaths—his and Karen's—and with Jonas Lemon lurking around somewhere and in control of the deadliest drone ever made.

The incoming call alarm sounded again. This time,

Xander knew who was calling, so he only activated the audio.

"Uh eh, Xander, what you can't see *can* still kill you," said the voice of Jonas Lemon. "I told you I'd be around. So, who was it that I just crushed?"

"It was me, you bastard," Hugh Barden announced over the intercom. Xander had linked the communication to the rest of the team, just in case Jonas gave away a clue as to his location.

"Now, that gives me great pleasure," said Lemon. "I'd say that other than Xander, you're the one I most wanted to beat the most."

"Is this still about Linda what's-her-name?" Hugh asked. "You know she never liked you anyway."

"No, she preferred pretty boys like you: brainless geeks with a flashy smile."

"Eat your heart out, you ugly fucker. If I recall now, she was the best I ever had, so you really missed out on something special."

"Keep at it, Barden, but now I'm filthy rich, and I just knocked you out of the game. So sit back and be quiet, like a good little boy, while I do the same to the rest of your Team Alpha. You see, Xander, that's been your major weakness throughout the years. You've always relied on others to help fight your battles. I only counted on me, so I became better than you."

"Yeah, and that go-it-alone attitude got your ass fired and your wife out the door with your daughter. I understand that she's remarried and that little Katie loves him, unlike the hatred she now feels for her real dad. Oh, I'm sorry … is it too soon?"

"Stop trying to bait me, Moore, it won't work. But I'll tell you what I will do. First of all, I'm going to take out the remaining stealth RPAs you have in Karachi, and then I'm going to take over one of Billy's little JEN-Tech drones outside your hiding place in Washington. Then, I'm going to kill all of you, and not just your machines, but your flesh and blood bodies. That will be a new experience. It's rare when we get to use our drones to kill a real enemy. So, let's get the preliminaries out the way so I can get on with the real contest. I'm in the furthest corridor to the north, the one marked with the large bronze flowerpot. There's a connecting tunnel between the south and north corridors. I shouldn't be too hard to find."

"Switch to backup frequency," Xander ordered, and a moment later, he spoke. "Don't take the bait, Karen. We're here to find the pilot's room, and that's it. Maybe after that's done, we can go after Jonas."

"I'm tempted," Karen said, "but I know to follow orders. I haven't found anything promising this way. I'm cutting south down another corridor. I assume most of these tunnels join—"

Xander could sense the dead air on the frequency. "Karen, are you there? Karen…."

The line crackled. "I'm here. Comm cut out after the two RPGs were fired."

"RPGs?"

"Yep. These missed, but I won't be leaving the same way I came in; the tunnel's collapsed. Where are you?"

"Hell, if I know. All the corridors look alike. Wait … this looks promising."

The corridor Xander was in suddenly expanded in width and height, and he rolled into a large circular room with three double-wide doors lining the far wall. All three were closed.

29

Charlie Fox was about to drop down and survey the damage to the control hangar when he was suddenly swarmed by half a dozen flag-colored drones. He spun the Goliath around and, in a fit of rage, gunned the throttle, plowing directly into the middle of the incoming flight.

His vision was jarred as two of the RDC drones bounced off the titanium frame of the Goliath and broke apart, spiraling to the ground a thousand feet below. Next, he whipped the Goliath into a vertical stall, coming to an abrupt stop in mid-air. The remaining four attack drones were caught off guard by the unexpected maneuver and shot past. Fox let the huge drone begin its fall tail first to the earth, yet a moment later, he throttled up again and leveled out. He fingered the trigger on his control stick, sending a spread of heavy-caliber slugs in the direction of the four RDC drones now ass-end to him. They shattered apart in a blossom of colorful debris.

The assault on the hangars at Andrews had been going on for over ten minutes, and Abdul-Shahid Almasi knew the batteries in the remaining forty-one combat drones under his command were nearly drained.

He also knew there were enemy UAVs in the underground complex, although from the security cameras and reports from his men, only two of the stealth units remained. The battle taking place on the surface was inconsequential. If the pilots in the control room could take out the hangars in America, then the attacking drones above would simply transition into hover mode, awaiting new commands, commands that would never come.

The flight command bunker was one of the most-isolated chambers in the complex and even more than that, Almasi had a secret weapon he didn't even know he would have: Jonas Lemon.

Originally, the Ninja 5 was for Almasi himself—if it was needed. With the presence of the American stealth drones, it was now a vital part of the compound's defense. Yet he was not in command of the deadly drone.

Jonas Lemon was still in Dubai, yet somehow, he acquired the necessary portable relay and control equipment necessary to link with Almasi's base in Karachi. With the proper access codes, Jonas could operate any of the units the terrorist had in his arsenal. With his guidance critically needed elsewhere—in coordinating both the defense of his compound plus the attack on the hangars in Washington, D.C.—Almasi gladly allowed the American access to the Ninja. With Lemon in control of the most advanced killer drone in existence and guarding the underground command post, Almasi had one less thing to worry about.

His main concern at this moment was the remaining battery life of the drones in America.

"Attention all pilots operating in the United States." His voice was loud and strong and got everyone's attention as it echoed off the walls of the huge control room. "Guide all your remaining drones directly into the two hangars. Overwhelm the few defenders they have, and once you impact the buildings, detonate your explosive charges. Their command center must be destroyed, and your batteries are running low. Line up and attack at will."

The pilots turned back to their stations. Camera gimbals were manipulated as visual contact with the target buildings was established. Courses were altered, and in a huge, seemingly choreographed movement, the attack aspect of the drones all pointed in one direction. They hovered for a moment as if taking a deep breath in preparation for the sprint to the target. And then, with one mind and one purpose, the flock of drones attacked.

Charlie Fox and the other six surviving defenders

noticed the momentary break in the battle. Now, they watched in horror as the drones performed their deadly ballet and then shot off toward the hangars.

It was an odd situation for Fox to wrap his mind around. He was in two places at once, and he fought the conflicting emotions that resulted from his split perspective. To the Charlie Fox sitting in a control pod in one of the hangars, he knew his death was quickly approaching. Yet from his perspective within the Goliath drone, hovering high above the hangars, he felt an odd detachment from the tragedy about to take place. In a strange way, he felt … safe.

Fortunately, the feeling quickly passed.

He ripped off his goggles. "All the drones outside are on a suicide dive towards the hangars!" he yelled at the top of his lungs.

Time in the hangar froze as shock and inevitability affected everyone in the building. No one knew what to do next.

No one except Xander Moore.

Back in Karachi, he throttled the Goliath, aiming it at the center doorway his deadly RPA now faced. The four wheels screeched before finding a purchase, and then the drone surged forward. The front prop rings struck the metal doors with a sound like a thunderclap. The matching panels separated, and Xander found himself racing along a short platform running along the elevated outer rim of a large, semi-circular room. Beyond the platform, the floor transitioned down into a series of steep steps, leading to a lower floor area packed full of control stations and startled pilots.

Even though the Goliath was in ground mode, it nonetheless took flight off the narrow platform. The two remaining lifting rotor rings managed to keep the drone from falling straight down. Instead, it dropped along a graceful, gentle arc toward the center of the control stations. With a slight grin on his lips, Xander Moore—with a steady gaze and sure hand—activated the detonate button on his console.

Abdul-Shahid Almasi reacted quickly when the odd, four-wheel drone crashed through the door of the command center. He was experienced enough with drone warfare to know what was coming next.

Brushing past a stunned General Burkov, Almasi shot through a small side door and dived to his left around a bend in the hallway—just as the explosion filled the command center.

Charlie Fox placed the goggles back on his head, choosing to watch his death arrive through the strangely detached perspective from outside.

With no way to defend against forty suicide drones, nearly all of the attacking UAVs hit the metal buildings unimpeded. At sixty miles per hour, even the light mass of the combat drones was enough to puncture the structure. Dozens of rays of light erupted from the dark roofs of the hangars as they were perforated by the crashing drones.

Although the red, white and blue UAVs were heavily damaged from the impact, with their prop rings and cameras sheared off, Fox knew the ordinance packages would survive—they were designed to survive. He heard the ear-piercing claps as the drones struck the building and then, without delay, crashed into the pods and other parts of the building's interior.

With his eyes focused on the outside overhead view seen through his FPV goggles, Charlie Fox waited for the inevitable.

But after a second … and then two, and still no explosion, he pulled off the goggles. He was suddenly in the hangar again, but this time in the middle of a scene of terrible devastation.

Even though none of the drones had exploded, the ballistic nature of their arrival did a number on the interior of the buildings. Several of the pods were in tatters, with bodies hanging out of the ones where the attacking drones made direct contact. Other parts of the huge room were in ruins as well, yet by a quick estimate, over two-thirds of the pods survived. Their shocked and confused occupants were looking about the room, just like Charlie Fox.

Yet Fox wasn't assessing the damage anymore; instead, he was looking for one person in particular. He climbed out of his pod and stood up, scanning the room. His knees grew weak—not from the shock of tragedy, but rather from relief and joy—when he saw Xander Moore standing next to a pod two rows over. He met Fox's laughing eyes with a pair of his own.

"You got 'em, didn't you?" Fox yelled at the senior pilot.

Xander gave him a wide, satisfied grin.

"You sure do like to blow up really expensive drones, don't you?" Fox said as he ran up to Xander and encased him in a powerful hug. "And, boss, nothing like cutting it close. That has to be the literal definition of *'the last second'*!"

"Helps to keep the suspense level up," Xander replied. But then the smile vanished from his face as he looked around the room. "What about casualties; any idea?"

"Still too early to tell ... but it could have been worse."

Heat and exhaust shattered the narrow door and flooded his escape route with smoke and fire, scorching his shoes and pant legs, igniting them. He slapped at the burning fabric, strangely oblivious to the pain as his survival instinct took over. Other pieces of burning fabric were scattered around him; they were the dark green of the Russian general's service uniform.

On his hands and knees, Almasi crawled down the corridor and farther from the inferno behind him. Vague thoughts of anger and frustration filled his mind, even if the full impact of the explosion hadn't yet been realized.

He managed to get to his feet and hobble, dragging his injured left leg behind him. He had escape routes already dug, so he knew he could get out of the underground complex and to a nondescript building outside the compound, even in light of the catastrophic failure of his operation.

Almasi's thoughts became clearer as he moved along the narrow, dirt floor of the escape tunnel. He didn't need to go back to check; he knew the loss was total. Even if some of the pilots and operators survived, the sensitive equipment in the room was now damaged beyond repair. Contact was lost, not only with the drones in the compound above but also in America.

The mission was over. All the missions were over. All that remained was his personal survival.

30

At a desk in the master bedroom of his suite at the Armani Hotel in the Burj Khalifa building in Dubai, Jonas Lemon saw the screen on his computer go dark, and the tense feel of the control stick vanish. The three men guarding him in the room saw it as well, and they now looked at each other with confusion on their dark faces.

"What happened?" Faisal Haddad asked.

"Looks like you're going to need a new boss," Jonas answered.

"Almasi's dead?"

"The control room back in Karachi has just been taken out, and the last I knew, he was in the room. You can draw your own conclusions from that." Lemon smiled at the bearded man.

"Fuck you, Lemon!" the man yelled as he pulled out

his cellphone and began to frantically dial numbers. The other two men watched with nervous expressions as Faisal dialed and redialed the number. All he kept getting was a recording saying that the number he was trying to reach was not in service at that time and to try back later.

"I sincerely hope you got paid in advance," Jonas said after the terrorist gave up trying to reach Almasi.

In a surge of anger, the man stepped forward and placed the barrel of his Berretta nine-millimeter against Jonas's temple. "I should just kill you now. I've wanted to since the first moment we met. What difference would it make now if I did?"

"He has a lot of money, Faisal," said one of the other men.

Haddad hesitated. "So, Lemon, how much is your life worth?"

"I don't know … why don't you ask *him*?" Jonas nodded toward the door to the bedroom.

The terrorist smiled, not about to fall for the old ruse —until he heard the *pop-pop* of two silenced gunshots go off. He'd managed a half turn toward the door when a dark hole suddenly appeared in his left temple. A torrent of escaping blood quickly filled the wound as Faisal Haddad collapsed on the carpet.

The gunman entered the room, unscrewing the suppressor muzzle from his Sig Sauer. "Just the timing of this fortuitous arrival should warrant another ten thousand dollars," said the man with the thick French accent.

"I would agree, Francois," said Jonas Lemon, "except for the fact that it was you who let them take me captive in the first place."

"The opportunity to free you did not present itself … until now."

Jonas smiled and looked back at the dark computer screen. "I'll give you the extra ten thousand—and another fifty grand—if you can locate and isolate Xander Moore for me. Don't kill him. Just get him ready for me."

"Seeing that he is far away in America and under the protection of the U.S. government, that may take some time. You know I do not rush these things."

Jonas looked around at the three bodies bleeding out on the floor of the bedroom. "No, you don't, but I must say, your timing is impeccable."

Jonas Lemon stood up from the desk. "Just do what I ask, Francois. I've waited this long for my revenge; I can wait a little longer."

31

Xander Moore and Billy Jenkins were in Nathan Hall's office in the secret DARPA building, located one block over from the Washington Mall and three down from the headquarters of the Federal Bureau of Investigation. Six days had passed since the dual-battles in Karachi and D.C., and Xander was livid.

"What do you mean Almasi wasn't there? Of course, he was."

"That's right—he *was*. Search teams located several escape tunnels within the complex, two even leading from the control room. He obviously got out through one of them."

"And Jonas?"

"We traced the calls he made to you to Dubai. He's gone, as well."

"So, both of the bad guys got away?" Billy summarized.

"For now, Billy, but you know how these things go. The whole world's out looking for them. Justice will be served."

A sharp knock came to the door, and the other person they were expecting entered the room. The three men rose to their feet when Tiffany Collins came in, dressed in professional broadcast-reporter attire, including a grey vest that struggled to mask two of her most prominent on-air distractions. Throughout her career, she'd fought to keep her ample natural assets from taking away from the seriousness of the words she spoke on camera. Unfortunately, the vest wasn't cooperating.

"What did they say?" Xander asked.

"Just a few minor edits, and it's ready to go."

"Well, Ms. Collins, this could be a big step for your career," Nathan Hall said.

"I want to thank you again, Nathan, for the access you've given me. I know a lot of people were against it."

"It's time more of the truth about drones—and our susceptibility to them—was better known. Besides that, your unique perspective on the events of last week will help counter some of the crazy rumors flying around out there."

"Frankly, I was surprised your people allowed me to be so open and forthcoming. I know I put a lot of personal spin on it, but I was there. I saw it with my own eyes."

"That's the best type of reporting—first-hand. Cuts

through all the he-said-she-said B.S.; however, I am sorry about the restriction concerning the Russian link to the crisis. It's better if we keep that part of the story under wraps until an official response can be worked out. Don't want to go start World War Three, now do we?"

Tiffany smiled and looked at the men. "I don't know; it sure would provide *me* a lot of job stability. You know what they say, *'Never let a good crisis go to waste.'*"

Billy turned to Nathan Hall. "So, did we save Christmas?"

Nathan laughed. "And then some! There's no denying the fact that Americans sure love to buy things, and they're out doing it with a vengeance. Of course, the retailers are cooperating. My wife is out right now, spending twice as much as we budgeted for but getting four times as much. My grandkids are really going to be spoiled this year."

It was Billy's turn to smile. "It's Christmas Eve, and with the hefty contract advance I got to build Goliaths, I might actually splurge a little myself this year. There are still a few hours left. Is there anything the two of you want in particular?" he asked, addressing Xander and Tiffany. By now, the two of them were standing very close to one another.

"I don't know." Xander began. "I kinda liked that Lear jet that brought us out here from California. But short of that, I could sure use a vacation." He looked into Tiffany's blue eyes as he made the non-verbal invitation.

"I've always fancied the South Pacific." Tiffany's eyes

locked on Xander's. "Never been there before, but there's always been something romantic about the word *Polynesia*."

"Consider it done!" Billy said. "And first class all the way; hell, I might even spring for a yacht charter. It's absolutely gorgeous down there, and the two of you would make for the perfect travel poster."

Xander nodded before breaking his gaze with Tiffany. He looked at Nathan and then to Billy. "Thanks, dude. Oh, and also, the surf down there is supposed to be pretty gnarly this time of year."

"In that case, I just might tag along." Billy then lifted his right hand, curling in his index, middle and ring fingers while extending the thumb and little finger. He wiggled the familiar gesture at Xander. "Cowabunga, dude!"

EPILOGUE

The snow falling over Moscow in late January had let up briefly, and the temperature climbed to a few degrees above zero; even so, Abdul-Shahid Almasi was not used to the extremes of the Russian winter.

His puppet masters had placed him in a small apartment not far from the Kremlin, with a sporadically operating steam heater, and then left him there for over three weeks before granting him the meeting with President Mikel Marko and his inner circle of advisors. The meeting did not go well, as everyone wanted to sweep the terrorist under the rug and pretend that their once warm and mutually beneficial affiliation had never existed.

Almasi knew there was nothing more the Russians would do for him, with the possible exception of sparing his life. To this end, he humbled himself before the leader of the Russian Federation, vowing to disappear from the world stage with the modest contingency funds he had hidden away. They wouldn't even have to give him money, just let him leave.

In reality, he had over twenty million American dollars stashed in various hidden accounts across Europe. He would, indeed, disappear from the world stage, but he would not remain so. Already, plans were underway to resurrect the now-disbanded Arm of Allah. And from the look of things, he just may get the chance to once more serve as its leader.

Marko escorted him out through a side door of the Kremlin and into a rectangular courtyard surrounded on all sides by four levels of gaudy-looking architecture. He shivered in the cold, even as the Russian shrugged off the chill while wearing only a bland blue suit and red tie. Six security guards stood in the courtyard while a screen of eight nearly silent sentry drones hovered near the roof line of the surrounding buildings. Almasi eyed the drones with concern. Even though he used the machines in his work, he never trusted them. They always made him nervous.

"So you will be taken to the airport and flown to Switzerland," Marko was saying. "At that point, we will have no further contact with you. Is that understood?"

"Yes, Mr. President."

"You came to us with a plan that ultimately failed,"

Marko continued. "Yes, our ultimate goal was to accomplish just as you said you could deliver, yet if you had not come to us, we would have proceeded along our own timeline and in our own manner. As it has turned out, I'm now receiving too many phone calls from the Americans with rather pointed and embarrassing questions. Of course, they know all, and now I may find myself having to make concessions to them just to keep the truth from being revealed." The tall, slender Russian glared down at Almasi. "I am the leader of the Russian Federation, and now I will have to bow down to the Americans simply because of public relations. Do you know how furious that makes me?"

"I'm sorry it has come to this," Almasi said. "The plan was sound, and it nearly succeeded, and if it hadn't been for the financial blackmail committed by the Americans, it would have."

"If's and blame will not salvage the situation, Almasi."

Abdul-Shahid continued to watch the hovering drones as the Russian spoke.

"And neither will your death—as long as you remain silent. Even as we choose not to follow that course of action, I wouldn't be surprised to read of your assassination sometime soon."

One of the hovering drones seemed out of place. Instead of looking outwards, scanning for threats, it had rotated until it now faced the pair on the cobblestone courtyard below.

"So I would take the money that you do have and use it to dig a very deep hole to crawl into. Even though Russia's involvement in the crisis will be used for pragmatic political advantage, the Americans will take immense pleasure in announcing your death to the world, just as they did with Bin Laden's."

Almasi stretched out one of his rare smiles, a gesture that caused the Russian President to pause and cast a quizzical look his way.

"Mr. President," Abdul-Shahid Almasi began, "I believe we will both share the same fate for what we have done recently; only in my case, I will find eternal life and peace with my God. What awaits you? That will be known any moment—"

The sentry drone arched forward and descended toward the pair, a heartbeat before the explosives aboard the quadcopter detonated.

President Hector Ortega looked over at Owen Murphy's sallow face and nodded.

"You're welcome," he said to the President-elect, a title Murphy would hold for another six hours. "Now, all you have to do is rebuild the United States of America … from the ground up. Good luck with that."

The ex-governor of Maryland remained silent, although a prominent swallow was seen traversing his thick neck. This was so much more than he'd bargained for when he set out to win the highest office in the land. Now, he would actually have to do … something. And at that moment, Owen Murphy had no idea where to begin.

The End

THE METHUSELAH PARADOX

Another technothriller by Tom (T.R.) Harris.

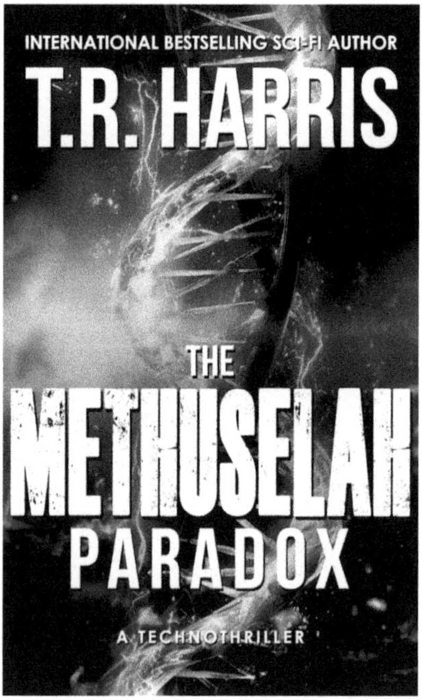
INTERNATIONAL BESTSELLING SCI-FI AUTHOR
T.R. HARRIS
THE
METHUSELAH
PARADOX
A TECHNOTHRILLER

AUTHOR NOTES

Thank you for reading **BuzzKill**. I sincerely hope you enjoyed it.

The evolution of this story goes back over ten years. The original version of the book was released in 2014 and was titled **The Day of the Drone**. It was one of my earlier works, having begun my publishing career in October of 2011.

The first release of the book could be termed mediocre at best, mainly because it was rough around the edges and possibly ahead of its time.

But now current events have caught up with the book, requiring an extensive re-edit, updating and a new title to **BuzzKill**.

Back in 2014, the original novel took much longer to write than my science fiction stories. It was my first technothriller, but not only that, it required tons more research to make it authentic. I would work on the book for a while and then set it aside before returning to the work after writing another sci-fi adventure.

At that time, the threat of terrorist strikes by drones was just beginning to hit the headlines, and numerous agencies and private organizations were struggling to come to grips with this new reality. As I researched the book, I had a hard time keeping up with all the changes. I kept starting and stopping because, seemingly, every week a new strategy was being proposed. This really screwed up my research and storyline.

However, like most imaginative people, I set my mind to work on the problem, extrapolating the next step in both drone attacks and ways to protect ourselves against them. I thought *'what next'* and then tried to come up with a solution. The methods I describe to protect shopping malls seemed logical, if—or when—the need ever arises. Let's hope it never comes to that.

And so the Rapid Defense Center was formed, if only in my mind. It seemed like a logical step in unifying a strategic defense under the banner of a central agency. After all, isn't that what government's answer is to everything, another agency?

Of course, I took a lot of literary license in creating the Center and the events described in the book. And it's my sincere wish, hope, prayer that *none* of this comes to pass. This is a work of fiction, first and foremost. I'm just trying to tell a good story.

I can't help it if reality catches up to my imagination. However…

But enough of that. If you've made it this far in the book, then you already have enough to think about.

I hope you enjoyed the book and will see fit to read my other novels. The full reading list can be found below.

Now, I'll let you get to sleep. If you're able.

Thank you,

Tom Harris
April 2024

FACEBOOK GROUP

I'm inviting you to join my exclusive, secret, Super Fan Facebook Group appropriately called

Fans of T.R. Harris and
The Human Chronicles Saga

Just click on the link below, and you—yes, **YOU**—may become a character in one of my books. You may not last long, and you may end up being the villain, but at least you can point to your name in one of my books – and live forever! Maybe. If I decide to use your name. It's at my discretion.

trharrisfb.com

Contact the Author

Facebook
trharrisfb.com

Email
bytrharris@hotmail.com

Website:
bytrharris.com

YouTube:
The Human Chronicles HFY

NOVELS BY TOM HARRIS / T.R. HARRIS

Technothrillers
The Methuselah Paradox
BuzzKill

Human for Hire Series
Human For Hire
Human for Hire 2 – Soldier of Fortune
Human for Hire (3) – Devil's Gate
Human for Hire (4) – Frontier Justice
Human for Hire (5) – Armies of the Sun
Human for Hire (6) – Sirius Cargo
Human for Hire (7) – Cellblock Orion
Human for Hire (8) – Starship Andromeda
Human for Hire (9) -- Operation Antares
Human for Hire (10) – Stellar Whirlwind

Human for Hire (11) -- I Am Entropy
Human for Hire (12) – Earth Blood
Human for Hire (13) – Capella Prime

The Human Chronicles Legacy Series

Raiders of the Shadow
War of Attrition
Secondary Protocol
Lifeforce
Battle Formation
Allied Command

The Human Chronicles Legacy Series Box Set

The Adam Cain Saga

The Dead Worlds
Empires
Battle Plan
Galactic Vortex
Dark Energy
Universal Law
The Formation Code
The Quantum Enigma
Children of the Aris
The Adam Cain Saga Box Set

The Human Chronicles Saga

The Fringe Worlds
Alien Assassin
The War of Pawns
The Tactics of Revenge
The Legend of Earth
Cain's Crusaders
The Apex Predator
A Galaxy to Conquer
The Masters of War
Prelude to War
The Unreachable Stars
When Earth Reigned Supreme
A Clash of Aliens
Battlelines
The Copernicus Deception
Scorched Earth
Alien Games
The Cain Legacy
The Andromeda Mission
Last Species Standing
Invasion Force
Force of Gravity
Mission Critical
The Lost Universe
The Immortal War
Destroyer of Worlds
Phantoms

Novels by Tom Harris / T.R. Harris

Terminus Rising
The Last Aris

The Human Chronicles Box Set Series

Box Set #1 – Books 1-5 in the series
Box Set #2 – Books 6-10 in the series
Box Set #3 – Books 11-15 in the series
Box Set #4 – Books 16-20 in the series
Box Set #5—Books 21-25 in the series
Box Set #6—Books 26-29 in the series

REV Warriors Series

REV
REV: Renegades
REV: Rebirth
REV: Revolution
REV: Retribution
REV: Revelations
REV: Resolve
REV: Requiem
REV: Rebellion
REV: Resurrection

—

REV Warriors Box Set – The Complete Series – 10 Books

Jason King – Agent to the Stars Series

The Unity Stone Affair
The Mystery of the Galactic Lights